Issue 8
April 2018

Lezli Robyn & Tina Smith, Editors
Shahid Mahmud, Publisher

Published by Arc Manor/Heart's Nest Press
P.O. Box 10339
Rockville, MD 20849-0339

Heart's Kiss is published in February, April, June, August, October and December.

www.HeartsKiss.com

Pleaee refer to our website for information on how to submit material for *Heart's Kiss* magazine.

Available by subscription (www.HeartsKiss.com) or through your favorite online store (Amazon.com, BN.com, etc.).

ISBN: 978-1-61242-408-8

Advertising in the magazine is available. Quarter page (half column), $95 per issue. Half page (full column, vertical or two half columns, horizontal) $165 per issue. Full page (two full columns) $295 per issue. Back Cover (full color) $495 per issue. All interior advertising is in black and white.

Please write to advert@HeartsKiss.com.

FOREIGN LANGUAGE RIGHTS: Please refer all inquiries pertaining to foreign language rights to Shahid Mahmud, Arc Manor, P.O. Box 10339, Rockville, MD 20849-0339. Tel: 1-240-245-2214. Fax 1-310-388-8440. Email admin@ArcManor.com.

Contents

EDITOR'S NOTE

by Lezli Robyn

*H*eart's Kiss starts off a new issue with a heart-felt thank you to our new readers out there who purchased Issue 7. Tina and I are committed to showing our readers how beautiful love is, in all its forms. This issue contains an erotic F/F story by new writer Kate Capulet, as well as a M/M romance, too, set in the Czech Republic, the ancestral homeland of the story's author, Olivette Devaux. Not only that, but L. Penelope is back again with another novelette in her *Before I* series, this time a new adult piece that is as erotic as it is sweet.

But as our romance readers know—love is more than what happens in the bedroom, Tina and I ensured our readers are immersed in stories of *all* heat levels, to show the full gamut of what the romance genre has to offer. The gentle, but evocative, story of abiding love by acclaimed author Juliet Marillier, is rich with Aussie spirit and written with such sensitivity that there is no doubt why Juliet's books have captured the heart's of so many readers. We also have another reimagined fairytale by Harlequin author Melinda Curtis, and the next installment of Anna J. Stewart's *Warden* series, where the second of a trio of sisters meets her hero for a chance at a happily ever after.

I can tell you now, I get paid to edit this magazine within my 9-5 work hours, but I often cannot wait for the next work day to devour a new story by one of our authors. The minute I hear that distinctive *ping!* of a new email I'm salivating and waiting for my first spare moment at the end of the night to curl up with a hot chocolate, a cuddly chiweenie and the latest submission to *Heart's Kiss*. Who could have thought my work as an editor could bring such pleasure to me as a reader?

Tina and I couldn't have been more delighted to buy our first story from D. H. Hendrickson, which shows us true love, even at first blush, doesn't care about physical limitations—nor should it. Our hero might be seeing his future partner for the first time while she's seated in a wheelchair, but all he sees is her strength—of character, mind *and* body. I wanted to read more about this couple.

An interview with the *New York Times* and *USA Today* bestselling contemporary author, Marie Force, along with an excerpt from one of her recently published books, *Delirious,* also enticed me to seek out more words by that writer; I was buying the full edition of her book before we had sent this issue off to be typeset. Add C.S. DeAvilla's list of Recommended Books to the mix, and Tina and I have no doubt our readers' To Be Read pile will be stacked higher by issue's end.

For there is one thing we're proud of, and that is the caliber of our writers. And you could not be of a higher caliber than Brenda Novak. Not only are we thrilled to be featuring her short story "Blood in, Blood out" in this issue, which ties into her *Bulletproof* series of novels, but will be publishing her first installment of *Date Night Recipes.* They say that the way to a man's heart is through his stomach. Well, who better to get irresistible recipes from than a *New York Times* and *USA Today bestseller* romance author? She was even just announced a finalist for the 2018 short form Contemporary Romance Rita Award. (Congratulations!)

On that note, I will leave you to devour this issue at your leisure. We hope you find the contents as delicious as we did!

L. Penelope has been writing since she could hold a pen and loves getting lost in the worlds in her head. She is an award-winning fantasy and paranormal romance author. She lives in Maryland with her husband and their furry dependents. Sign up for new release information, updates, and giveaways on her website: http://www.lpenelope.com. We welcome her to the pages of Heart's Kiss.

BEFORE I FALL

by L. Penelope

Head pounding along with the bass line, Renee crossed the congested living room dance floor and disappeared into the darkened hallway. She was still sober and couldn't blame alcohol for the haze that covered her mind. In the shadows, a couple writhed in one another's arms. She looked away—they obviously didn't care about privacy, but maybe if she'd averted her eyes a few weeks ago, she wouldn't have discovered Khalil in basically the exact same position, sticking his tongue down another girl's throat.

Jesus, what if he was here?

Part of her had felt relief when she discovered them. Khalil's hands on her own body had never quite felt right. And his tongue caressing hers had never made her quiver the way she always hoped she would.

Oddly unsteady in her five-inch heels, she carefully negotiated the uneven wooden floor. This old Victorian on the edge of campus had seen better days. It had at least a dozen drafty rooms. Paint peeled from the walls in patches that looked like water damage. She hoped it wasn't mold.

Students carved up these houses and split the outrageous rents among as many as ten people. They made great party houses now that so many of the fraternities were on lock down for hazing. This wasn't the same house in which she'd discovered Khalil playing tonsil tennis, but at a certain point, all the turrets and peaks ran together.

Thinking about all the parties she and Khalil had attended made Renee's stomach clench. Her heart wasn't broken, but her pride was. They'd been a super couple, that's the only reason she'd put up with his bullshit for so long. His heavy breaths always panting in her ear, the way his cold fingers slid up and down her skin. She shook off a chill thinking about it. She had no idea how she'd lasted almost a year with him. Whoever that skank was giving him mouth-to-mouth, she could have him.

But now Renee felt adrift. Their friends had intermingled and since Khalil was slightly more popular—being a starting attack on the lacrosse team—he trumped whatever Renee's family, looks, and reputation brought to the situation. Now, she'd been on her own for the past few weeks, something she wasn't accustomed to.

The thump of the beat made her head spin. Everywhere she turned there were people grinding, or making out, or playing some kind of drinking game. Instead of oblivion, tonight she craved something she couldn't quite put her finger on. She could have stayed home, but staring at the four walls of her single room for almost a month had gotten old. Being naturally social, she wanted to be around people—she just needed to figure out who, exactly.

An Asian girl with purple dreadlocks brushed by her, bumping her shoulder. "Sorry," the girl said, giggling. The little bells strung into her locks jingled merrily. Her purple, glittery eyeshadow matched her lipstick.

Renee took a step back. "It's okay."

The girl grinned and then raced up the steps in a cloud of fruit-scented shampoo.

"And I thought *my* heels were high," Renee muttered. But her stilettos had nothing on the other girl's insane purple platform boots.

Renee looked up the darkened stairwell, then behind her at the party she didn't want to be at. After a moment's indecision, she climbed the creaking stairs. The old wood shifted worryingly under her feet.

She was disappointed to find the second floor only slightly less crowded. A line snaked out from the bathroom, and the distinctive sounds of people hooking up rang out behind at least two of the doors. Another staircase led to a third level, but the purple dreadlocked girl was marking it off with yellow police tape reading: CAUTION! DO NOT CROSS!

"What's up there?" Renee asked, craning her neck to peer up into the dark.

The girl turned and shrugged. "Dunno. But it must be something really bad considering the tape and all."

"But you just put the tape there." Renee pointed.

The girl scrunched her nose and tilted her head to the side. "Did I?"

"I just saw you." Renee turned to see if anyone else was hearing this, but nobody was paying attention to the two of them.

When she turned back around, the girl was gone.

There was no way Miss Dreadlocks could have gotten by Renee, who was standing directly in front of the steps. But she couldn't have gone up either, not in less than a second—not in those shoes, without making any noise, when every section of the floor in the house creaked. It was like she'd vanished into thin air.

Renee considered the tape. If nothing else, it should mean fewer people going up there. The most likely explanation—that didn't involve the girl beaming back onto the starship she probably arrived on—was that Miss Dreads' room was upstairs and she just didn't want anyone bothering her.

But Renee wasn't going to bother anyone. She was just going to have a look around, maybe enjoy a little quiet for a few minutes and then head home.

She slipped off her shoes and climbed under the tape.

The third floor was small, there were only three doors off the hallway, and it was thankfully empty. She pushed the first door open to find a tiny bathroom, its sloping ceiling meant you'd have to either be really short to shower in here or be okay bending over and hunching down. But the porcelain pedestal sink looked original and so did the black and white tile, only slightly chipped.

There was a bottle of combination shampoo and conditioner in the shower and not much else. No evidence that a girl used this bathroom.

The second door off the hallway was missing a doorknob so she passed it on the way to the third. She paused outside, listening. The music from below still vibrated through the walls, but was muted up here, it could have been happening outside or down the street just as easily.

The curiosity that had overtaken her could be explained by the fact that she was a naturally nosy person. One of her nannies had nicknamed her Harriet, after Harriet the Spy, and Renee hadn't even protested.

So she blamed her natural inquisitiveness as the reason she turned the knob and pushed open the door.

From the corner of the stairwell, Delilah watches the human girl enter the bedroom. She has temporarily traded in her physical body, with all of its color and pretty decorations, for her natural form—a smoke-like wisp of elemental energy. Though she would much prefer to be purple, stealth is necessary to observe the progress of her mission. A disembodied wisp of colorful smoke would not be incognito.

Her first assignment for the Guild did not exactly go well. Delilah can't afford another mistake, or the dream she's had since her inception of becoming a full-fledged member of the Cupid Guild will never come true.

The roll of yellow tape she acquired from the Requisitions Department hovers in the shadows next to her insubstantial body. At least she had anticipated her target's nature correctly. All the girl needed was a push. Delilah's elemental form cannot smile in satisfaction, though she imagines herself doing so.

Not until the bedroom door eventually closes does she fade into the darkness and leave.

Milo looked up when the door opened. The lock had broken just that morning and he hadn't had a chance to fix it. He figured he'd be flooded with drunk kids busting into his room, but hadn't had any interruptions—until now.

The girl standing in his doorway didn't look smashed. Straightened, black hair fell past her shoulders and the dress she wore was form fitting, but not a cry for attention. She was barefoot, with vicious looking heels clutched in one hand, but she didn't wobble or sway. She just stared at him with wide eyes.

He had an assortment of sarcastic statements at the ready for these instances, but they all fell out of his head.

"The bathroom's across the hall." He pointed behind her. She looked over her shoulder then turned back and stepped fully into the room, closing the door. Milo's eyebrows shot up.

"Um, sorry to bother you," she said. She had a cheerleader quality about her—small bones with a perky nose, like an ebony-skinned pixie—but instead of the high-pitched, girly voice that her frame suggested, she spoke with a pleasant alto. He bet if she broke into song, she would enrapture any audience.

"But?" he asked.

"What?" She squinted.

"You're sorry to bother me, but you will anyway?"

She ducked her head, looking apologetic and he felt a little bad, but seriously, what was she doing barging into his room? He couldn't stop his roommates from hosting these crazy parties, but he'd learned after being in college for two years how to survive them. Just stay away.

"Why aren't you at the party?" she asked, inching closer. She didn't recognize him, that much was clear, so what was with her? Why was she even interested?

He shrugged. "Not my thing." He closed the book he'd been reading and turned fully to face her. "What about you?"

Her face shuttered. She was standing in the middle of the room looking lost—he wasn't sure why she was there but suddenly he didn't want her to go. He had an overwhelming need to know what had brought her here into his room in the middle of one of the campus's epic parties.

"It used to be my thing. But lately…" She shrugged and looked around, then sidled closer to his bookcase and pointed to the light switch next to it. "Do you mind?" she asked, but flipped the switch before he could answer. The overhead light came on, the one that flattened the entire room making everything looked washed out.

Milo popped up and flicked on the floor lamp, then went over and turned the overhead light back off. She stood next to him looking up and up. It was true he towered over most people, but he felt like a giant next to her. She must be a full foot shorter.

She smiled and bent down. When she rose back up she was much closer to his height—she'd put on her shoes. Though they still only brought her up to his chin.

"Renee." She held out her hand. He stared for a second before grabbing it. She shook his hand firmly and fireworks shot off under his skin. The sensation was so surprising, he took a step back. She tilted her head at him, and his face flamed. He cleared his throat and squeezed her hand again before letting go. No fireworks this time, maybe that was a low blood sugar thing.

"Milo."

Her face cracked into another grin. "Milo," she repeated. "Cool name."

"Thanks."

"Not boring and normal like Renee. When I was younger, I wanted to change my name to something more dramatic…"

"But?" He was suddenly interested in everything about her.

She shrugged, running her finger across the spines of the books on his shelf. "I couldn't think of anything. My parents wouldn't have let me anyway. Names have power they always said."

He watched with fascination as she traced his books. Her nails were sparkly and blue, but short, not the fake claws lots of girls wore. "Renee means reborn. It's a good name."

She looked up at him and he noticed her eyes were a clear light brown, lighter than her brown skin. He swallowed.

"What does Milo mean?"

"Nothing."

The corners of her lips turned up and her brow furrowed. Her expression was a contradiction, sort of the way she was shaping up to be. "It has to mean something."

He turned slightly so he wouldn't stare at her; for some reason he couldn't tear his eyes away and didn't want her to think he was a creeper. Though he felt like one. Especially since he'd do anything to keep her here longer, to talk to her more. The thought scared him.

"It's based on the name Miles, which means either soldier or merciful, but in and of itself it's sort of just made up."

"So you can make it mean whatever you want it to?"

"I guess. I never thought of it that way."

"What do you want it to mean?"

Stuffing his hands in his pockets, he leaned against the closet door. He stared into space but his gaze kept coming back to her, looking up at him. "I don't know. What do you think?"

She cocked her head to the side and placed a finger on her lips, scrutinizing him. What did she see? He was ridiculously tall, light-skinned, and curly haired. Nothing really special, nothing that stood out except maybe his height and he tended to slouch to make it less of an issue. His T-shirt and sweats weren't from any kind of designer. But this girl, this beautiful girl, kept staring at him like she was seeing something more. He had no idea what that could be.

"Milo," she said, her voice cutting through the silence like a knife impaling him. "I think it should mean *solitary scholar*."

A chill went through him. Maybe it wasn't profound—he *was* sitting in his room alone studying in the middle of a party—but it felt profound to him, like she'd seen something true about him, even if it was obvious.

He looked away from her crystal gaze. "Sounds about right." His cheeks heated and he hoped she didn't see. But most of all, he hoped she wouldn't leave.

He was blushing. It was the most adorable thing she'd ever seen. Actually, *he* was the most adorable thing she'd ever seen—he had this sort of shyness to him, that wasn't really shy. He didn't seem to have a problem talking to a strange girl who'd invaded his space, but there was something *solitary* about him.

That was really the best word for him. He wore aloneness like a cloak. She envied him while at the same time, felt sorry for him. But standing here talking with him was like being alone *with* someone in a way she'd never felt before.

She'd always been surrounded by people. As an only child, she'd never had the opportunity to be lonely because her parents were always bringing people around. Their employees and assistants, staff, party guests. Renee's house was a bustle of activity one hundred percent of the time and she'd copied that once she'd gotten to college. Surrounding herself with roommates and girlfriends and then her boyfriend.

Khalil had come with ready-made friends and they had all become a huge crew. She never had

a moment alone and hadn't minded. Or had she? Had she really felt suffocated by the only life she'd known? So suffocated that it was actually a relief discovering Khalil's infidelity.

Milo stood there awkwardly. Did she make him nervous? She certainly didn't want to.

A pulse of pain shot through her toes. She'd put on her shoes so as not to have to strain her neck looking at him, but now her feet hurt.

There were only two places to sit in the room, the chair at his desk and the bed. It was just a double bed, and she didn't see how he could fit in it. Maybe he just slept crossways. The thought made her giggle.

He raised his eyebrows and she tried to get herself together, but the giggles turned into a full laugh and soon she was cracking up so hard she bent over.

Milo was at her side with a hand at her elbow, leading her to the bed to sit down. Then he stood towering over her looking concerned.

"I'm okay. For god's sake, sit down."

He looked around like he wasn't sure where he should sit in his own room, so she slid over to make room on the bed for him. The expression on his face when he sat next to her was priceless—both frightened and pained. She wanted to package it up and save it for all time. She also felt bad for invading his space but no way was she leaving now.

For the first time in weeks, she felt comfortable. Both in her skin and in her solitude. Being alone wasn't so bad if you were with someone like Milo.

"I was laughing thinking about how you fit on this bed."

His confused expression sent her into a fit of giggles again. She grabbed his arm once she'd collected herself. "How tall are you?"

"Six five," he said, looking at her like she was a little crazy. Maybe she was, she felt a little crazy.

"Do you, like, have to sleep diagonally?"

He looked at the bed then back at her and a grin spread across his face. "I just curl up. Isn't that how most people sleep?"

She tilted her head to look at him and shrugged. "I have no idea."

"Why is that so funny?" He didn't look annoyed just perplexed.

"Again, no idea. I'm sorry, I wasn't really laughing at you. I just…I haven't laughed in forever. Sorry."

She was still touching his arm, and it was warm beneath her fingers. He was thin, being so tall, but not reedy. There was a cord of lean muscle beneath her fingertips that she had the sudden urge to stroke. She wanted to see him without his shirt on, she wanted to find out what he felt like, how hot his skin was and if she could make him moan. She really wanted to hear him moan.

An image of him crowded into that tiny shower popped into her head. Water on his body, muscles bunching as he crouched.

"What are you thinking about now?" he whispered. She didn't know how much of her thoughts had made their way to her face, but she was at a loss for words.

Gazing at him, she kept getting caught on his lips. They were full and kissable and suddenly she couldn't think of anything else.

She leaned forward, his lips the only thing in her vision. But he backed away.

"Oh shit. I'm sorry." She shook her head, mortification spreading over her. "Fuck." She pulled her hand away and ran it through her hair before hiding her face.

"You have a girlfriend," she said at the same time he said, "Were you drinking?"

His expression was concerned, not angry. She checked her breath. "No, do I smell like alcohol?"

He shook his head.

"So why did you ask me that?"

"I don't know, for a second there you seemed… drunk?" He lifted a shoulder, his gaze on her lips as well.

Understanding dawned and she felt a rush of affection for him, even more than before. "So, I'd have to be drunk to kiss you?"

His eyes widened and his mouth opened but nothing came out.

"Do you have a girlfriend?"

He shook his head.

"You just don't want to kiss me?"

Once again, his eyes betrayed him by roaming to her lips and staying there. "It's not that."

"What is it?"

"I don't even know you."

"I'm Renee. I crossed the police tape to see what was up here that was so precious we weren't supposed to find it. I found you." She leaned into him and felt his breath on her cheek. He smelled like peppermint and it only made her want to kiss him more.

"Police tape?" His eyes were guileless, so open and innocent.

She waved the question away. "Don't ask." She wasn't sure what it was about him, but she wanted to find out. "So?"

"So?" he whispered, a hair's breadth away. It was like they were being towed together by an invisible line.

"Can I kiss you?" Her lips were nearly brushing his they were so close. The peppermint invaded her nostrils and somehow turned her on even more.

"If you want."

There was no distance to close. His lips on hers were warm and sensual. A trill rippled up her spine as they came together. She wrapped her arms around him; his hands moved tentatively to her waist. Sparks erupted under her skin where he touched her. Even through the fabric, his fingers felt right and strong. She slid over into his lap and straddled him. His shock transmitted through the kiss, but he recovered quickly and his palms slid down to cup her ass, bringing her closer. Now she was flush with his growing erection. He swelled against her panties, drawing a gasp from her.

Her dress had ridden up to her thighs leaving them cold, but the rest of her body was hot. He kissed like she imagined he did everything, with focus and deliberation. With one hundred percent of his of himself and extraordinary attention to detail. He was thorough. Her mouth was plundered. His tongue stroked hers so completely, it was like she'd never experienced a kiss before today—this was so different.

Heat shot through her and her exposed thighs finally warmed as the pressure of his hands on her ass increased when he tilted her down. Her back hit the mattress and he was on top of her, keeping the weight off her body with his knees. Legs wrapped around him, and the fever between her thighs was growing. She broke her mouth away and gasped for breath.

"Take off your shirt."

He licked his lips and rose to do as she asked. She missed his hands on her butt, but it was worth it when he lifted his shirt to reveal cords of lean muscle on his slim frame. She sat up, running her hands down his chest then kissed everywhere she could reach. And then she got what she wanted, a moan. A deep one pulled from his diaphragm that shot her panties with moisture. He moaned so good. It should be illegal.

Milo had made out with a few girls—in the closet while playing Seven Minutes in Heaven, on couches in basement rec rooms, beneath the bleachers at high school dances. His freshman year, before he started avoiding large gatherings of people, he'd had too much to drink one night and made out with his roommate's sister, which had been a mistake.

But making out with Renee made him feel like whatever he'd been doing before should be classified as a different activity altogether. Her skin was so soft and smooth, she smelled like sunshine and happiness. He couldn't believe how responsive she was, her whole body shuddered when he touched her.

He drew back to look down at her, hair spread on his pillow, and took a mental picture. A part of him was convinced this was some kind of hallucination. He needed to remember it accurately once he returned to consciousness.

She smiled drowsily and he rested his head next to hers, breathing heavily. Within a few moments, she'd rolled into him, forcing him to lay on his back with her tucked under his arm.

She drew lazy circles on his chest with her blue-tipped fingernail. "So why don't you do parties? Don't you like fun?"

He lifted a lock of her dark hair and rubbed it between his fingers. "You got it, I hate fun. Death to all fun. What, do you think I'm the Grinch?"

She giggled and the sound shot through his bones, filling him with warmth.

"I like certain kinds of parties, but these huge, faceless crowds that invade every corner of the house, those aren't the right kind."

She turned on her side and looked up at him, her eyes bottomless and open. "So what kind of parties do you like?"

"Smaller ones. Where you can actually talk to people. Where you can dance without crashing into everyone, and hear each other, and get to know people."

"You dance?"

He shifted, cupping her shoulder and kissing the top of her head. Hoping to avoid the topic. But, of course, Renee was having none of that.

She hopped out of bed and held out her hands. "Dance with me."

The music from downstairs bled through the walls, a driving, EDM track he suspected you had to be on Molly to truly enjoy. "To this?" He shook his head.

"You don't have any music playing devices up here?" She turned on her heel and crossed to the desk, then bent to inspect the shelf under the window. He couldn't help but look at her ass, pointed in his direction, and suppressed a groan. His dick was still painfully hard and embarrassingly visible in his sweat pants.

She tossed a glance over her shoulder and smirked when she caught him staring. A snap of her fingers draw his attention back to her face. "You have vinyl?"

He nodded and sat up, scrubbing a hand over his face. Adjusting his pants as best he could, he rose and paced over to her.

She kneeled in front of the shelf full of records, flipping through them. "Why vinyl? Do you have a record player?"

He chuckled. "Of course I have a record player. You think these are decoration?"

"These aren't even new, they're antiques."

"They were my dad's."

When her gaze hit him, he realized he'd let too much emotion into his voice. This girl was perceptive as hell. He held his breath, waiting for her to ask, but after a few moments she went back to scrutinizing the albums.

"We can dance to this," she announced, holding up a sleeve featuring a woman looking out a window expressively.

Milo paused, surprised. This had been one of Dad's favorites. The model on the cover resembled his mother, and he remembered sneaking down the steps, long after he was supposed to be in bed, to spy on his parents dancing barefoot to this song in the kitchen.

He pulled the album from her hands and their fingers brushed. Though she'd touched far more of him, the contact still made his breath catch. To cover his reaction, he turned quickly and crossed to the stereo, which really was an antique, but it was his dad's too and he'd never give it up while it still played. Maybe not even afterwards.

The opening organ of Percy Sledge's "When a Man Loves a Woman" filled the little room. Renee's arms wrapped around his waist from behind. He turned into her embrace and slid his hands down her back.

"I should get my shoes," she said. Though she was pint-sized, she fit him perfectly. He shook his head. When she went to pull away, he grasped her waist and hauled her up. Her legs came around him, her arms circling his neck. Her body pressed against him was sweet agony, and they danced like that, her clinging to him, attached to him, chest to chest, heart to heart.

"See," he said into her hair. "This is my kind of party."

She laughed and squeezed him tighter. His hands grabbed her butt to keep her in place, and she sighed against his neck.

"Mine too," she whispered so soft he almost didn't hear.

Renee woke up warm. It was odd because she was never warm when she woke up alone, but a wall of heat burned at her side. She pried her eyes open to find the sun shining into her room from the wrong side—then last night came rushing back to her.

Milo was still asleep, his face slackened and peaceful and beautiful in the morning light. She couldn't see his hazel eyes, but his lips beckoned to her. She kissed him gently, and he smiled in his sleep.

Her bladder was full, so she slipped out of bed to the bathroom across the hall. The cold, wood floor stung the bottoms of her feet. She ran back into his room to find him rubbing his face, staring at the spot where she'd lain as if confused. A huge grin broke onto his face when he saw her.

"It's freezing in here in the morning," she said, rubbing her arms.

"Then come back to bed." He opened the covers to her. She dove in on top of him, settling into the warmth of his arms, resting her head on his chest.

"Sorry I conked out on you," he said.

She didn't know how long they'd danced. Record after record had gone by and she hadn't wanted to stop, but at some point they'd fallen onto the bed and, apparently, into comas.

An apology was written on his face and she kissed it away. "Milo. Why haven't we met before?"

He brushed a strand of hair off her forehead before tracing her lips with his finger. "Cause you're not real."

"I'm not?" She raised her eyebrows.

"Nope. Not real. Just an imaginary girl who showed up at my door last night trying to escape the best party of the year."

"That must make you imaginary, too." She trailed a finger up his chest then stroked the emerging stubble on his chin.

"Why? I'm not impossible."

"What makes you say that?"

He lifted his shoulders. "I'm just Milo."

"And I'm just Renee."

"No, there's no such thing. You're like the sun, full of light. I've seen you out there. You always have a bunch of people around you, hanging off everything you say. You have a campus radio show, you write for the newspaper, you feed homeless kids on the weekends. You're a force of nature, Renee."

"How do you know so much about me?" She tilted her head to regard him anew. Last night he hadn't given any indication that he recognized her. How had she not seen him before? She would have remembered someone like him, so tall and beautiful.

He shrugged.

"We've never had any classes together, have we?"

"Freshman English. Econ last semester."

"You were in my Econ class?" She was incredulous. He nodded. "With Professor Akanbe?"

"Yup." He smiled a half smile and looked away, his hold on her loosening.

She thought back. Khalil had been in that class with her and she'd been so wrapped up in him, so wrapped up in who they'd been she hadn't noticed anything outside that little world. Shame filled her.

"That just proves I'm real. I'm a jerk. I don't know how I couldn't have noticed you."

He'd grown far away. Even though she was right there with him, his heart only inches from her lips, he was retreating. She could feel it.

"Why would you have?" His voice was hushed.

She forced him to look at her, sliding a hand to cup his cheek. With an unwavering gaze, she kissed him, slowly, remembering their first kiss and how she'd never felt anything like it before. He kissed her back just as thoroughly as before, with just as much focus. It thrilled her. She would make sure he knew how real she thought he was.

She slid her hand underneath his boxers and stroked him. She kept stroking until his throat vibrated with a rumble that made her bones melt. Then he pulled his lips away.

"What?" she said, chest heaving.

He shook his head and before she knew it, she'd been flipped onto her back with him on top. She was still in the dress she'd worn all night. He slid up the skirt, hands grazing her thighs until her hem was at her waist and her panties were revealed. Then he kept pushing the dress up, helping her out of it until she lay in her bra and panties blushing under his perusal.

He didn't seem to know where to look first. He took her in with tiny darts of his eyes; an eternity passed before his mouth descended onto her breasts, pulling her nipple between his teeth with the fabric of her bra as a barrier. She shifted to undo the clasp, pulling it away from her body to give him better access.

He licked her nipple, then bit it gently and the sensation shot straight between her legs. She trembled with need as he savored her breasts with his tongue. Propped on one elbow, his other hand caressed the underside of her thigh, then pulled it around him as he leaned his weight into her, his erection pressing at her core.

She was aflame, the well of arousal running deep until she couldn't take it anymore. Ripping at the waistband of his boxers, she pulled them down along with his sweats, wanting him inside her so much she was unwilling to wait through any more foreplay. She was so wet, responding to his slow, methodical tongue which pulled pleasure from the deep recesses of her body.

"Condom. Now," she ordered. Eyes unfocused, he shifted to the nightstand and pulled out an unopened box. She tried to be patient as he ripped open a packet, but couldn't keep her hands off him. Her fingers roamed his chest, his back, his dick, be-fore he swatted her hand away so he could sheath himself.

She swallowed as the cold air hit her wet nipples—wanting to pull him back down on top of her, inside of her and keep him there. Both her legs wrapped around him, she arched her back to get closer. All too slowly, he guided himself home. As he sunk in, a flutter built within her chest and needed to escape. She let out a sound she never had before as he seated himself all the way inside her. It was more battle cry than groan and vibrated in her throat as it came out.

Thankfully, Milo muted her with a kiss, his hands on her ass cheeks, spreading them apart as he drove into her. Though her eyes were open, she couldn't see anything. She could only feel the way he slid in and out, feel his fevered skin beneath her hands everywhere she touched. Hear their labored breaths mingling as they both struggled for air. The gentle roars escaping from him spurred her on. She clawed down his back, begging for more with her body, unable to speak coherently.

She reached up to grab the headboard and isolate the movement of her lower half, pushing up to meet him thrust for thrust, the trembling in her legs making its way up her body. Her hair even trembled.

The orgasm built from inside, nurtured by Milo's deep thrusts, which impaled her in the best possible way. He demanded more from her. The unassuming boy she'd stumbled upon, who'd focused on her exclusively, required that she meet his demands. She rose to the challenge. Right before she flew apart, her vision returned and she found his gaze on her. Tears sprang to her eyes and then she was subsumed in pleasure that was felt in each strand of her hair. It pulsed outward like a supernova, infinite energy and blinding light. A star being born inside her.

Milo's own shouts brought her back to herself. He shook above her and collapsed, mingling their sweat and breaths. Her body thought it had run a half-marathon. She'd never put this much effort into sex, though this hadn't been a chore—it was effortless—but took everything from her. She was stripped bare, literally and figuratively, and the look on Milo's face showed he was similarly affected.

She felt cracked open like an egg, like everything was seeping out of her and melting into goo right there on the bed. Though it was a long time before she could move, she knew she had to leave as soon as possible.

Milo saw things no one had seen before. His knowing gaze sent shivers through her spine, and she couldn't escape. Solitary scholar was right. He'd been studying her all night. Half of her wondered what he'd found, but the other half did not want to find out.

Renee walked through the campus in a fog, looking over her shoulder every other minute, sure she'd seen a glimpse of a tall form from the corner of her eye. But he was never there.

It was stupid. She was the one who had left. Crawled out of the warm, comfortable bed, afraid to admit how too much comfort was uncomfortable. In that moment, she couldn't handle whatever had just happened and thought it better to leave a one-night stand before she was asked to leave.

But would Milo have asked her to leave? She knew the answer in the marrow of her bones, but ignored it.

The cold seeped into her skin. She drew her coat closer and pulled out her hat, but it didn't help.

Khalil had always hated her hat, specifically he hated hat-head and wasn't that stupid? She used to walk around letting her head get cold because of someone else's preferences. But Khalil had also never looked so deeply within her that she felt exposed and vulnerable. She never would have thought she'd want that, until Milo.

The shiver that came over her was immune to wool and down lining. It was from the memory of his hands over her, gentle and exploring, testing her, requiring things she wasn't ready to give.

She ducked into the Communications building and took the elevator down to the basement. Right before she stepped into the campus radio station, her phone rang. She tensed—hope surging from some hidden place inside her. Had he found her number somehow? But no, it was her dad. Or rather his assistant, since he rarely had time to call.

"Hi, Gloria."

"Renee, how is everything?" Gloria's voice was warm but clipped. Dad kept her really busy, but she could always get anything Renee needed. Too bad she couldn't get her a new brain.

"Good, everything's good. What's up?"

"Haven't heard back from you about your parents' annual white party."

Renee sighed. Senator Brookes's charity event got a lot of press in the social pages and it always looked best if the whole family was in attendance. Renee paused, leaning against the wall, her head in her hand.

"I don't know if I can make it this year," she said, not knowing exactly why she was hesitant to go. The glamour and buzz of her parents' parties had always appealed to her—or had they?

She was struck by the thought that she'd rather hang out with Milo in his third-floor sanctuary than be at any party ever. But she pushed the idea from her mind. That wasn't her life—she was out in the world and not hidden away like a hermit.

Gloria exacted from her a strong promise to try, and Renee said she would.

"Glo," she said as the woman began to get off the call.

"Yes?"

"How are they?" Her voice caught in her throat. She hadn't spoken to either of her parents in weeks, only to their proxies—either Gloria or her mom's personal assistant, Dean.

"They're good."

"Of course they are." Renee hung up, sighing. The Senator and his wife were always good, no matter what.

Her radio show's producer, a senior who she wasn't sure ever left the station, greeted her when she entered. Renee sat at the board, staring at all the blinking lights, willing her stray thoughts into place. Over the course of the next hour, she played nothing but classic soul: Otis Redding, Sam Cooke, Wilson Pickett, Carla Thomas, Mary Wells.

She kept her banter light, even though her heart was heavy. When it came time to take listener requests, she perked up. Milo had known about her show. He didn't say he listened, but he might—and maybe he'd even call in? What would she do if she heard his voice live on the air?

But as the show came to a close with no calls from him, her spirits dimmed. She'd left after all. What did she expect?

She packed her bag as the outro ran, then slipped out of the studio passing the next host on the way in. He was a guy that had been in their circle of friends—he and Renee used to be cool. But he got Khalil in the breakup and now they didn't even speak.

Outside, she stopped to zip up her bag. Awareness tingled up her spine and she turned around slowly to look up, and up. She couldn't release the smile that wanted to form—anguish caught her in a stranglehold.

Milo stood next to the door to the stairwell. He looked just as he had in his room, hands stuffed in his pockets, shoulders hunched a little, his beautiful mouth twisted into a wry grin. But his eyes were sad.

Her body longed to launch herself at him, but she held back. His melancholy gaze was still sharp. He saw more than she wanted, and she longed to cover herself, to hide in the crowd the way she always did, avoiding the scrutiny.

"Hey," she said, stuffing her hands in her pockets, mimicking his stance. His face fell as he withdrew his hands. He thought she was mocking him.

"Hey."

Silence hung thickly between them. He was staring at a space behind her on the wall, a frown creasing his forehead. He pulled something from his pocket and held it out to her. "I guess you left this." He held out a tiny gold hoop earring.

She touched her earlobe. She could have sworn she put both of those earrings on this morning. And were those even the ones she'd worn to the party? But her left ear was bare.

When she reached out for it, Milo dropped the earring into her hand, careful not to touch her.

"Thanks." Their gazes locked, but she didn't know what else to say.

He shrugged. "No problem."

"Renee!" a voice called from behind her. She turned to find the station manager standing in the hallway. "I need to talk to you about next month's schedule."

"Okay, one sec," she said then turned back to Milo. But he was already half-way down the hall, making fast time with those impossibly long legs. Her heart sank, and she forced the tears back from her eyes.

Delilah's purple painted fingertips scratch at the fabric of her skirt. She smooths the material before brushing one of her long dreadlocks from her shoulder. When she looks up again, her supervisor, Neenah's, expression has not changed.

"You were doing so well," Neenah says, with a sigh. Delilah nods, she *had* been particularly pleased with herself.

"You'd done your research and executed a plan that was simple but effective."

Delilah smiles. "Humans are naturally curious, and often the ones who follow all the rules are the same ones who justify breaking them."

"Yes, yes, breaking the boy's lock and predicting that the girl would be compelled to cross the police tape was all fine. Unusual, but perfectly within regulations." Neenah's green eyes narrow. She's gotten the hang of taking on human form now and almost never slips into her elemental form unless she plans to. She's even mastered the art of controlling her facial expressions to convey specific meanings, like intimidation.

Neenah leans across her desk and motions to the tablet sitting there with the latest progress report on Delilah's mission. "But how long has it been since they last saw each other?"

"Well, technically Renee *saw* Milo yesterday coming out of the library. You see, I arranged a little accident to befall his laptop so he would be forced to—"

"Not. What. I. Meant."

Neenah's command of anger is also exemplary. Delilah blinks rapidly, almost without thinking. These motions have become second nature given all the time she's spent on Earth lately.

"It's been a week since I rematerialized her earring in his room," she offers.

"Your window of opportunity is narrowing." Neenah shakes her head, a little too jerkily to be considered natural. "Close this case in the next three days or you will be assigned a Field Coordinator."

Delilah's shudder is one hundred percent natural. "Yes, ma'am. I—I won't let you down."

Neenah nods and de-manifests, dissipating into column of smoke.

Delilah pulls the tablet toward her, and engages the communication mode. "Requisitions Department? Yes, I'm going to need a couple of invitations."

Renee debated going to her parents' white party up until the moment she got in her car and started the drive home. It wasn't like she was doing anything else, but the thought of being around so many people, of smiling and glad-handing and turning on the Renee Brookes the world expected to see was exhausting.

For the entire forty-five-minute drive, she considered turning around and heading back to her room on campus and spending the night with the Bennet sisters and Mr. Darcy. But she stayed the course, and all too soon she was pulling into her family's gated driveway.

Her mother's assistant, Dean, greeted her at the door. "You're late, and the missus is in a state."

"When is she not?" Renee responded with an eye roll.

Dean shrugged just as his cell phone rang. He shook his head and answered his Bluetooth all while shooing her up the stairs.

The decorators were putting the finishing touches on the house, fluffing flower arrangements, and hiding the cables for the festive but moody lighting they'd added. Mouthwatering scents wafted up from the kitchen, where the caterers were making their magic.

Renee's bedroom hadn't changed since she went away to college. The walls were plastered with photos of her and her friends—the people who constantly surrounded her all through school, but who she barely even talked to anymore. The images staring down at her only served to underscore the gnawing ache in her middle.

The grandfather clock struck. Guests would be arriving soon and Renee needed to get ready.

She'd picked out the dress months ago, when the idea of the party was still exciting and didn't fill her with dread. The vintage, off the shoulder gown was classy but still sexy, with pearl buttons and ivory lace covering the skirt. After pinning up her hair, she took a selfie, but wasn't sure what to do with it.

She wanted to send the photo to Milo. Would he like the dress? If she posted it online, would he see? Did he lurk on her Instagram account? She stared at her phone until the screen went off.

A knock at the door jerked her back to the present. She called out and Dean poked his head in and whistled. She smiled, giving him a little twirl.

"Honey, you look fierce tonight. Jaws will definitely drop." He squinted and tilted his head. "What's wrong, sweetie?"

Before she could answer, his cell phone rang again. Renee shook her head. "Nothing." The shrill ring tone set her teeth on edge and this time it was her doing the shooing.

"I'm fine, promise," she said. He gave her a long look before closing the door.

She turned to her vanity mirror. If she was going to get through this, she needed to put her game face on. She hefted her makeup kit onto the table and proceeded to paint on the perfect girl.

Fully armored and shielded with a thanks to whatever god had created Sephora, Renee went downstairs to face the firing squad. She was a bit more than fashionably late and was immediately set upon by family friends, important donors, respected constituents, and other guests, all cooing and telling her how happy they were to see her. She smiled and posed for pictures with people she didn't know. The responsibility of being a Brookes was so deeply ingrained, she did much of it on autopilot.

In fact, her whole life felt like it had been on autopilot since leaving Milo's room a week ago.

Her parents expertly flitted through the crowd. Through the mass of partygoers, she got brief glimpses of her father's distinguished, bald head and her mother's elegant coif, but didn't actually see them up close until the speech-slash-photo-op where the Senator thanked everyone for attending and spoke briefly about whatever charity this year's party supported. Refugees from a war-torn country or school lunches for deserving, but impoverished young children, or something. Renee's mind had wandered, though she made sure her smile was perfectly welded into place.

After the applause died down and the music started up again, her mother cornered her. She wasted no time with a greeting, gave no acknowledgement that this was the first time Mary Brookes had seen her daughter in months. She just went straight in to the topic on her mind.

"Honey, where's your date?"

Renee frowned. "Date?"

"That boy you were dating? Carl? Chris?"

"Khalil, mother." Saying his name didn't even bring the bile it used to. "And we're not dating anymore."

"Hmm." Her mother flashed a smile at a passing attendee and drew Renee a little closer. "I could have sworn he was on the guest list."

"I promise I didn't put him there." And neither Dean nor Gloria would have, Renee was sure of it.

Her mother waved her wrist around as if it made little difference, then dashed off when someone more important called her name. A sick feeling took hold in Renee's gut.

She wasn't even surprised when she turned and saw Khalil coming toward her, walking with his usual swagger. Anger welled up inside.

"Renee," he said, greeting her like they were still friends, like they were still anything. She stalked away to the kitchen where the staff were preparing the dessert trays.

Khalil's presence behind her was wrong. She whirled to face him, taking in his handsome, bland features, wondering what had ever drawn her in. "What are you doing here?"

He grinned. "I got an invitation. Great party."

"Why did you even want to come?"

"The Brookes' annual white party? Who wouldn't want to come? Besides," he said, moving closer to stroke her cheek with an ice-cold finger. "I think we should clear up our little misunderstanding."

She jerked away but found herself backed against the counter. "What misunderstanding?" Her skin was literally crawling, trying to get away from him.

"The one where you thought that girl meant something to me. She didn't. It was just a fuck."

"And I was just your girlfriend. You don't get to fuck other girls when you have a girlfriend."

"Well, to be fair, I don't think we ever specified that."

Renee's eyes widened. "You can't be serious."

"But if that's the way you want to roll, then I can handle it. I promise, it will never happen again."

"Renee!" Someone called her name. She peered around Khalil to find a photographer pointing a lens at her. Why there was a photographer in the kitchen, she had no idea, but this particular paparazzo was familiar.

Though the camera covered the young woman's face, her purple dreadlocks were unmistakable.

Khalil stepped to Renee's side and put an arm around her. Though confusion swirled in her mind, the smile was automatic, ingrained from years of charm school and cotillions and that one summer her mother had believed models could be five feet three inches tall. Whenever a lens faced her, whenever anyone's attention was on her at all, she smiled. *I'm like a trained dog.*

"Great shot!" the strange photographer said and then turned to disappear back into the fray.

"Wait!" Renee called, too late. She started after her, but Khalil's hold on her shoulder pulled her back. His touch sat on her skin like cold grease.

Then another thought stopped her short—what if Milo saw that picture? Suddenly, she feared she may throw up.

"So, baby," Khalil said, sliding his arm around her again, like he had for the pose.

She pulled away and turned on him. "Don't call me baby. We're never getting back together."

His brows drew down. "Why?"

She stepped as close to him as she could stand to whisper, "Cause you never gave me an orgasm I could feel in my hair, that's why." And then she walked out of the party and straight to her car.

It had been a week, so Milo decided to wash his sheets. They didn't smell like her anymore and it was pathetic to keep sniffing, trying to catch a whiff of her scent in them. The house's washer worked only twenty-five percent of the time, so he headed out to the laundromat on the corner.

A few other students lounged in the chairs or laid across the wide tables, either studying or sleeping. The TV on the wall played the local news. As he filled his washers, the newscasters engaged in what they must have thought was witty banter. Milo was only half listening until the words "Senator Brookes' white party" pricked his eardrums.

He sat heavily, transfixed by the screen, as stills from the event rolled by. Not only were her parents black royalty, they also looked like movie stars. His breath caught in his chest when a photo featuring Renee popped up. The newscasters hurried on to the sports report, but Milo couldn't get the image of Renee out of his head.

It was almost easier to believe he'd made the whole thing up than think for a moment she had been with him last weekend, dancing to classic R&B from his dad's collection.

If it had all been a figment of his imagination, then he just might be a creative genius. He should give up engineering and study art instead—painting, or maybe he could learn to play the saxophone. That way he could use the swept up pieces of his heart for something useful, not just pining over a girl who was never real in the first place.

When the laundry finished, he stuffed it back in the bag and headed home. The house was quiet, no parties tonight. A few roommates lazed on the couches downstairs, playing video games or texting. He almost wished for the chaos and the noise of the week before. It would have been a good distraction from sitting in his room alone—something that had never bothered him before. Not before she appeared in his doorway, like some kind of fallen angel.

He climbed to the third floor, vaguely aware of soft music coming from up there. Maybe from the phantom roommate who kept vampire hours. He pushed open his bedroom door—he should get around to fixing that lock—and stopped short.

Renee stood next to the record player in a heavenly white dress. If Milo had taken anything stronger than Ibuprofen that day, he would have thought he was on some kind of trip.

Her expression was sheepish. She looked up at him through lowered eyelashes. He stepped fully into the room and dropped the laundry bag. And stared.

Her phone was plugged into the stereo. The song that had been playing ended abruptly and she was pulling up another.

The opening chords of Sam Smith's "Stay With Me" filled the room and broke him out of his fog. He closed the door and crossed over to her, without feeling his feet move.

She swayed slightly, still in her angel dress, barefoot again, a pair of white heels next to his desk chair.

She held out her hands and he grabbed hold of them, this time ready for the electricity that pulsed through him when their skin touched. He pulled her closer until her head rested on his chest.

And then they began to dance.

Every feeling he'd been trying not to feel for the past week came out full force, threatening to break him. When the song ended, he stepped back. She looked up, eyes overflowing with tears.

Milo cupped her face in his hands and brushed away the wetness with his thumbs. "I saw you on TV tonight."

A look of horror and regret crossed her face. "I don't know who invited him."

"Invited who?"

She shook her head. "My ex. I wasn't sure if you saw—if they showed…"

"No. I mean, I'm not sure. But that's not—"

"Listen Milo, I wanted to apologize. I'm not used to people really seeing me. Nobody ever seems to. There's this girl who's an extension of her parents' brand, whose picture gets in the paper but the caption only ever says 'and daughter'. You said I wasn't real—you were right."

Her tears came faster now, and shame punched him in the gut for the fact that he'd had any part in putting them there. "That's not what I meant."

"No, it's okay. I mean it's not, but you know that." She sniffed. "I left that day because it hurt too much, being seen. It felt like standing naked in the middle of campus."

He couldn't *not* pull her into his arms then. But she was still too far away, so he lifted her, and sat in the desk chair with her on his lap. "You weren't naked in the middle of campus, you were just naked with me."

That brought a little smile to her face. "I know. And…." She swallowed before meeting his eyes. "It's kind of the only way I want to be."

"Naked?"

She laughed and nodded. "With you."

Her eyes were hopeful, staring up at him. He was speechless. He leaned in to kiss her and fell all the way down. The kiss was slow, full of things unsaid. Full of hope and care and tenderness.

She rested soft against his chest. He held her tightly, breathing her in.

"So…" she said, tracing a pattern on the exposed skin of his neck.

"So?"

"About that naked part? Can we start now?"

He laughed and carried her to the bed.

Delilah backs away from the window and floats down to the ground. In a shadowy alley surrounded by trash cans, she transforms into her human form, scaring a patchy gray cat who squawks and bounds away.

"Sorry," she calls out, the bells in her hair tinkling merrily.

She approaches the purple Volkswagen Beetle parked on the corner and turns back to Milo's house with a smile. "I love my job," she says, before hopping into her car and driving off to her next assignment.

Copyright © 2018 by L. Penelope.

Juliet Marillier is a multi Aurealis, Tin Duck, and Sir Julius Vogel Award winner and recipient of the Le Prix Imaginales for her historical fantasy fiction. Her novels are published simultaneously by major publishers in United States and Australia and are translated into other languages all around the world. Known for combining folkloric fantasy with historical fiction, her novels are often filled with sensitive depictions of the transformative journey a person can go through, metaphorically and physically, to protect their family and future partner—even characters who once thought themselves too broken or incapable of love. Born in New Zealand, Juliet now resides in Western Australia with a delightful menagerie of elderly dogs.

JACK'S DAY

by Juliet Marillier

The waves wash in at my feet, lapping against the rocks that cradle me. The sun is making its slow dive into the inky waters of the Indian Ocean. No surfers linger at the Point.

I'm starting to feel chilly and thinking a glass of red would go down nicely. But something holds me. A voice whispers, *DON'T GO YET, BETH. STAY WITH ME A WHILE LONGER.*

The wind stirs my hair, intimate as a lover's breath. Oh, Jack. If you'd stayed longer with me, how different things might have been. You could have seen all our son's milestones: the first ride without trainer wheels, the first day at school, the first football match. The first girlfriend—I'm glad she didn't last—and the first holiday with his mates. Goals kicked, exams passed, graduation day…. "You might have had a daughter, Jack," I murmur as the sun touches the water. I imagine a little girl with his curls and dimpled chin. "You might have had the dog you always talked about. You might have coached Rick's team and gone fishing on the weekends. We might have grown old together, loving each other a bit more every day."

Gulls fly over me, their harsh comments mocking my flight of fancy. Might have, could have…what's the point of that? Suddenly the beach feels empty, the rocks too big, too dark, the ocean immense and powerful. My footprints make a track down from the dunes and along the sand to this, my thinking place. A lonely track.

The sun's setting. Time for the ritual. I stand, lift my arms, hold my head high. I think about the two of them, Jack and Bill, mates serving together in a war most of the country didn't understand. Jack was a shooting star, one of the SAS's youngest, lauded, decorated, sent off on one secret mission after another, doing things he never talked about, though I saw them slowly darken his eyes. Bill was a plodder, an infantryman, three tours of duty in a hell-hole of swamp and jungle and snipers in the dark, till the day they wheeled him off the transport with a head full of monsters and one leg blasted to nothing. Jack never came home.

I whisper into the wind. "Happy Birthday, Jack. I love you. I miss you." A last sliver of gold flashes at the rim of the world and is gone. The beach is full of shadows. Time to go home.

The driveway's empty, the house deserted. Inside, I take a quick look in the fridge. Outside, magpies exchange evening warbles. The sound of a car, passing, fading. Jack's photo on the wall: Trooper John Miller, SASR. Strong shoulders under the camouflage. Sunset hair under the sandy beret. Sea-blue eyes, bright as diamond and hard as steel. February 1940—August 1966. I wonder what you'd have been like now, Jack. I wonder if you could have borne the time when it all had to stop. How would it have been to wake to a day with no rushing adrenaline, no life-or-death choices? I wonder if you could ever have slowed down.

Old grief stirs in me; old weariness wraps around me, a familiar garment. It was hard in those first months after Jack was killed, when Rick was a tiny baby and my Mum got sick. I hadn't known a person could be so tired and still go on. But you do. Help comes from the least likely places. The kids grow up, and you look back and think, maybe I didn't do such a bad job after all.

I put on the kettle, get out a mug, pop in a bag of Earl Grey. Turn on the TV news to swallow the silence. Catch a glimpse of myself in the mirror and chuckle. Look at me, Jack: picture of a lonely old woman, drinking tea in the dark. At least it's not whisky.

Light flashes across Jack's handsome features as a vehicle turns into the car port. Another pulls up be-

hind it. Doors slam; kids chatter. They're here! Sally marches straight in, dumps a laden platter on the table and switches on the light. "What are you doing sitting in the dark, Mum?" My daughter-in-law casts her eye over the empty table. "You didn't forget the salads, did you?"

As Natasha comes in the door, carrying a wriggling baby and an immense pavlova, I open the fridge and start getting out the food I prepared this morning, before the heat of the day. Nat's older kids, well trained, set the table. I hear clinking sounds as the men unload bottles from the cars. By the time Rick and Matthew join us, the meal's ready. A summer feast; a celebration.

I glance at Jack's stern image. We're a tribe, I tell him. There's your son, Captain Richard Miller, SASR, enjoying his leave, pouring wine and promising his niece and nephew he'll play beach cricket in the morning. If he has shadows in his eyes, he's learned to deal with them. There's the daughter you never had, and there's her man Matthew. There are my beautiful grandchildren. I hope that doesn't make you sad. I hope it makes you smile.

"We talked to Tom on Skype last night," Sally's saying. "He's looking well. He sent his love. We don't know when he'll be home."

I ask no questions. She and Rick have just the one son: Private Thomas Miller, twenty-one this year and on his first overseas deployment. Back in the sixties, when Jack went away, I played a lot of mind games. Made crazy bargains with God. I pray Tom's girlfriend never has to go through what I did.

"I'm glad Tom's well," I say, but I feel the weight of it all.

After we've eaten we sit and talk awhile, exchanging our news. Rick proposes a toast to the father he never knew; we raise our glasses. To Jack! Happy Birthday!

The girls do the dishes. Matthew and Nat gather up their yawning kids and head for home, a five-minute drive away. Sally and Rick are staying over. We linger over our last drinks, not saying much. Beyond the fly wire, the shrill sound of cicadas overlays the wash of the waves.

"Shame Dad couldn't be here," Rick says, glancing at me. "You all right, Mum?"

I nod and we say our good nights. Later I stand on the veranda in my pyjamas, letting the sea breeze cool my skin. A familiar sound breaks the quiet, the engine of an old Holden ute. Headlights pierce the night. Home so soon? My heart clenches tight. What's happened?

The car lights go off, and he's opening the door and getting out, awkward with the prosthesis. Blue jumps down and bolts ahead to greet me with a doggy kiss. And here's Bill, limping towards me with a big smile on his tired face.

I throw my arms around my husband, loving the warmth of him, the roughness of his work-worn hands, the way he lays his cheek against my hair, still so tender after all these years.

"I wasn't expecting you back until Monday!" I say. "What happened? What about the boys?"

"The boys will cope without me this once," Bill says. "I know you said it didn't matter if I wasn't here for Jack's Day. But it felt wrong, somehow. And… well, I missed you."

I stand on tiptoe and kiss him; he smells of wood smoke. He's been at the annual reunion, a bunch of vets out bush, taming their demons and sharing the stories nobody else ever gets to hear. Bill doesn't need it any more, not for himself. But he has to go. He's the one who makes it all happen: organiser, chauffeur, counsellor and best friend. The brother they always wanted; the comrade they don't lose.

"Hungry?" I ask as we go inside. "Your daughter made her special pavlova."

Bill shakes his head. He's standing in front of Jack's photo, looking into his old friend's eyes. I expect him to wish Jack a happy birthday; that's our ritual. But what he says is, "You saved me, Beth. You know that? You pulled me out of the swamp." His voice is hushed in the stillness of the sleeping house.

I lay my hand against his back. "You saved me," I tell him. "I've been so lucky, Bill." Without him Rick would have had no father. There would be no Natasha, no Matthew, no laughing children in my life. I'm blessed with the best husband in the world, a man who lost so much and still had love to give. "I'm glad you came home."

An award-winning author and an Amazon bestseller under a different pen name, Olivette Devaux writes LGBT contemporary and paranormal romance. Her novel Like a Torrent, *book 2 of the Disorderly Elements Series, has won a Honorable Mention in the 2017 Rainbow Awards. She enjoys swimming the rivers in Pittsburgh, PA.*

I AM HERE FOR YOU

by Olivette Devaux

The Prague International Airport guided Adam into the "Arrivals" hall without his luggage, without local currency, and with a bank card that's been cut off by the overactive Fraud Prevention Department.

His guitar strap dug through his thin, short-sleeve button-down shirt. Its weight was comforting, as was the knowledge that both the cord and the small amp were securely nestled in the soft case's side pocket. His current duffle bag was stuffed to bursting with basic necessities, and for that, he was grateful.

He tried so, so very hard to keep his usual upbeat attitude, but considering he couldn't even buy a cup of coffee, optimism was a little hard to come by.

Adam searched out the exit sign. Ten in the morning meant it wasn't sweltering hot yet, not even in this hotter-than-usual June. The one-hour time change from London had left him alert even though he had to get up at an ungodly hour to make his flight.

You're not jet-lagged. Count your blessings. Although that cup of coffee wouldn't go amiss. Even instant would do.

No drummer, no luggage, no money. His parting words with Seth had been bitter—because what kind of a drummer gets drunk two days before a concert and breaks his arm at a party?

He turned on his phone, resolved to swallow the massive roaming charge and call their manager with a plea for help. As soon as his screen lit up, however, a new text came in.

I am here for you.

Adam could've cried with relief. Finally, after the nightmare of the last two days, with the money issue and the luggage issue and his severe caffeine withdrawal, his phone showed evidence of his vocal coach's undying, ever-present support. The phrase was as familiar as it was welcome. Adam wondered whether he and Maurice shared some kind of a psychic connection.

He wasn't alone, marooned in a coffee-deprived center of Europe. There was a sympathetic baritone out there who had his back. Not quite sobbing with relief, he responded immediately.

Thank you. Your support means so much to me, especially now! I'm going through a terrible time over here.

After he added a suitably sappy emoticon and pushed "send," he realized the message had not come from a known number. Slowing down this time, he typed another message.

Your name isn't showing up in my contacts. Who is this?

He pressed send, then shifted mental gears to solve his transportation issues. Before he made it to the information counter, however, his phone dinged again.

Adam stopped mid-stride and dug it out of his jeans' pocket to have a look.

I am your driver. Come out door 2 and look for a red Skoda.

Embarrassment warred with relief as he pocketed his phone and headed for the one of the many glass doors. The good news was, they sent him a driver. The bad news—he couldn't tip him until he could communicate with his bank, or unless he could break a big bill from his emergency fund.

Martin put his phone away and grinned. It looked like the star singer and lead guitarist of Sylvan Breeze had a rough morning. He had all of their music memorized, he knew all their YouTube videos by heart, and now he wondered what Adam Vanek would be like in person.

Adam's voice always made his stomach flip-flop, as though the American stranger was signing to him personally. The conceit was, of course, ridiculous. Adam had probably never heard of Martin, nor of his percussion obsession. There was no reason for him to know that Martin had played with folk groups from Iceland to Mongolia, nor that the hammer dulcimer his grandfather had built for him was now surrounded by a collection of percussion instruments from around the world.

When Martin found out that Sylvan Breeze's rhythm guy broke his arm in London, he was all too happy to double up his gigs and make use of his skills.

Not that he needed the exposure—but he'd get to play with his internet crush. Which is why he was now circling the short-term parking, hoping to pick up the amazing and almost-legendary Adam Vanek without scoring a ticket.

On his next crawl past the passenger pick-up area, his eyes honed onto to a tall, blond figure with a duffle bag and a guitar. He pulled over, turned on the hazards, and jumped out. "Adam?"

When Adam turned to him, Martin waved him over, and opened the rear door. "Hurry up! I'm not allowed to park here!"

Adam jogged over, tossed his duffle in the back, carefully set his guitar on top of it, then turned and attempted to shake his hand.

"Hurry, hurry!" Martin saw a police car creep in their direction.

They darted for their doors, hopped in and buckled up.

The police car flashed its lights, and Martin got his idling car in gear and pulled away from the curb. "Sorry," he said. "Parking here is impossible." He glanced at Adam. "You have no suitcase?"

"I do. It's in Lisbon right now." Adam let out a long, controlled exhale, and sank into his seat. "Thank you for picking me up," he said slowly. "My name is Adam."

Martin turned to him while driving, offering his hand. "I'm Martin Sklar," he chirped. "I'm your new drummer."

Adam's shook his, letting go right away, presumably so Martin could drive. That was kind of too bad, because Martin would've eagerly traded down to an automatic transmission car, just to be able to hold Adam's hand for a while longer.

His warm, smooth palm.

His long fingers, so skilled and sensuous on the guitar. Adam's callused finger-pads were a testimony to his dedication to music.

With his peripheral vision, Martin saw Adam shift in his seat and rearrange his long limbs to have a better look at him. He felt heat rise up his neck and to his cheeks. Being carefully studied by his idol made it hard to pay attention to the convoluted traffic patterns.

"Oh. Okay." Adam wrung his hands. "I take it they sent you because you're the newest member of the band?" He was looking ahead now, and a glance told Martin that Adam was gripping the sissy strap above the door pretty hard.

"Oh, no! I insisted." He downshifted, letting the engine rev before he switched lanes and passed a trailer that had been slowing the traffic in their lane. "And I am not in your band, not really. I am only volunteering for the duration of the festival."

He felt, rather than saw, Adam's head whirl back toward him. "Volunteering?"

"Yes," Martin said happily. "I'm a big fan."

There was no mistaking Adam's groan. In retrospect, Martin realized his error. No luggage, no drummer, a festival far away from home—and one of the band's key positions was being filled by an unknown entity who was "a big fan." Martin swallowed hard. "Don't worry," he said, trying not to wince. "I know all your songs, and I know how to drum a little bit." He phrased it like that, because the Czech culture had beaten boasting out of every little boy by the time he reached third grade.

Boasting was unattractive.

He couldn't very well say that he was a kick-ass percussionist on anything and everything that caught his eye. Hell, he could play a set of garbage cans and make them sound good—but again, that would be *boasting.*

He saw Adam settle into a deep, almost deliberate breathing pattern. Weird, that. It was as though the guy was trying to meditate. When they were well outside of Prague city limits, Adam broke the silence unexpectedly. His sexy baritone was as mellifluous as Martin remembered it from all his songs. "Thank you for volunteering, Martin," he said with smooth confidence. "I'm sure we'll be great!"

The little hotel near castle Tocnik was booked solid. Even Jennie, his bassist, and Aleeta, a vocal-ist who played the keyboard, got lucky when two German jugglers offered to share a room with them. "This is Greta and Frieda," Jennie introduced them. "I'm sorry, Adam. I have no idea what to do. I asked the others, but everyone's slammed!" She twirled her braid nervously and leaned in. "Even the local farmers have their hay lofts packed. Some performers are staying up at the castle, camping. But our gear's safe, and there's a drum set. You can find it all in here."

Adam nodded grimly and accepted a business card with a numerical code hand-written on the back. "This is the portable storage unit number, and that's the combination to get to our stuff. And Martin here knows where things are, too."

No luggage, no money, and now, nowhere to sleep. Time to visit a local farmer and ask Martin to be his interpreter. Martin and his "I'm a big fan, I can drum a little" can-do attitude, and his crazy driving habits.

"Okay." Adam nodded. "Let's meet for a quick rehearsal after..." He glanced at his phone and thought a bit. "At four? Let's cut those drum solos out so we'll have a bit of slack tomorrow."

Martin nudged him from the side. "We already played a little. Don't worry, it will be okay." His English was oddly accented, as though he had learned the British version, but was smooth from frequent use.

"But the solos," Adam started intently. "Did you… can you…."

Their eyes met in a fierce clash of wills, of doubt and confidence, of fear and joy.

"I can! Don't worry. I made no changes." Martin's face lit up with an accommodating smile. "If you don't mind, you can stay with me. I have an extra sleeping roll."

Somehow, Adam found it hard not to smile back.

On their way back to the car, as the reality of having to camp at a major music festival began to truly sink in, Adam realized he began to let go of his preconceptions and of the tenuous pretense of control he maintained at most other times. He was willing, unusually, to wing it—I mean his luggage was already in another country. Once he gave in to the crazy, spontaneous flow of unlikely events, the knot in his stomach began to transform into that light, pre-show buzzy feeling he knew and loved. Yes, it was adrenaline, but his jitters mellowed from worrying about logistics into a more positive vibe, the sort that came with the anticipation of a good run and a receptive audience.

Looming emergencies no longer threatened to tear his composure apart. The girls were set, the gear was secured, he had his guitar and a change of clothes. What could go wrong?

"Is there coffee where you live?" he asked Martin with a hopeful gleam in his eye.

Martin doubted Adam had even absorbed any of the countryside around them. The rolling hills, the small villages they had passed through on the way from the airport, the narrow country roads lined with the public fruit trees whose apples and cherries were still too small, and too green, to pick.

He doubted that even now, Adam was paying attention to the spectacular approach to Castle Tocnik itself. The gravel road curved up the hill topped with an old granite cliff, the peak of which rose above a steep gulley, creating a sheer drop higher than a six-story office building.

"Wow." Adam's exclamation was almost lost in the roar of the little car's engine and the spitting gravel as Martin made the best of his manual transmission, and he cut a curve a bit too tight. "Is this where we're performing?"

"Yeah!" Martin yelled, then cut to the right, toward the woods. "And here's where we sleep." When he pulled the car to the edge of the road, he jerked his head at Adam's gear. "Take everything. I have to move the car, and the carpark is far away."

Adam rolled out of the cab of the car and stretched his long limbs. "Thank you for driving me," he said unexpectedly. "And thank you for drumming for us. I'm sure everything will work out just fine."

Ah. So that's where his mind had been when he should have been playing tourist and soaking in the sights—worrying. "My pleasure," Martin said with a slow smile. "Now let me show you my place."

Adam followed him with his guitar slung over his back and a duffel in his hand. Once Martin veered off the road and into the woods, however, Adam stopped behind him. "Where are we going?"

"You'll see," Martin said. "Don't worry, you'll be comfortable, and it's not too far away."

At first, Adam had hoped they would sleep in the castle. From across the moat, the ancient structure looked hard and unforgiving, however, and he had soon changed his mind. The tower on the far right was partially broken and rebuilt. A wooden draw bridge across the deep, dry moat looked newly maintained. Even though he would be happy to perform there, the rough-hewn, gray castle stones would, most likely, make for an uncomfortable bed.

As they made their way through the woods, the trunks of the firs stood far enough apart from one another to leave ample space for them to pass. A few more trees in, he came upon a group of small structures. The little houses were barely taller than a man, and were made of rough, weathered lumber with an opening for a window in one end and a hole instead of a door in the other.

"What are these?" Adam asked. He poked his head into one of the rustic, tent-sized houses. The door opening didn't go all the way down. He would have had to climb over a foot and a half of boards to get inside, but once he looked, he knew why.

The small structure was filled with hay.

"This is where some of the festival-goers sleep," Martin said. "Others pitch tents, but that's not as comfortable."

Adam raised his eyebrows. When their eyes met, he was drawn into the warm hazel of Martin's gaze. There was something welcoming in it, something sweet and hot, and...dammit, they were here just to play music.

"My place is down by the creek," Martin said. "Come on! I got here early just to claim it."

As he followed his new drummer through the sap-scented shade of the forest, Adam couldn't take his eyes off his broad shoulders, nor off the way his nut-brown hair stayed long in the back and curled up over the neckline of his red T-shirt.

In the disoriented stress of his situation, Adam had been thinking only of the logistics of their festival gig, and his luggage, and the issues related to replacing Jared. He had not really *looked* at Martin until now. Ducking branches and weaving between the boles of trees had him notice the slight, swishy looseness of Martin's movement.

A familiar looseness of someone who was comfortable with who he was, someone who felt safe within his surroundings. Someone out, like himself.

A slow smile began to tug on Adam's lips. Fate might have just sent him a new drummer he could talk to without faking an interest in team sports.

Few minutes later, the hill dipped away from the castle and toward a creek. A lone shack stood on what must have been the only flat area on this bank. Its roof looked new, its boards sat tight together, and the door and window openings were barred with a rustic, green fabric.

"Welcome to my secret hiding place," Martin said as he gestured at the shack proudly. "I always get here first to make sure nobody squats in here."

"Oh, it's not first come, first serve?" Adam asked with amusement.

"Well." A crafty expression crossed Martin's face. "It just so happens that we aren't on the castle's property anymore. This forest is private, but my cousin is the owner's forester and game-keeper. He made sure it was okay to build this here. The owner knows—his kids camp in here sometimes. We're farther away from all the fans this way, but we're still close enough to all the parties. With the lay of the land, we'll even be able to hear other people's music!"

A brief tour got Adam acquainted to his new "home away from home." The inside was hung with fabric alive with exotic patterns. A small, shell-shielded candle lantern hung off the ceiling, and the soft hay on the floor was covered with a lush, rich-patterned knotted rug. A lump of bedding was rolled up in one corner, and a painted wooden box sat by the door. "This is amazing," he said, realizing that Martin was sharing his special place with him.

A safe place.

A private place.

"The latrines are downstream," Martin said. "I'll show you later. But the best part is the swimming hole."

"The swimming hole?" Adam perked up. Even though the heat abated in the shade of the forest, a cool dip sounded like heaven on earth.

"It's upstream, under a small waterfall. I use it instead of a shower." Martin shot him a bemused look. "What do you want first, the water hole, or some fresh-brewed coffee?"

First, coffee.

Half an hour later, Adam was sitting on a small carpet outside Martin's shack ("Carpets are more comfortable than needles",) watching him use a rock-and-brass, coal-fired brazier ("My cousin says this is safer than a campfire in the woods,") as he roasted green coffee beans in an exotic-looking brass pan.

"Where did you learn to make coffee like this?" Adam asked in wonder as he watched Martin pulverize the fragrant, roasted coffee beans using a mortar and a pestle while the water was slowly heating in a brass kettle.

"I spent a good bit of time all over the Middle East." As Martin said that, Adam's heart leapt at the adorable blush that rose up his neck. "I learned this from one of the Bedouin tribes in Morocco," he said, nodding at his exotic set-up. "Do you mind if I add some spices?"

"No, go right ahead." Fascinated, Adam let the percussive thump-and-grind of the mortar and pestle draw him into a trance of sorts, a state during which he was always transported to *that place*, a place where cultures clashed, and music collided, and where new words and melodies sprang to his head unbidden.

On any other occasion, he would've dived for his notebook and started jotting down rhymes and phrases, fleeting impressions of *that place* and its melody and its particular colors and scents. Now, however, for the first time in quite a while, he desired to linger. He wanted to share this quiet, hypnotic moment with the beautiful man sitting cross-legged on the other side of the carpet and making an unheard-of, original, one-of-a-kind cup of coffee just for him.

The water bubbled to a boil, adding its own music, and in due time Martin had poured it into a small brass pitcher chased with fanciful designs that spoke of faraway places, and was scented with cardamom.

"Now we wait," Martin said with an air of happy complacence. Because here, in the middle of the woods where the brook next to them sang of eternal life, and where Martin had opened his sanctuary to an utter stranger and played his coffee-music for him, he was obviously happy.

Their eyes met. They exchanged a smile that stretched across centuries. Not knowing anything else about Martin, Adam came to an unlikely and startling realization.

He was dangerously close to falling in love—which was, of course, impossible.

The exterior battlements of the castle enclosed a space that fit a stage and ample space for a mosh pit. Booths with carnival foods lined the wall, separated by spaces where visitors could peer through the narrow archery slots into the woods, and at the flat lawn across the moat. That's where most of the campers would settle down tomorrow on their blankets, equipped with picnic baskets and ample supplies of drink.

"The acoustics in here is amazing," Martin said as he gave Adam a tour of the venue. The scent of roasted sausages began to drift on the air, and with it the sweetness of cinnamon pretzels as the first food vendors started setting up to sell to the casts and crews of many performing groups.

Adam didn't know where to look first. "So...we stay out here?" he asked. "Can we go inside the rest of the castle?"

"Yes, and the great hall is even being reconstructed." Martin's enthusiasm was palpable. "This is the only castle that had never fallen to the Hussites and their siege engines," he said as he beckoned Adam through an underpass.

The ancient stones met in a crest of a gothic arch that supported the weight of the structure overhead. Adam wondered at the craft that had created something so strong, and so lasting.

The washed-out, old frescoes were being restored on the walls, the ancient well's wheel had been rebuilt, and the chambers seemed as hard and inhospitable as Adam suspected they would be. "Do people ever sleep in here?"

"Only if they're drunk," Martin said with a laugh. "This is a major party area for the musicians. And

look, the new roof isn't even finished yet. Nobody wants to risk a nighttime shower."

They grinned at each other. The few people that rushed past them were with the festival, lugging cables or fastening signs for tomorrow. "We should go get our instruments," Adam said, trying not to let his regret show. Spending time with Martin was nice, and his enthusiasm for the old place was infectious. "You'll have to show me where things go, since this is your stomping ground," he said, bowing to Martin's experience.

Martin stumbled over a cobble stone. A curse flew, spoken in a language Adam didn't recognize, and Martin righted himself.

"Are you okay?"

"Yes." Martin bit off. "Fine."

Only once Adam caught up with him, he saw the flush of embarrassment rise up his cheeks.

Martin could've kicked himself. Adam Vanek gave him a compliment—a true, heartfelt compliment—and he almost face-planted on the hard cobblestones. Even though Martin had high confidence in his ability to deliver musically, a swarm of butterflies began to rise as time wore on as he saw Adam-the-tourist grow into Adam-the-musician.

He had been kinda cyber-stalking this guy for the last two years like a love-sick fan-boy. None of the few boyfriends he had during this time measured up, because despite their undeniable assets, they lacked one key quality: they weren't Adam Vanek.

Martin settled behind his drums, adjusted the set to his reach, and began to twitch in tempo as the familiar songs of Sylvan Breeze ran through his head. The band was doing a sound check, working with the stage crew, and tuning their instruments. Ironically, the mosh pit attendees would get to see the stage, but it was the crowd out on the meadow, who would see them only on a huge screen on the castle wall, that would benefit from the castle's unique acoustics.

"Go ahead. Feel free to warm up!" Adam's words broke his flow. Martin was in mid-piece while thinking sideways. He looked up. Adam's overgrown hair was darkened with sweat and slicked back, and he had that focused, feral look on his face.

Just like in his videos.

And he was staring at him.

Once again, Adam nodded. "Go on!"

The sound of his drums reverberated throughout the courtyard as Martin ran through a few sequences, but under the weight of Adam's seething gaze, not even his drumsticks managed to retain their composure. His left one spun out of his grip on rebound and sailed up, flipping through the air.

He thought he would die of embarrassment. As he scrambled to the ground to hunt down a part of his instrument, he noticed a pair of familiar brown shoes under his nose.

He slowly looked up. This is where Adam would decide that Martin wasn't really needed. Hell, the base could play the beat. So could the keyboards.

To his surprise, Adam squatted so their faces were on the level. "Relax, okay? This will be fine." He still had that intense, wild look in his eyes, one that made Martin think of old berserker fighters that had, no doubt, died assailing these walls. His intensity spoke of confidence, though. Confidence in himself, in his band, and also in Martin, their fan-boy volunteer. "Sit up and take a deep breath," Adam whispered so only Martin could hear. "And then, when you're ready, we'll start with *Nightshade*."

Martin nodded. "Thanks," he whispered. He didn't know what was happening to him. He had played on so many stages around the world, with so many bands, not understanding their languages and trying hard to fit into their cultures—and he had a boyfriend with him here and there, as the local conditions allowed—yet never did he freeze the way he did when Adam Vanek fixed his dark, heated gaze upon him.

Adam only nodded, squeezed his shoulder, and took his place on the small, open stage.

The touch of his hand had seared a mark into Martin's consciousness. Soft and hard, hot and cool, calm and full of inexplicable energy. He wanted more. Hell, he was ready to play himself into utter exhaustion to earn another squeeze on the shoulder—but the next one would be one of recognition and praise, if he had any say in it.

"One, two—one two three four!" Adam counted out the beat and music exploded, washing over Martin like an irresistible wave. It cleansed him, it passed around him and through him, and as he rolled with the complicated syncopations that had once been Seth's trademark, Adam's resonant voice joined the cresting wave of the melody.

The magic took Martin to that other place, the one where he felt no pain and only the oneness with the universe pulsed through him with every riff, every beat, and every wail of the guitar.

The set ended so abruptly, he felt the absence of music as physical pain. As he looked up, though, Aleeta and Jennie's exuberant expressions stilled any concern that had might have threatened to wiggle its way back in. Then Adam's eyes met his with a gaze that took his breath away.

Oh yeah. Tomorrow's concert would be just fine.

Martin would have sat there, basking in the afterglow, if a stage hand didn't prod him along. "Hey, the Black Arrow needs the stage, dude. You ready to go?"

❖

Hours later, Adam stumbled through the woods by the light of the moon. They had a dinner of the traditional Czech dumplings, pork, and sauerkraut at the pub down in the village, chased by excellent local beer, and they had walked the girls to their hotel.

Good rehearsal, great food, awesome company—

A dry branch snapped underfoot. He tripped, but Martin grabbed his elbow and yanked him back. Adam stumbled, his shoulder hitting Martin's as they grabbed for each other.

Martin's sweat smelled of the sun, of hard day's work, and of the last remnants of his aftershave. It was a warm, clean scent that reminded Adam how physical drumming was, the result of which was the fine shape of Martins arms and shoulders.

It also reminded him that Martin was a man, the kind of man he liked. Adam leaned forward and inhaled, not overthinking it after all that beer.

"Adam?" Martin's quiet, even voice joined the breeze rustling in the trees.

"Martin," Adam echoed. Martin's face was darkened by shadows, but their arms were still tangled. Neither made an attempt to move away.

Slowly, gently, Adam let his fingertips circle on Martin's back as he repositioned slightly. The gesture was just this side of friendly, but it left room for interpretation. The warm, muscled back stilled under his touch, tensed, then relaxed.

Joy thrilled through him when Martin's fingers grazed up his arm and to his neck.

A fling. This would be just a casual fling with a fan who happened to volunteer on a gig gone adventurous. This wouldn't have any repercussions at all, Adam rationalized as he pressed on Martin's back, moving them together.

Their chests touched, their heads drooped forward like flower heads in the breeze, close, and closer still.

Adam let Martin's firm hand on his neck guide him. Their lips brushed, setting off internal sparks that seemed to have been accentuated by the darkness of the forest. Lips that were soft yet hard, expressive, supple, often smiling.

Martin's lips, amazing and tempting even as his sharp jaw stubble attacked Adam's chin. Martin's tongue ventured out with a languid flick along the seam of Adam's mouth, and, obligingly, Adam let him in.

His eyes closed as their tongues met in an explosion of want. He didn't resist when Martin steered him back, forcing him to take a step, then another. Rough pine bark dug into his shoulder blades. The sensation ran counterpoint to the delicious storm of their kiss, and Martin's hard-day scent was now punctuated by pine sap and a desire for something more.

He wrapped his arms around Martin's strong body, surprised when it went all supple against his own. When Martin wedged his thigh between his legs, still latched mouth to mouth, and now hip to hip, Adam gasped.

The desire that he had been holding back longer than he cared to admit rushed through him like a firestorm. He didn't care that his drummer pressed him into a tree in a dark forest. He didn't care he was far away from home. He didn't care that the running of his band had him strained to the breaking point, and that his creative energy was spreading dangerously thin.

All he cared about was this feeling—yes, he was *feeling* again—and Martin's hard, hot arousal, which

he felt through layers of fabric against his hip, had a lot to do with it.

He was alive, dammit. He was *alive.*

If it hadn't been for Adam's strong grip, and the fact that they were pressed against a tree, Martin just knew he would have slumped to the ground. Was it possible he was in a death-grip with Adam— *that* Adam, wild-eyed and fierce, with a smooth voice that could talk him into just about anything? Were they *KISSING?*

Once that light-headed feeling passed, and Martin realized he had been pressing the evidence of his need against the object of his affection, he thought he was going to die of embarrassment. But then Adam's hot mouth landed under his ear.

"I want you." The low growl came with a bite-and-suck on his neck, on a place where it was sure to show—yet Martin's knees threatened to give out, and not falling took priority.

He leaned deeper into Adam and that's when he felt it, the seething and familiar hardness that was pressing into his belly, an evidence that he wasn't just imagining things. That he wasn't alone.

He wanted to do something about it—anything, really, anything Adam wanted—but scratching his back against a tree was hardly a way to show his adoration. "Let's go," he whispered, appalled at how breathy his voice had become. "Let's get more comfortable."

Walking through the woods while holding hands in the dark may not have been the smartest thing. They made it to camp all sweaty and scratched by stray dry branches, but intact and suppressing bubbles of laughter.

"I'm so hot and sticky," Martin heard Adam say as he was lighting the candle inside. So was he, with sweat pouring off his brow as the warm night became muggy and stifling.

"We could dip in the creek. Here, let's bring some light with us." A flash of inspiration, a moment's improvisation, and Martin pulled out a spare votive candle and a wooden bowl out of his supply box. He handed the towels to Adam. "You take these. I'll carry the light."

And carry the light he did, a glass-enclosed flame that cast just enough light for them to find safe footing by the creek. He set the candle in the bowl by the bank, and began to strip.

"I don't have a bathing suit," Adam said behind him, as though he was letting him know that he was about to flaunt a social convention. Ah, that's right, Americans. They didn't skinny-dip much.

"You're in Europe now," Martin said, unable to hold back a smile. "Nobody cares." He thought. "Well, except for me," he corrected himself, which he perhaps shouldn't have, because almost immediately the familiar, hated heat rose up his neck. At least Adam wouldn't see him blush in the dark.

The creek water was cool and fresh, and the swimming hole was still waist-deep. "We could use some rain," Martin said. "But the low current will let us do this." He set the wooden bowl on the water like a boat. The candle's flame danced steadily as Martin sent it in Adam's direction.

The illumination showed Adam in all his glory, with the dips and valleys of long, lean muscles leading down to his unslaked lust. Adam peered at him with hooded eyes, then he slowly stepped into deeper water and dipped all the way under, washing off the dust of the day.

Quickly, Martin did the same. When his head broke the surface again, he saw the bowl of light wedged against the stone dam. The soft glow was magical. He turned to Adam—but Adam wasn't there anymore. Only the water surface rippled in the golden light.

Then warmth surrounded him, the soothing comfort of Adam's long limbs as he came from under the water with a mischievous grin on his face.

Not hesitating, Adam pulled him into an embrace. "I still want you."

"Let's see if we can do this without drowning," Martin said lightly, peering around. "Ah. See that rock?" And there it was, right next to the thin waterfall. A rock to sit on with a boulder to lean against.

Things happened fast after that, a mosaic of questing fingers, mapping hands, and stifled moans in the night. Martin found himself straddling Adam, facing him as they pressed together in an exhilarating overload of sensation. "Let me," someone said,

either Adam or himself, and their hands met below their waist.

They both wanted the same thing.

Aligned for the best way to feel each other's satiny soft, hot hardness, they shared as two fists joined with each stroke. Two voices gasping with each thrust, each scintillating explosion of pleasure. Of unexpected emotion, too, because he was here with *his* Adam, swallowing *his* rushed exhale as they kissed, as the singer took care of *his* pleasure. A warmth of unaccustomed affection swelled in Martin's heart.

It had never been like this before—

Not with anyone else.

"Martin!" Adam's shout split the forest silence as slick heat covered Martin's hand.

Martin followed, teeth buried into Adam's neck as pleasure flooded his body in a wave of sizzling, coruscating heat.

He bit hard.

Adam's gasped in response and shuddered, then buried his face in Martin's neck and kissed him in what could have only been sated approval.

A silvery flash lit up the sky, followed by thunder overhead. Soon thick, fat drops of warm summer rain susurrated against the canopy of the trees overhead.

Still languid, Martin nuzzled Adam's neck. "We should get out," he said. "This isn't safe now."

"None of this is safe," Adam said, but Martin heard the smile in his voice. "You're gonna waltz off to some far-away country to sub in another gig and break my heart."

"Or I'll drag you to my shack and tell you about a drummer who knows all your songs. Even the ones you haven't written yet."

Slowly, they rinsed each other off, retrieved the floating bowl and the candle that was still alight, gathered their clothes, and made their way to Martin's special, quiet place.

As Martin dried off and climbed inside to spread their bedrolls, he heard Adam hum a snippet of a tune. It wasn't one he recognized.

They soon snuggled under a light blanket as the drumming of the rain on the roof increased. "It's just one of those summer showers," Martin said. "It's supposed to be clear tomorrow, don't worry."

"I'm not worried," Adam said, laughing and humming all at once. "I have a tune, and all I need is a beat. One like the rain, and like thunder, and like you."

"I can give you a beat like that," Martin said, smiling into Adam's still-wet hair. "And I can keep it up forever."

❖

November 11ᵗʰ, 2018—NEWS FROM THE GREEN ROOM: Five month after Seth Jones left the rising alt-rock phenom "Sylvan Breeze" under strained circumstances, Czech percussionist Martin Sklar takes the stage as a permanent band member for the first time. This weekend, Adam Vanek introduces their new surprise album, "I Am Here For You," to a growing international audience.

D. H. Hendrickson has published two hockey romance novels, Body Check *and* No Defense, *as well as four other novels (writing as David H. Hendrickson). His novel* Offside *has been adopted for high school student required reading. His short fiction has appeared in* Ellery Queen's Mystery Magazine, Pulphouse, *and numerous anthologies, including multiple issues of* Fiction River. *His story "Death in the Serengeti" has been selected for* Best American Mystery Stories 2018. *Hendrickson has published over fifteen hundred works of nonfiction, most recently "Travis Roy: Quadriplegia" and a "Life of Purpose". He has been honored with the Joe Concannon Hockey East Media Award and the Murray Kramer Scarlet Quill Award. Follow him at www. hendricksonwriter.com.*

A WHEELCHAIR AND A UNICYCLE AT FANEUIL HALL

by D. H. Hendrickson

Julie O'Reilly saw the crooked-nosed creep wearing an old gray hoodie half an hour before he actually did anything. But though she'd thought it odd, *really* odd, that anyone would wear anything so suffocatingly hot, with the hood pulled up, no less, in sweltering ninety-five degree weather, she pushed it out of her mind because she was already rather tired of being spooked out.

This was, after all, Independence Day. Not the real Independence Day, July 4. It was only July 1, a Saturday, close enough to be called July 4ᵗʰ weekend, but not the actual holiday. But she'd chosen it as the day she would set herself free from the prison of her apartment's four walls. A prison she'd locked herself in for the past eight months, a jail of lost dreams and sadness, one erected on the night of the car accident when everything changed.

She could get around in her wheelchair—her physical therapist called her a workout warrior—but Julie worked from home, writing software, and let her mother bring her groceries and other necessities, all so she didn't have to go *out there*. And if she did venture into the outside world, it was never alone, it was always with her parents, and as far away from crowds as possible.

Never alone. Never exposed.

Until today. Independence Day.

How fitting.

And so, freshly showered, her long, rust-colored hair hanging down over the back of her wheelchair and her sandaled feet squarely on the footrests, she had taken the elevator down to the ground floor of her apartment building, and felt the blast of heat as she exited the air-conditioned foyer. Bad as it was—ninety-two degrees and it was still just eleven o'clock—it wasn't bad enough to make her regret wearing jeans instead of shorts to cover her stick legs, once athletic and beautiful according to the constant compliments by her friends that were now carefully omitted during their conversations. Now they were weak, the muscles atrophied from disuse no matter how faithfully she followed her therapist's exercise program. Almost as awkward as her overdeveloped shoulders and forearms, out of place on her otherwise petite body, and the decidedly unfeminine calluses on her hands, all of which made her feel like a freak. She'd almost worn long sleeves to cover her arms, instead of the short-sleeved, blue flowered blouse she was wearing now, but the mid-to-high nineties and high humidity forecast had won out.

She wheeled herself the three quarters of a mile to the local T stop, and, blinking rapidly to keep the stinging sweat out of her eyes, boarded the screeching subway into Boston—the Haymarket stop on the Orange line, to be exact. Then after taking the elevator up to the ground floor, she wheeled herself another half mile to the Faneuil Hall Marketplace, beads of sweat forming almost instantly on her forehead and soon tasting salty on her lips.

It had been a favorite trip she'd made often with Shawn before everything changed. This would be the first time she dared return. But she'd been spooked from the start, surely a bad omen. On the way from her apartment to the T station, she'd noticed a tall, thin man walking briskly behind her for several blocks, sure he meant her harm even though it was broad daylight. He'd slowed when she slowed. He'd picked up the pace when she did. Her heart had pounded and her palms had grown moist, but then he'd suddenly walked briskly right past her, paying her no attention at all.

Then after she got off at Haymarket and took the elevator to the ground floor, she'd wheeled herself along the god-awful bumpy, brick walkway, and once again became sure she was being followed, this time by a short, squat, middle-aged man she'd seen eyeing her on the train. Her chair placed a big bullseye on her back as an easy mark, she knew, and she felt her mouth go dry and her pulse again quicken. But he'd turned off a side street, and she never saw him again.

Good grief, she thought. You're acting like a four-year-old in bed, pulling the blankets over her head, convinced there's a boogeyman in the closet. Grow up! The whole world isn't out to get you.

Julie tried to laugh it off—*silly me!*—and mostly succeeded. Except her heart kept pounding, as if to call her own bluff.

So when the crooked-nosed creep in the sunglasses, faded jeans, and gray hoodie strode beside her for a few heart-stopping seconds before moving quickly past as she approached the section of the Faneuil Hall Marketplace known as Quincy Market—a fifty-foot high, forty-foot wide, granite edifice to overeating and shopping—Julie decided she'd been weirded out twice already and she wasn't going for the hat trick. Maybe the guy, thirty or so, scrawny and a shade under six feet tall with a nose that clearly had been broken in the past multiple times and never set, was trying to sweat off a few pounds.

Whatever. It wasn't her concern.

As the wheelchair clattered along the brick walkway and she neared the entrance, laughter and applause erupted off to her right where a street performer rocked back and forth on a ten-foot-high unicycle, juggling four flaming torches.

For just the slightest nanosecond, Julie turned away, mentally yawning at a juggler on a unicycle. Big deal. Eye roll material.

Then she looked again.

Ho-leee crap!

Sitting high atop on the unicycle was the most gorgeous man she had ever seen. Dark, thick, wavy hair. Probably Italian, she guessed. Maybe Greek, as in the Greek God Adonis, but her money was on Italian. Piercing blue eyes and a killer smile he was sending her way.

But what made her stop short—making a pedestrian behind her bump into her chair, knock it forward, and then rush away, apologizing profusely—was the performer's perfect body, one straight off a fitness magazine cover. His bare chest—tanned, chiseled, and undoubtedly shaved—glistened with sweat in the noonday sun. Julie didn't find attractive the excessive, vein-popping musculature of a competitive bodybuilder, but this...this Italian Stallion was perfection at just the right notch lower! He wore only red, white, and blue starred shorts, appropriate for the holiday, showcasing legs like tree trunks, tanned and strong, just like his gorgeous inverted triangle of a chest.

Wow.

Julie's legs didn't work anymore, but everything else down there did, and everything else down there liked what she saw.

"Hey, pretty lady," he called out and waved. "Come over and join us."

Julie looked around. Who was he talking to?

Was he...?

"Yes, you," the Italian Stallion said, again flashing the killer smile.

Julie felt her eyes go wide and her face grow hot, even hotter than it had been wheeling her chair over half a mile of brick sidewalks. She realized for the first time that the crowd circled around this...this Adonis...was five or six deep.

And almost all of their faces had turned to see her, eager with anticipation, until—

Until they saw the object of the Italian Stallion's attention—they saw her—and their smiles froze. Their faces fell and they looked away, uncomfortable. And what Julie saw in almost every single eye was what she hated most about what she had become. What she feared seeing more than anything else.

Pity.

Even before the accident, she'd never been comfortable in the limelight. In high school, she'd always played team sports, never individual, blending in with her teammates, instinctively deferring to the stars. In college, the very thought of a presentation in front of a classroom caused her to break into a cold sweat. So she chose team projects in which she could do the grunt work and someone else presented it, getting the attention she wanted no part of.

After the accident, that need to blend in grew even more intense. She didn't want to be seen.

And she definitely didn't want to be stared at, like now, by close to a hundred people.

Julie shot the wheelchair forward as fast as she could get it to go, bumping across the dark red brick surface, hearing the Italian Stallion call out after her, "No, don't go, don't go! Come back."

She got to the foot of the granite stairs and froze.

There was no handicapped ramp! The landing in front of the double doors had to be thirty feet wide with four steps leading up to it. But there was no way for her to get up there. One of the most popular locations in downtown Boston, and there was no way for her to get inside.

Could that be?

Humiliation and anger washed over her. She barely realized that the street performer had fallen silent, or rather, had continued on with his act and thankfully taken her out of his sights.

But she still felt all eyes on her. On her helplessness.

And when an unseen man behind her with a deep, Southern voice, said softly, his mint-scented mouth next to her ear, "I could lift you up there, miss, if you'd like," she almost screamed.

Julie shook her head violently, unable to speak as the tears welled up within her. She closed her eyes and tried to calm her shaking hands.

It was probably only a second or two before she realized the building's wheelchair ramps must be on the sides, but it felt like forever.

Tony Gianino felt awful. He'd spotted the cute redhead in the wheelchair looking at him, and instantly been struck by something about her. Not just her petite beauty, though he was a sucker for redheads, especially ones with bright cinnamon-colored hair like hers.

There was something about how she carried herself. An almost contradictory mix of toughness and fragility. And even at a distance of twenty yards, he was sure her eyes were emerald green.

Definitely Irish. Probably a Shannon or an Erin.

Whatever it was, something about her hit him between the eyes. It was like in *The Godfather*. (What Italian boy from the North End didn't know at least the first two movies by heart even if they reinforced the stereotype that all Italians were gangsters, not just the few guys from the neighborhood like Vinnie Sarducci and Paulie Numnuts who really were connected?) There was that scene when Michael Corleone sees for the first time the Sicilian girl who will become his wife, and he's instantly thunderstruck.

Yeah, thunderstruck. That was how Tony felt about this girl. This Shannon or Erin or Kellie or whatever her name was. This girl he'd embarrassed without intending to, an outrageous blunder, pushing her away when he'd only wanted to draw her near, so he could perform for her and maybe even....

What? Win her heart?

How silly was that? He'd seen her all of fifteen seconds, twenty-five tops, and sent her rushing away. Yet here he was thinking of winning her heart? What was wrong with him?

And an Irish-looking girl, no less. Of course, not every redhead is Irish, but this was Boston, and if she wasn't Irish, he'd eat his unicycle. More to the point, she sure wasn't Italian. And his old-school mother had a bird anytime he got serious with any girl who wasn't Italian. (God forbid if she were anything but a Catholic, though surely that wouldn't be a problem for this Shannon or Erin or Kellie; all the Irish here were Catholics.) But his mother had a bird over lots of things these days. Especially him trying to make it as a full-time street performer instead of getting "a real job."

"You have so much potential!" she whined. "You can do so much better than this!"

Mio Dio. Tony almost crossed himself, although that would have been disastrous, what with him juggling four flaming torches atop his ten-foot high unicycle.

Get your act together, he told himself, and brought his focus back to his performance and the hundred or so people surrounding him in a wide circle, five or six deep.

Normally, he could go through the whole act purely on instinct, and get automatic laughter from all his punch lines even while entertaining the silliest of ideas, of a lasting love with an Irish beauty he didn't even know. And most of the times while performing, he wanted to stick with all his instinctive moves, burned into muscle memory, instead of consciously thinking about them, which was always a disaster.

Normally, he could think of this Shannon or Erin—could he *stop* thinking about her?—and only the most perceptive audience member would notice the slightest lost edge in his delivery. But he'd hit a rocky patch the last few weeks, what with a string of mean-spirited hecklers and even a slashed tire on his unicycle. This wasn't a time to be distracted.

Besides, every audience still deserved his total focus. He would give it to them.

Unless, of course, the Irish beauty returned, and he got the chance to make up for his blunder, and maybe get her real name so when he thought of her again she wouldn't be Shannon or Erin or Kellie. She'd be the *real* her.

Inside the building was even worse than outside. Julie found a side, wheelchair-accessible entrance, but soon found herself in a sort of pedestrian gridlock. The main aisle here was wide enough for perhaps five people total going in the two directions, but between people standing in line at the most popular food kiosks like Pizzeria Regina, Boston & Maine Fish Company, and MM Mac N'Cheese, others just stood there trying to decide between what were probably fifty eating choices spread out over a length of about a hundred yards.

Julie would creep forward a couple inches, then have to stop and wait.

A few more inches.

Stop.

Wait.

It was worse stop-and-go traffic than on the Southeast Expressway at rush hour. Julie felt like honking a horn, if only her wheelchair had one. This was what it must be like to be a sardine. It took what felt like half a lifetime to make two purchases.

She bought an outrageously priced lobster roll at a place that pandered to the tourists, exaggerating the Boston accent on their menu so, according to it, she had actually purchased a *lobstah* roll. She could have alternatively chosen the combo with clam *chowdah*, corn *chowdah*, or even *lobstah chowdah*. Julie didn't think she or her fellow Bostonians actually sounded like that, but figured she probably was tone deaf to it all, having lived in neighboring Somerville—*Summahville*—all twenty-two years of her life.

She salivated thinking about her lobster roll, remembering its succulent taste from a little over a year ago, big chunks of fresh lobster with just enough mayo and little bits of celery, all on a bed of crisp lettuce inside a fresh, soft roll. She'd eat it outside along with *Galactobouriko*, a Greek custard-filled pastry with a soft, flaky crust, topped with honey that was her old favorite among the many sweet treats.

She bought the *Galactobouriko*, and wheeled herself toward the front door, the two small, white bags of food on her lap.

Inch forward. Stop. Wait.

Inch forward. Stop. Wait.

She pushed through the doors, felt the blast of heat hit her in the face, and saw the crooked-nosed creep with the gray hoodie and sunglasses.

He was standing on the thirty-foot wide landing off to the side, watching the bare-chested street performer with the perfect body. Maybe, Julie thought, the guy was admiring the hunky view, which was perfectly fine with her. She could understand anyone staring at the Italian Stallion.

But why was the creep sweating his ass off in the thick hoodie, even to the point of having the hood pulled up, covering tufts of brown hair sticking out on the sides? And that frown on his face was intimating, if not menacing. Maybe this guy wasn't appreciating her Stallion at all.

Realizing she was holding up foot traffic, Julie pushed further out on the landing before realizing she'd come out the same door she'd originally tried to enter, only to find no ramp. Any further and she'd go tumbling down the steps. For a brief moment, she panicked that someone would accidentally bump into her and send her sprawling down every last hard, granite step.

But people brushed past her on both sides and others came up the steps as well. Face burning, Julie turned to reenter the building and play stop-and-go for the next five minutes until she got to the side wheelchair ramps. She scolded herself for her stupidity in coming out here. How had she forgotten that there wasn't a ramp? Hadn't that fact been memorable enough?

Only then, as she moved back inside the doors did she realize the creep was gone.

❖

When Tony saw her emerge from around the corner off to his right, the side where the Cheers replica bar extended a hundred feet toward the back, he bolted from inside the circle of onlookers awaiting his next show. He had just finished drumming up interest, clapping his hands above his head and calling out to passing pedestrians to join in the circle; the show was about to start, and the circle had begun to form.

"This will be the high point of your day," he had called out. "The high point of your year. The high point of your life! If you keep on walking and miss this opportunity, you will never forgive yourself!"

It was the kind of bombast that got people, especially those conditioned to watch street performers in this square, to at least consider joining the audience.

As he sprinted toward the girl in the wheelchair, some onlookers broke into expectant smiles, sure this was a part of the show.

But this was no show.

"I am so very, very sorry," he said when he got to within fifteen feet of her. At first, she seemed to shrink away from him, and that made him despair that he'd ever make things right. "My name is Tony Gianino, and I never, ever meant to embarrass you."

He held out his hand, but she just looked at it warily so after a few uncomfortable seconds, he put it down.

"I'd like to make it up to you," he said. "Please come watch my show." A wave of inspiration hit. "Be my assistant."

Astonishment came over her face. "Your assistant?"

"Sure! It'll be fun!"

"What...would I do?"

"Whatever you want."

❖

She almost told him to leave her alone. She didn't want his attention or anyone else's. Or at least that's what she'd thought.

But the truth was, she did like his attention, this Tony Gianino, even if she wanted no one else's. Just wanted to blend into the background and be no different than anyone else. She didn't have to be pretty and admired and flirted with like before the accident. She just wanted to be normal, and not a spectacle for others to see.

But that ship had sailed, hadn't it? She and her bleeping wheelchair weren't going to blend into the background. Not now. Not ever.

So maybe she should just see what this gorgeous hunk was all about, him and his glistening sweat covering that most magnificent tanned, shaved chest of his.

Did that make her shallow? She supposed it did.

Perhaps it even made her as shallow as Shawn had been eight months ago, dropping her like a hot potato after just one visit to see her in the hospital. *It's not like we're married,* he had said as he cast her aside. *We were probably going to break up anyway when I leave for grad school.* And then he'd coldly taken up with Katie Flowers with scarcely a guilty look behind.

Behind at what he clearly considered damaged goods.

No, she wasn't being that shallow, not even close. After all, wasn't this how relationships often started? Two people mutually attracted to each other, at least partially based on superficial, purely physical attraction? And then something more substantial forms from that?

Not that she and the Italian Stallion were going to have a relationship, of course. She wasn't that foolish. What was there for him in all this? The wheelchair was just the beginning of her baggage.

And maybe he, too, was just showing her all this attention out of pity.

Julie felt like spitting the word out. Of course he was. He wasn't thinking, geez, she reminds me of Gisele Bündchen. I've got to get to know her!

But…couldn't it just be guilt at embarrassing her earlier? She looked again at that magnificent chest and said to herself, screw it! Whatever the motivation, maybe it would turn into something beautiful. Or perhaps she'd just have fun. Wasn't it worth taking that chance? What did she have to lose?

And maybe she had everything in the world to gain.

A girl could dream, couldn't she? Even her. Even with this contraption she huffed around in.

So Julie wheeled herself over to the circle that had already formed, took the front row position Tony made for her, and once the show began, became thoroughly enthralled.

"Come close," Tony yelled to passersby, gesturing for them to come over. "Free Wi-Fi!"

It was a totally nonsensical joke, yet she found herself laughing along with everyone else.

Her eyes widened in surprise.

She…was…laughing!

Laughing!

How long had it been since she'd heard the sound of her own laughter?

Too long.

It hadn't been eight months. That barren stretch hadn't been entirely without a single smile, chuckle, or full-out laugh.

But it had been close.

She sure had enjoyed a more buoyant sense of humor back in the good old days. When it was so easy to be happy. When *everything* was so easy, though she hadn't necessarily appreciated it.

Yet now, after all the crap that had happened since the accident, she was laughing anyway to a stupid little quip like, "Come close! Free Wi-Fi!"

She'd assumed her days of free laughter had been in her past.

"Hello, my name is Tony Gianino," he began loudly, spreading his hands wide in greeting before starting to juggle four simple bowling pins. "I'm an Italian from the North End whose given name is Anthony, but I go by Tony. I'm a walking stereotype. And like all Italian men, I'm a great lover."

The audience chuckled mildly and a couple hearty wolf-whistles rang out.

"All true," Tony said, still juggling. "Except the lover part."

Stronger laughter.

He shrugged, still juggling. "Hey, no one's perfect. I just need more practice."

He began to clap while continuing to juggle.

"Like all magicians, jugglers, and con men, I need an assistant," he proclaimed loudly. "I lost mine during the last performance, so I need an adult volunteer."

A few scattered hands shot up. Julie frowned. She thought she was supposed to be the assistant. What was going on here?

But Tony shot her a glance and winked.

"I am legally required to disclose that the assistant I just lost wasn't my first," he announced. "I've kind of had a string of bad luck." He shrugged while keeping the pins moving. "I've lost five assistants in six performances. Hey, no one said juggling chainsaws is easy."

Julie laughed heartily, joyously along with the rest of the crowd.

"So, I see no one is still willing to be my assistant," he said.

Picking up on what she thought was her cue, Julie shot her hand up and said, "I am!"

"We have a sucker!" Tony said. "And what is your name?"

"Julie."

Tony tightened the muscles in his magnificent chest, drawing her instant attention.

"Um, Julie." He pointed to his eyes. "Up here, Julie. My eyes are up here."

Everyone broke into laughter, Julie even more than most.

And amazingly enough, she had a great, great time.

"You're a natural," Tony said after the show when the two were by themselves. The audience had dispersed, and the two had moved off to the side of the courtyard for a little more privacy.

Julie beamed, feeling a warm glow inside. "Thanks. It was fun." Remembering her food, she said, "I've got this lobster roll here that I better eat before the sun ruins it. And a Greek pastry." She slid the lobster roll from its small white bag and held it out on a bed of napkins. "Would you like half?"

"No, I'm all set. Go ahead and eat." His left eyebrow raised. "Would you like to stick around for the next show? Be my assistant again?"

"Um…" It sounded like fun, even though Julie was sure the jokes would all be the same.

"I promise I won't add the chainsaw trick," Tony said, and flashed his killer smile.

How could she say no? Good God, she loved to look at this man, and talking with him was even better.

"And if you think you can put up with me, how about dinner and a movie some night next week?"

Julie broke into a broad smile.

Until she saw the creep in the hoodie.

Sneaking up behind Tony.

Only now, the creep had pulled a black ski mask down over his face and that oft-broken nose. And he held in his right hand a sawed-off baseball bat he'd just pulled out of the hoodie's pouch.

Almost in striking range.

Julie opened her mouth, but nothing came out. It felt as though all the air had been sucked out of her lungs.

She pointed with her left hand, her free hand, the one not holding the lobster roll, but the creep had shifted his position to line up just behind Tony, who now blocked her view. She could barely see the creep at all.

Tony looked at her with a curious, uncomprehending smile, and pointed to his bare chest as if to ask, "Me?"

She couldn't see the creep. Just his hand, clenching the sawed-off baseball bat. Drawing it out wide. Poised to swing.

Julie drew back her own right hand.

And with all her might, threw the lobster roll at Tony's head.

For a split second, his eyes widened. Then he ducked.

The lobster roll hit the creep squarely in his ski-mask-covered nose. Behind the mask, black except for the newly applied white smear of mayonnaise, his dark eyes blinked. For a moment, he stood like a statue, his arm extended to strike, but frozen in position.

Then he took a step forward.

And swung.

At Tony's head. Arms. Chest.

Each time, Tony stepped aside, dodging the blow or at least deflecting it. Each time, the creep moved in closer.

"Help!" Julie screamed, her lungs finally cooperating, and belatedly she thought to throw the bag holding the container of *Galactobouriko*. It hit the creep on the side of the head, but stopped him no more than a split second.

Tony lashed out with an acrobatic leg kick aimed at the creep's midsection, but the creep was just fast enough to avoid it, stepping back then slamming the bat into Tony's side.

Tony fell to one knee with a gasp. *No!* yelled something inside Julie's mind.

She shot the wheelchair forward, screaming like a banshee.

The creep froze.

Narrowly missing Tony, Julie plowed the wheelchair into the stunned creep, slamming into his right leg and knocking the sawed-off bat to the ground.

The creep, eyes wide behind the ski mask, turned and fled.

The police took their statements, but help from passersby had been too slow to arrive and the creep had gotten way. There'd be no tracking him down. There were any number of his kind in the city with oft-broken noses: true thugs, boxers and MMA fighters, and plain old-fashioned barroom drunks. None of whom was in short supply.

It wasn't until they were waiting in the hospital emergency room, waiting for Tony to get X-rayed, the smell of disinfectant in the air, that Julie remembered the blur of red.

"I thought you were bleeding right from the start," she said, as the waiting room TV droned on thirty feet away. "I thought he'd hit you."

"No," Tony said, shaking his head and wincing. "Not till the end."

"But I saw red, I'm sure of it," Julie said. "The more I think about it, the more sure I am. Right from the start. Just not the same color as your blood. Lighter and brighter."

"From the start?"

"Yes!"

"Red, but not the color of blood? Lighter and brighter?"

"Yes. On his hands or wrist. Somewhere like that."

"Was there some kind of shape to the red?"

Julie thought about it. "I guess so, now that I think about it. But I'm not really sure how to describe it."

"Try."

Julie closed her eyes and tried to bring up the image. "There was, kind of like a thin red line across the wrist. Then once when a sleeve of the hoodie slid up, I could see…I don't know…I guess it was a shape with some kind of a sharp edge to it. Does that make any sense?"

"An inverted triangle, perhaps?"

"Yes! I think that's right. An inverted triangle!"

Tony closed his eyes and swore softly. "You mean, like half a diamond on a playing card?"

"Now that you mention it, yeah."

"Paulie Numnuts," Tony said softly.

"Who?"

"It's a nickname. He's a crook who fancies himself the King of Diamonds. He has a red diamond tattooed on his wrist. He fits your description. In his thirties. Scrawny. Had his nose broken more times than he can count."

"Why would he want to hurt you?"

"I don't know, but he's connected. I'm not sure I want to know."

Two nights later, Julie and Tony sat at a table in the back of a small North End Italian food restaurant. Not well known, it was located on a side street off the main drag, and in truth had a plain sort of ambience. Plain white tablecloths. Plain wooden walls. And a menu on plain white paper.

But the smells of tomato and cheese had just about driven Julie mad until the food arrived. Then they were even more mouth-watering. And the taste was to die for!

Best of all, though, was who she was eating the meal with, despite the crazy story he was telling her, one that had led to the ugly, purple-and-black bruises on his arms and side, covered now by a long-sleeved light blue shirt, but reluctantly shown to her earlier when he'd picked her up outside her apartment. They both considered him fortunate not to have broken any bones.

"So it was all your mother's fault?" Julie asked, incredulous.

"Not really."

"But I thought you said—"

"Only because she talks too much and tries to run my life," Tony said.

"I don't understand."

"She was complaining to one of her friends about how I was wasting my life being a performer," Tony said. "I needed to stick to my real job, which is here."

"Here?"

"This is my parents' restaurant. I work here some to make ends meet and to help out, but they want me here full time, which means sixty hours a week. I give them twenty, so I can work on my show."

"Oh, I see," Julie said, though she didn't really.

"My mother said to this friend that she was so upset with me, she'd do anything to get me to stop 'this juggling nonsense.' Those were her words. *This juggling nonsense.* It's my dream, but to her it's nonsense."

Julie nodded.

"But the key word is actually 'anything,'" Tony said. "When she said she'd do anything to get me to stop, she meant one thing. But after a friend repeated it to a friend who repeated it to another friend…well, by the time it got to Paulie Numnuts, he thought I needed the full Tonya Harding treatment."

"That's sick!"

"My mother was, of course, horrified," Tony said. "She never meant that at all. She's so horrified she actually hasn't said a word to me about getting a real job for all of two days now."

"But this Paulie Numnuts guy sounds scary. How could he have put two and two together and gotten forty-nine?"

"Paulie ain't exactly Harvard material. He's a graduate of the School of Hard Knocks. Well, maybe not a graduate. More like a dropout. But you get the picture."

Julie took another bite of her gnocchi. She didn't want to ask the question, but had to. It might be insulting—she hoped he wouldn't take it that way—but she had to know.

"Tell me the truth," she said tentatively, wondering if she should stop right there, wishing she could. But the cat was already halfway out of the bag. "Are you…connected?"

Tony laughed heartily and shook his head. "About the furthest thing from it. Swear to God."

Julie breathed a sigh of relief. She knew instinctively that Tony was telling the truth. That he would always tell her the truth.

"Now order a whiskey, Irish," he said. "You're gonna need it for when you meet my mother."

Julie felt her heart beat a little faster, and a warm glow filled her chest. "When is that going to be?"

"She'll be here in five minutes," Tony said. "If that wheelchair of yours has a seat belt, you might want to buckle up."

Julie smiled. With Tony here, she could face anything. She hadn't wasted a perfectly good lobster roll for nothing.

Melinda Curtis is an award-winning, USA Today *bestselling author of over 40 romance titles. She writes sweet romance for Harlequin, sweet romantic comedy, and fun, sexy sports romances. Sign up for her book release newsletter and download two free reads.*

CINDERELLA FELL FOR A FELLA

by Melinda Curtis

ONCE UPON A TIME

Do you believe in fairytales and fairy godmothers?

You should.

If you come to the farmer's market in Brody Falls, you'll see an old woman sitting at a card table. She dresses in red. Magical apple red.

In winter, she wears a woolen red cape. In warmer months, a red scarf flutters around her silver hair like silken butterflies. Her purse is a large red satchel with a crocheted rose hanging on the side (red, of course).

Unlike other vendors, the woman in red offers no fresh produce or handmade goods. She hangs no professionally made banner and puts out no painted sandwich signs. She sits behind a simple card table with a piece of pink notebook paper taped to the edge. Her sign has two simple words on it: Love Advice.

Young or old, no one in Brody Falls can remember a farmer's market without her. Ignore her invitation if you like. She'll remain a mystery. Those who've sat on her folding chair won't discuss what's been said.

They don't call her odd.

They don't call her old.

They simply call her their Fairy Godmother….

CHAPTER ONE

They say that women who aren't in love fill that void with chocolate and shoes.

Cindy Carlisle was single, enjoyed gourmet chocolate, and owned too many shoes.

Too many shoes? How could that possibly be?

She had shoes for every occasion and situation. Power pumps for court. Flirty sandals for nights out with the girls (rare though they might be). Flip flops for bumming around. And boots and sling backs. And, oh, let's not get started on sneakers. Cindy had more shoes than Kim Kardashian had thongs.

Or maybe that was just the way it felt, because she was schlepping sixteen shoe boxes up the steps, over the stoop, between overgrown brambles, and through the door. Cindy had bungee-corded the boxes together, thinking it would be easier to move them out of her apartment in San Francisco, and into her new apartment in Brody Falls.

In her end-of-the-move packing frenzy, Cindy hadn't factored in her short arms, a narrow stoop with two-foot high, bramble-tentacled walls, or an apartment door that wouldn't stay open. It'd been drizzling since dawn and to save herself more frustration, she'd tucked her glasses into the outer pocket of her blue jacket. Now the world looked like a runny watercolor painting.

Cindy reached the front stoop without being snagged by thorny vines, adjusted her load, and reached for the door handle. It was wet and she couldn't get a grip.

This was her last load of boxes and her most drool-worthy—the five-inch gold Cleopatra gladiator heels, the spangly, bright-colored shoes from every time she'd been a bridesmaid, and her grandmother's wedding shoes (a vintage pair of white satin pumps with rhinestone buckles).

The spring drizzle turned into a steady rain, fat drops that threatened to drench Cindy's boxes, her hair, her morale.

I should never have left the city.

But she'd had to. For her own sanity. After losing a heartbreaking court case, the odds of her making a difference in Brody Falls were ten times better than in a big city's overworked court system.

She gripped the door handle tighter, bending her knees, and trying to ignore the sharp digging of box edges into her arms. The old brass doorknob turned, but not far enough to click free of the latch.

Something in her bundle shifted. Four boxes slid forward, threatening to dump onto the narrow porch, and a fall to ruin. The eggs Cindy'd had for breakfast shifted in her stomach as if they'd been pancake-flipped.

A fuzzy figure ran down the interior stair toward her, hand to ear as if talking on a cell phone. She took a step back within bramble-striking distance, but the boxes shifted again and she lunged forward, pressing her stack against the door to straighten them out.

The broad-shouldered, blurry figure on the other side of the glass had turned and was backing toward the door.

"Hey," she said, shuffling back a step on the stoop.

The door swung open, bumping against Cindy's load and forcing her closer to the low brick wall and the brambles.

"I'm meeting him this morning, Dad." A deep voice. A sexy voice.

Clueless to a damsel in distress.

He opened the door wider, nudging her closer toward trippable walls, a briar patch, and a short, painful fall.

A thorn pierced her skinny jeans. And then another. "Ow." It was soft as exclamations went, not her court-appointed attorney voice. And then she wobbled backward, teetering precariously above.

Her mind whirled through options like her last secretary leafing through her ancient round rolodex. She could drop the boxes down the stairs. She could toss the boxes over her shoulder. She could save the boxes and fall into the brambles herself. Any way she looked at it: *ouch.*

"Wait!" she exclaimed, hoping the man would realize he was about to bowl her over.

No such luck. He was the kind of guy who needed to open the door wide and make a grand entrance. Or in this case, a grand exit. "I'll take care of it, Dad."

The thorns were a team of acupuncturists now, yanking her toward a complete body treatment. And that sexy voice was going to be the last thing she heard before she fell.

She tilted backward, reaching for her lawyer-voice, finding instead her little-girl-lost voice. *"He-eh-eh-elp!"*

Chunk-chunk. Splat-clatter.

"Hey!" Strong hands grabbed her arms and pulled Cindy upright. "I've got you."

Mr. Sexy Voice saved her. But in an attempt not to fall, she'd squeezed her load too tight. A box launched toward Cindy's savior.

"Oomph." His grip on her arms wavered, and then the box fell down the steps. *Plop-splat.*

Cindy's stomach did another pancake flip.

"Put your boxes down, lady."

"No." Was that her voice? It sounded like a waifish wail.

Somewhere, bells chimed the eight-o'clock hour.

Another box popped out. This time with less punch. Cindy clutched the outer row of shifting boxes, afraid to move lest the entire bundle tumble down the puddle-filled steps.

"Lady…miss…." He was a blur. A tall, impatient blur.

Plop-splat. There went another box.

"For the love of…." He yanked the front door back open and swept her inside.

The boxes tumbled into the foyer, Cindy on top of them. Wet cardboard gave way as she fell. And then something in her vest pocket crunched.

My glasses.

Cindy scrambled to her feet and rushed back into the rain to save the fallen boxes. One had spilled open. A shoe balanced on the walk. A white pump. Her grandmother's wedding shoes.

Cindy's breakfast shifted. Upward this time. Toward Cindy's throat.

The man was already picking up boxes and Grandmother Drusella's shoe, along with other items. A coffee cup perhaps, and—

"My phone is a total loss." Gone was his emergency-mode impatience. In its place was a weary resignation, as if his luck had been bad for far too long. He handed her the boxes and her precious pump.

Cindy retreated to the foyer, stacked the boxes on the floor, and wiped the pump dry on her T-shirt as if it was a genie's lamp. Something didn't feel right. She brought the shoe within inches of her face. "It's missing the buckle."

The man stood facing her in the rain. Without her glasses, Cindy had no way of knowing if he was handsome or homely, scowling or bewildered, well-dressed or frumpy. All she saw were black jeans and a royal blue jacket.

"My grandmother's shoe is ruined without the buckle." She squinted at him, wanting her glasses. But if she pulled them out and they were broken, she might cry. And divorce attorneys were not supposed to cry. Ever. "I can't see…. Can you look around for me? The buckle must be out there somewhere."

She didn't have to see the color of his eyes to know one thing. He wasn't married. She could tell by his bachelor-weary sigh. "What does it look like?"

She rummaged through the soggy, flattened boxes and produced its mate. "Like this."

He dutifully searched the stairs and front walk. "I didn't see it. Maybe it fell in the bushes."

Cindy's shoulders drooped as low as her morale. Those brambles were thick and probably hid a treasure trove of lost items—keys and wheat pennies and broken promise rings.

She sniffed.

Do not cry. A buckle is not a lost child.

He patted her shoulder awkwardly. "You could take it by King's Shoe Repair around the corner. He works miracles."

The rain let up and a glimmer of sunshine reached the stoop, illuminating him and his short, blue-black hair.

"You must be 3B. I'm 3A." He extended his hand to shake. Or he could have been handing her a business card.

Cindy couldn't tell. Their hands touched. There was no card. Just his hand. Big. Warm. Meltdown erasing.

"I'll carry these boxes upstairs for you." He knelt at her feet and bungeed the ruined boxes together.

"I'm sorry about your phone." Cindy followed him up the stairs, clutching her grandmother's shoe to her chest.

"I was going to upgrade it anyway." Mr. Sexy Voice now had the patience of the pope.

"I'd offer to make you a cup of coffee." And offer to bear your children. "But I don't think I could find the box with my coffeemaker."

"No worries. I have a meeting at The Local Grinder. I'll grab a cup there."

He was so understanding, completely opposite of the angry, impatient, demanding lawyers and judges she normally dealt with. Maybe he was worthy of Grandmother Drusella's shoes.

And fairy tales do come true.

Was this why she'd failed in the courtroom? Because she was a hopeless romantic?

They reached the third floor landing. Lucifer let out a loud complaint. He had the most distinctive meow, like a baby's cry.

"Coming, baby." Cindy rushed to the door.

"Hey, uh, 3B. I've got a meeting. Can you take it from here?" Her neighbor deposited her shoe boxes at her feet.

"Thanks again," she called after his retreating back.

She was thankful. Not just for his catching her when she would have fallen, but for the reminder that she could deal with setbacks with dignity, not tantrums or tears.

CHAPTER TWO

Mack Prince was always in a rush to be somewhere.

This morning that meant meeting a potential new client in a coffee shop around the corner.

Too bad his run in with his new neighbor—the pretty, sight-challenged, blue-eyed blonde—had resulted in his phone's untimely death.

A few months ago, the collision with his neighbor and resulting losses (coffee, phone) would have been tantrum-inducing, a dark cloud over his mood for hours, if not days. But that was before his father had a heart attack at age fifty-five and nearly died. Before the doctor warned dear old dad that his cutthroat law practice was killing him. Before that same doctor had looked at Mack and said, "I hope you're listening. In a decade or two, this will be you."

Mack Sr. may not have taken the doctor's warning to heart, but Mack Jr. had. He'd enrolled in an anger management class. He'd installed a small aquarium in his office to make him less stressed. He'd made a "stop doing" list of things that made his chest feel as if he was being buried alive. And he'd taken up running.

He should have introduced himself to the blonde. She was sweet, and made him forget his reputation as a heartless divorce lawyer at King, Prince & Prince. On the other hand, 3B had a child, which meant there was a guy around somewhere—a husband or boyfriend or jealous ex-lover. Mack didn't do messy.

The rain had let up and the farmer's market was just opening for business on Main Street. The original downtown had brick buildings, gas lamps, and a sense that time stood still.

The old woman in red, the one with the handmade *Love Advice* sign, waggled her plump fingers in a familiar wave. "You need to slow down. Love takes time." Her sing-song, bird-like voice carried over the noise of the growing crowd.

Mack delivered his retort with a retort-softening smile. "Any slower and you'd be giving my eulogy."

"Any slower and you'll bore me to death." She winked, on top of her game today. "Wouldn't want that on your conscience, would you?"

"I'm a divorce lawyer. I have no conscience." Mack continued down the sidewalk until he reached The Local Grinder, the neighborhood coffee house. The door was open, and the rich scent of coffee mingled with the buzz of caffeinated customers.

A blond man with a goatee waved him over to a wooden booth. "Recognized you from your website, Prince. I'm Eddie Tremaine." Eddie's limp fish handshake took points off Mack's initial character assessment.

Mack waved at the barista for his usual shot of espresso and took a five out of his wallet. "What can I do for you?"

"You came highly recommended." Eddie stroked his goatee as if it was his favorite pet. "I…uh…I'm thinking I need to get a divorce."

"Thinking?"

Eddie grimaced. "Decided." And then he added, in a firmer tone. "She moved out, and I decided it's time."

More likely, his pride had been hurt by her leaving. "Kids?"

"Just one." A slight upturn of lips. Perhaps he cared for his prodigy.

"Complications?"

"What?"

"People usually hire me because they expect complications." His new neighbor was a complication. She must be legally blind. He admired her independence, but he wondered about her living alone, especially with a baby. No mistaking that cry he'd heard from the other side of the door.

"I want custody of our son," his latest client was saying. "I suppose that's what you mean."

"Mr. Tremaine…Eddie." He was momentarily distracted by the woman in red across the street enticing a sucker to her table. "Unless we can prove to the court that your wife is a risk to your child's safety, it's highly unlikely that we'll win full custody. More likely joint."

"She'll treat him like she did me."

Mack quirked an eyebrow.

"Look at my hands." Eddie held them palms up. They were pruney and the skin was peeling from his fingers. "She had me scrub the apartment all the time. The floor was never clean enough. The sink was never clean enough. She sniffed our sheets before bed each night and if they didn't smell laundry fresh—"

"I get the idea." This was why people should live together before they got married. "But still, being OCD isn't enough reason to be granted full custody unless she's abusing your child."

"My son is three. He has a play set of cleaning tools. It's only a matter of time before she makes him scrub the house." The barista delivered Mack's espresso, ignoring Eddie's leering gaze and earning her big tip.

"I'll see what I can do for you, Eddie." If only people could be normal, divorce would be more civilized.

"Talk to me about your assets.

CHAPTER THREE

"Why did you move into a building with a broken elevator?" Cindy's step-sister, Anna Tremaine, always seemed to enter a room with a toss of her hair and a toss of a put-down. "I had to leave Teddy's stroller downstairs." She set her toddler on the hardwood floor. "It's a mess in here."

"I just finished bringing all my stuff in this morning." Cindy snatched a soggy shoe box from Teddy's reach. Her glasses may have been broken, but she could see shapes and sense a boy with mischievous intent. "I haven't had time to unpack." Or burst the hero-worship bubble Mr. Sexy Voice had left in her.

"Maybe you should wait until everything is organized before you invite people over." It was easy to be contemptuous. Harder to do it in a way that made it seem like Anna's duty was to point out the failings of others.

They'd grated on each other's nerves growing up in the same house and weren't on the best of terms now, but Cindy would stand by family. Even if she had to nail her soles to the floor.

Cindy took a deep breath, refusing to lose her temper. "You invited yourself over."

"Only because I need you to start my divorce as soon as you can." Anna leaned against the door. "Who was that hunk I saw coming down your steps just now?"

"Blue jacket? Black pants?"

"Louis Vuitton loafers. Designer jeans. Expensive haircut." Cindy could almost hear the smirk in her step-sister's voice.

"He's my neighbor. Nice guy." Cindy sidled closer to her red-headed step-nephew. "Teddy, how about a story?" A nice nap-inducing story.

"No," Teddy said.

Anna huffed by the door. "Of course he was nice to you. Just look at you." Her distaste was palpable. "Your hair is frizzy, you're squinting like a mole, and there's a weed on the back of your pants leg."

Just as Cindy was about to sweep Teddy into a bear hug, Anna's words sunk in. Her shoulders cramped, her jaw clenched, and Teddy crept out of reach.

"I mean…." Anna and her need to clarify. "Don't get any ideas and embarrass yourself. He's way out of your league."

Cindy hadn't dated in so long, she didn't know what league she was in.

Teddy disappeared behind a large suitcase. The little guy had a sixth sense for trouble. And Lucifer had been quiet since Anna and Teddy had arrived. The cat wasn't the friendliest beast on the best of days, but he was a crank-monster from this move. If Teddy surprised him or yanked on his tail or tried once more to eat the "treats" in Lucifer's litter box….

Cindy navigated the maze that was her living room, trying to spot either lost party behind the stacks of boxes and suitcases. A change of subject was in order. "Why a divorce? I thought you loved Eddie. I thought he treated you like a queen."

"He complains about everything, and—"

"Okay, divorce it is." On second thought, Cindy wasn't in the mood for a laundry list of Eddie's faults. Eddie was a pretentious pill. *Where had that rugrat gone?* "You can afford my fee, right?"

"You'd charge me? I'm family."

"I'd charge my father for services rendered." Okay, maybe not Dad. Cindy sighed and moved into the kitchen. No rugrat. No raccoon-sized black kitty. Her doom-o-meter pinged into the red zone.

"I need to get out, Cindy. Being a single parent is exhausting." Anna's voice sounded as if she'd already shattered and had taped herself back together, but without enough tape.

"You've been a single parent for one day." She was letting Anna get to her. Cindy took a breath and tried again. "That's a healthy perspective." Cindy bent and squinted to check under the sink.

"I knew I could count on you. Teddy's things are in the stroller downstairs."

And then Cindy heard the front door open and close.

"Hey, wait." Cindy returned to the living room, but Anna was gone.

Teddy giggled.

Cindy whirled around to find the little bugger had opened the suitcase with her lingerie. He wore a purple Wonderbra strapped onto his head like a ski-cap, her lime green polka dot bathrobe sash around his neck, and was using a pair of her red sport socks like mittens. Without her glasses, Teddy looked like a Skittle-sprinkled snowman.

"Photo opp." Someday, Aunt Cindy was going to use that shot as blackmail.

Teddy giggled and tugged on the bra straps, beeping with every tug as if he was a truck driver.

Sadly, that was the most male attention that bra had ever received. Being a workaholic cramped her dating life. Cindy hoped that moving to Brody Falls would change all that.

Teddy smiled at her and for a moment, Cindy saw another young face. Big grey eyes. A ponytail of thin brown hair.

A tough child custody case related to a divorce she was handling had nearly broken her. She'd been unable keep her cool under pressure in the court-room, unable to remain detached. She'd let her client down. In the worst possible way.

Things would be different here. Things *had* to be different here.

"Okay, Teddy. We're going out." Cindy needed a change of scenery, even if it was only a watercolor world she saw.

And maybe if Teddy got some fresh air, he'd crash until Anna came home. And since Mr. Sexy Voice had mentioned the shoe repair shop around the corner, Cindy decided to take her grandmother's shoes.

She wrapped the delicate pumps in a clear plastic bag, and led a now braless Teddy downstairs—one careful step at a time (since he insisted on walking). The rain had stopped and the sky was beginning to clear. She carried the stroller to the sidewalk, strapped Teddy in, and searched the front stoop, the steps, and as much as she dared poke around the brambles for the missing buckle. No luck.

"Auntie, go-go-go!" Teddy kicked his little sneak-ered feet.

Cindy pushed him around the corner toward the farmer's market, her grandmother's shoes resting on the stroller's hood.

She'd never been to the market, but it was a well-known feature of Brody Falls and she'd been looking forward to experiencing it. She rounded the corner and took it all in. There were more people than expected. They milled about, pausing in front of stalls with what looked like produce and fresh flowers and other unidentifiable stuff. *How am I going to move in that crush with the stroller?* It was more crowded than Disneyland in July.

Something caught Teddy's eye. "Truck, auntie. Truck!"

"No truck."

"Truck!" His legs kicked out and one of his sneakers flew off. "Puh-lease…." He tilted his head back and smiled angelically.

What was an auntie for if not to spoil her only nephew? "Okay, truck." Cindy picked up Teddy's shoe and pushed into the melee. Miraculously, the crowd parted. Pushing a stroller wasn't such a bad thing after all. "Where's the truck, Teddy?" Hopefully some other little darling hadn't brought one from home. One not for sale.

"Bring the shoe to me." The words reverberated around Cindy as if she was in a cave and the voice of God (as a woman) had come to her.

Cindy stopped in the midst of the crowd and squinted in all directions.

"Red!" Teddy cried, pointing to an older woman wearing a red sweater and scarf, sitting at a card table.

The woman gestured for Cindy to come closer. Try as she might, Cindy couldn't see a truck near the woman.

"Red, red, red," Teddy chanted, reaching toward the old lady.

Did she have a red truck in her lap? Cindy paused in front of the card table, uncertainty tickling her earlobes, the way it did when a client wasn't being totally honest.

"Give me the shoe." The woman extended a hand.

Cindy handed over Teddy's shoe, and then bent, squinting at the pink page hanging from the woman's table. Was it…did that say…*Love Advice???*

Cindy stood so quickly her lower back twinged in protest.

"We can start with the boy's shoe," the old woman said in a voice as high and clear as a bluebird's. "But he has years yet."

"Decades," Cindy deadpanned, not exactly clear on what would come after Teddy's shoe was discussed. Was this a sales pitch? The lady didn't look like she was selling time shares. She looked like someone's grandmother—gray hair beneath a red scarf, a round pink face, and a slash of red lipstick where her mouth should be.

"Sit." There was a stern tone to the old woman's voice that made Cindy obey like a well trained Labrador. Red lipstick curled upward, kind of like the Cheshire Cat's floating grin on a pink oval. "This one will marry his childhood sweetheart."

"I'm going to find out who you've been kissing in pre-school, my friend," Cindy said to Teddy, taking back his sneaker.

He kicked his feet and giggled. "Girls are yucky!"

"And now for yours, my dear."

Cindy squinted at her pink pinstriped Keds.

"Your satin slippers, love." The old woman pointed toward Cindy's vintage heels on top of the stroller.

"Oh." Cindy handed them over. "Is this the shoe repair booth?" Finally, something was going right today.

The woman didn't answer. She removed the pumps from the bag and held one up. "It's the shoe."

Ah, she was nutty. Cindy glanced about for the nearest form of help, just in case she'd need reinforcements to reclaim her treasures.

"This shoe will lead you to true love." The old woman stroked one shoe and sighed. "You won't recognize it, of course. But in the end, the shoe will triumph…. Well, the buckles will triumph. The clock is ticking already." She cocked her head. "Listen. Your prince is coming."

Somewhere nearby, a clock tower chimed the hour. The same bells she'd heard earlier during the shoe incident with Mr. Sexy Voice.

"Red," Teddy said reverently. And then he yawned.

Cindy reached for her shoes, somewhat nervously, and was relieved when they were safely in the plastic bag.

"That will be forty dollars." The red slash of lipstick curled up in a smile.

"Forty?" Cindy should have bypassed the old woman and headed straight for the person selling red toy trucks.

"I didn't charge you for the boy."

"Truck!" Teddy cried.

CHAPTER FOUR

"What's *she* doing here?" Eddie said as he shook Mack's hand outside the coffee shop. "That's my kid." He hurried off.

The blond woman in 3B, the one who'd been the cause of Mack's broken phone, was pushing one of those jogging strollers with a red-headed little boy away from the Love Advice table.

This was Eddie's soon-to-be ex-wife? No wonder she had Eddie clean house. She couldn't do it, being practically blind.

Briefly, Mack considered rejecting the case. But only briefly.

The kid waved hands as Eddie neared, clearly pleased to see his daddy. And then the little dude kicked so hard one shoe flew off.

And 3B? She crossed her arms and scowled at Eddie.

Disappointment filed a grievance in Mack's gut. He moved on to the shoe repair shop. The bell over the door clanged as he entered. The smell of leather and oil were like the smells of home. "Grandpa King? What's up today?"

"Nothin's cookin' if you ain't been lookin'." Laughing, Grandpa King turned from his workbench to greet Mack. It was hard to believe a man so small and slight had contributed to Mack's gene pool.

A cowboy boot was mounted on a cast iron cobbler's last, its sole half removed.

"Looks like you're busy, Grandpa."

"I could use a hand." His grin invited Mack to put off drawing up the paperwork for Eddie Tremaine and play hooky. Grandpa King could afford to play hooky. He'd started the family law firm, brought in his son-in-law, Mack Prince Sr., and then retired to run his father's shoe store. He'd never had a heart attack and would probably outlive his father.

"I need to get a new phone and then head into the office."

"Manipulating the law is not what you should be doing on a Saturday."

"You'd rather I make an honest living repairing shoes on my *day off*?"

Grandpa's grin created more wrinkles in his already smile-wrinkled face. "I would, wouldn't you?"

"Well, maybe for a little while." Mack sat at the smaller workbench and began to remove the worn heel tips on a pair of racy red high heels. He bet the owner of those shoes was someone he might want to meet, if the owner looked like the woman in 3B. He refused to think of her as Mrs. Tremaine.

Down, Prince. That path only leads to trouble.

"Grandpa, didn't you meet Grandma King at a farmer's market?"

"It was the street fair back then." He shaped a leather sole on his work bench. "A woman at a booth, at the fair, told me to slow down and look around. I thought she was nuts, but I turned and bumped into your grandmother, knocked her off her feet. One of her shoes came off." He glanced up toward a wooden shoe box on a shelf above him. "She wore those shoes the day we were married. She taught me a lot about slowing down and enjoying life."

"History repeating itself," Mack murmured. He wasn't much for believing in fate or coincidence. "Don't tell me the woman in the booth, at the fair, was the same lady as the one out there with the Love Advice sign."

Grandpa chuckled. "I sense Cupid's arrow has finally struck my grandson."

A buzzer sounded in the back.

"That'll be Hank with my delivery." The old man moved with measured steps toward a curtain separating the storage room from the front of the business. At eighty, he was finally slowing down. "Can you watch the shop while I sign for my delivery, Mack?"

"Sure."

A few minutes later, the bell over the front door rang and who should enter but Mack's new neighbor with her son, who was sucking on a sippy cup with eyes half closed.

3B's bright blond hair was still in its utilitarian pony tail. It fell in a thick mass over her shoulder. Her baby blue T-shirt matched the color of her eyes.

Despite her vision challenges, she strode confidently in and parallel parked the stroller next to the counter. "Hi. I know this is probably an impossible request, but I'm looking for a replacement buckle for my vintage shoes." She brought out the heels, setting them on the table as if they were made of porcelain.

Mack met her gaze. She didn't seem to recognize him. "Uh, 3B, right?" He sure didn't want to tell her his name now that he knew who she was.

"You're my neighbor." She smiled and it was like a punch to Mack's gut.

She was pretty. Really pretty. But there was more to her than that. She didn't carry a cane to indicate she had a disability. Or have a guide dog. That took guts. Nothing was going to hold this woman back. How he envied her casual and steady approach to life. She seemed to hold onto it easily, as if the upheaval of her impending divorce was a blessing.

Mack relaxed just standing across the counter from her. He wanted to ask her out for lunch or coffee. But as soon as she learned he was representing her husband in the divorce, she'd hate him.

"The lady in red showed me where your shop was." Her cheeks bloomed a soft pink. "How long has King's been here?"

"Sixty years. My Grandpa runs it now." Mack handed her a claim slip. "Name and phone number is fine."

"Could you…uhm…just write 3B?" A deeper shade spread across her features, an indication that she was embarrassed by her disability.

"Of course. No worries."

The kid had conked out. His sippy cup had fallen to his lap and was dripping onto his pants. 3B probably couldn't see it. Mack came around the counter and moved the cup to a holder.

The curtain to the back room slid noisily along its rod. "That's what an old man likes to see." Grandpa tottered in from the back. "A pretty lady. What are we doing for you?"

She explained her dilemma. Grandpa assured her he'd find something.

Mack hurried to hold the door for her.

She hesitated next to him and then hesitated with her smile. "See you around 3A." And then she left.

He hadn't been on the receiving end of a sucker punch since the seventh grade. He watched her walk away, taking his time to collect himself.

"You should ask her out," Grandpa said. "Pretty lady. Nice kid. Good taste in shoes. She's a keeper."

"I'm representing her husband in their divorce." Oh, this was not going to be pretty.

"You could still ask her...." Grandpa tsked. "If you become a cobbler."

CHAPTER FIVE

"Where is your mommy, Teddy?" It was after six and getting dark. Anna wasn't answering her cell. Cindy needed a break and not just from her nephew. Mr. Sexy Voice hadn't been far from her thoughts all day.

She'd let Teddy play drummer with her pots and pans, while she wondered when Mr. Sexy Voice would get home. She'd played peek-a-boo while she wondered what Mr. Sexy Voice liked for dinner. She'd chased Teddy through her apartment, wondering if Mr. Sexy Voice gave foot massages.

It wasn't Teddy's fault that she was tired and preoccupied. Her nephew deserved an upbeat, happy aunt. It was just that aunts were supposed to have fun with their nephews and then actually return them, weren't they?

Cindy was starting to wonder if Anna was coming back tonight.

She tried Anna's number one more time with no success. "That's it, Teddy. We're going for a run before it gets completely dark or starts raining again."

Soon she was pushing Teddy through the park, up hills and down, on paths through thick foliage and beneath bridges. The terrain was new, but the pea-graveled path was wide and clear.

She loved it in Brody Falls. Everything was going to be all right. She had her first client and was opening her office on Monday. The divorce rate was at its peak. And private practice promised to be civilized and safe.

It began to sprinkle. She headed back the way they'd come.

Soon she began to hear footsteps, but every time she looked back, she saw no one. The world was a shadowy blur. She picked up her pace, again and again, until she was practically speed-walking and her quads threatened to cramp. She withdrew her mace from her fanny pack, ready to protect Teddy at all costs.

The bells chimed the half-hour.

"Stop," Teddy whined. "Stop, stop, stop." He began kicking. One of his shoes flew off.

Someone came up behind them. Fast.

Cindy screamed, whirled, and sprayed the large figure with mace.

And then she ran all the way home, leaving Teddy's shoe behind.

CHAPTER SIX

Coming up behind 3B without announcing himself was stupid.

Mack's eyes stung. He took his water bottle and poured the cool liquid over his burning, watering eyes. He counted backwards from one hundred. He steadied his breathing. He told himself accidents happen.

But that didn't stop his eyes from puffing up or his head from pounding.

He'd seen 3B ahead about half a mile back and thought she'd be safer waking with an adult companion, this close to night. But she started rushing off and he'd had trouble catching up without running. And then, just as he was about to catch up, he'd seen the kid's shoe fly off, and she'd turned and maced him.

On the one hand, it was his fault. He should have said something like, "Your kid dropped his shoe." Or, "Passing to your right, 3B." Instead, he'd been watching the powerful movement of her legs.

Grandpa King would have said that was a sin and he got what he deserved.

Dad would have filed a lawsuit in the morning.

Mack was neither of those men.

When he could shapes again, Mack stumbled toward home and tripped over the kid's shoe.

The Mack Prince of a couple months ago, the heartless divorce lawyer who worked all hours of the day and night, he would have left the shoe and avoided 3B forevermore.

But the Mack Prince of today felt the need to apologize for scaring her. He didn't want anything bad to keep 3B down.

CHAPTER SEVEN

The realtor who'd helped Cindy find an apartment in a safe part of town had another thing coming. First thing in the morning Cindy was calling her and giving her a piece of her mind.

Cindy dried Teddy off from their rain-capped stroll, and put him down on her bed. He was unaffected by their scare, and rolled over, closing his eyes. She changed into dry clothes—pajama pants, a Pooh-bear T-shirt, and fuzzy pink slippers.

The room was a little stuffy, so Cindy opened the bedroom window a few inches. As soon as she let it go, it fell back down and latched. She propped it up with an aspirin bottle.

There was a knock on the door.

"It's about time, Anna." Still jittery with adrenaline, Cindy was itching for a fight with someone. How could Anna leave Teddy all day? This was followed almost immediately by a guilty thought—that Anna might need more than some time alone. She might need professional help.

But it wasn't her step-sister. It was a man. A tall man. Mr. Sexy voice? The man from 3A?

Whoever it was, he wore jogging clothes and handed her Teddy's sneaker. "Sorry for scaring you."

That voice!

He turned to go.

"Wait," Cindy whispered, trying not to wake Teddy. "Did I…I maced you?" Thoughts raced through her head like a large flock of blackbirds swooping for a place on a very short wire. Was he a pervert? Or a hero? She hoped the latter. "You scared me."

"I know. I saw you and tried to catch up."

"And I heard you and tried to run away."

"By the time I caught up, I was out of breath."

It took a special kind of man to show his face after he'd been maced.

Her heart softened. "I am so, so sorry. I was raised in New York City. Even though I've been in California for years, old habits—like going on the offensive—die hard." Cindy wished she could see his face clearly. How much pain was he in? Tentatively, impulsively, she reached out and laid her palm on his cheek. It was warm and damp. "Can I help?" A trip to the urgent care clinic? "I read somewhere that milk works well in reducing the effect of mace. If you come inside—"

"You've done enough for one day," he said with humor in his voice, covering her hand with his. Then he pulled her palm to his lips, kissed it, and let it fall between them. "Good night, 3B."

Cindy closed the door and leaned against it, heart pounding.

Someone knocked on the door again.

"You came back." Cindy flung it open, but it was only Anna.

After she and Teddy left, Cindy did the dishes. She was dying of curiosity to know what 3A looked like. Tall, blue-black hair, and humble. Were his eyes as dark as his hair? Was his smile as warm as his touch? Her new glasses wouldn't be ready until Monday.

And his name! She *still* didn't even know his name.

It didn't matter. He could be a Beufort or a Marvin, and she wouldn't care.

Lucifer meowed from the bedroom.

"What's wrong, kitty?"

Movement near the window caught her eye. The sill shifted up and down.

Had Lucifer slipped out?

Cindy's heart leapt up her throat. Cats were notorious for trying to find their way back to their old neighborhoods if they were let outdoors too soon.

Cindy rushed over, raised the window higher and poked her head outside. "Here, kitty-kitty." Her elbow knocked the bottle of pain reliever to the floor.

She couldn't see a thing. The night was as black as ink, even the shadows melded into the shadows as the wind whispered through the tree branches.

Maybe Lucifer would come to her if she stepped out on the fire escape.

Cindy swung her legs over the window ledge and stepped onto the metal landing. It'd stopped raining. She hoped Lucifer had gone no further than the fire escape. She could use a little luck.

"Here, kitty-kitty-kitty."

The window slammed closed behind her.

CHAPTER EIGHT

Mack sat on his leather couch with a milk compress over his eyes.

3B had been the cause of his broken phone. She'd maced him. And he still couldn't get her out of his head.

He was just starting to feel better when he heard a noise on the fire escape. Cats sometimes used the metal system, so he didn't immediately do more than register there'd been a sound.

But then there was another noise, like a whisper, followed by a loud thud.

Burglar. The familiar heat of righteousness filled his chest.

Mack charged over to the window, eager to defend his home, his building, his new neighbor.

He flung open the window and said, "Hold it right there."

He'd been right to hurry. A shadow slunk beneath 3B's window. Mack may not have been able to escort her on her stroll earlier, but he could protect her now.

"3A?" came a tentative voice.

The bell tower over at St. Anthony's struck the hour. Moonlight spilled through the clouds to shine on her thick blond hair.

Mack sighed. "What are you doing out here?"

"I think my cat slipped out the window. You don't see a big black cat, do you?"

He scanned the fire escape, both up and down. "No. Go back inside. I'm sure your cat will come back."

"I can't. The window's stuck," she said miserably. As if needing to prove it, she stood and tried to lift it to no avail.

A child cried softly from her apartment.

3B gasped. "Oh, my gosh. It's Lucifer. He's still inside."

Along with her son. "Come over here. I've got a key."

"To my apartment?"

"To every apartment. I'm the emergency back-up if the super isn't available." He held out his hand. "Come on."

She edged along the wall, as if afraid she'd fall. "I think I saw your name on my rental agreement, although I don't remember what it is." She reached out and he took her hand. "Maybe it's time we moved beyond calling each other 3A and 3B."

"Let's not take off our masks just yet," Mack joked softly, guiding her in the window. "We need to get you safely inside."

Her foot hung up and her slipper fell. She tumbled into the apartment and into his arms.

She tilted that sweet face toward his, and Mack couldn't resist. He lowered his head and kissed her.

It was a gentle kiss, a getting-to-know you kiss, a wonderful-wonderful kiss.

The clock chimes faded away.

"We…I…." Mack cast about for the right thing to say.

"After what happened earlier, I wasn't expecting that." She smiled dreamily. "It was lovely."

Mack was in some deep doo-doo. He wanted to tell her his name and that he'd happily clean house for her if she'd kiss him, and only him, for the rest of her life.

But in a few days, when he requested a meeting of the divorcing parties and their lawyers, she was going to find out who he was and then she'd never speak to him again.

CHAPTER NINE

"Boss, I found out who Mrs. Tremaine hired as her attorney." Lovey Burney entered Mack's office on Monday afternoon. She'd been Grandpa King's secretary and was a pistol at the ripe age of seventy. "Cynthia Carlisle, from San Francisco."

Mack had been reviewing a particularly tricky new law related to the division of marital assets. He'd been reviewing it for the last hour, unable to get beyond the first paragraph. His thoughts kept turning to 3B.

"That's not good news," he said to Lovey.

"For Mrs. Tremaine, you mean." She sat in the chair opposite his desk, her shoulders slightly hunched from years of secretarial work.

"Of course, of course."

Divorce attorney Cynthia Carlisle had suffered a well-documented meltdown a month ago in a San Francisco courtroom when a judge had deemed her not to have provided enough evidence that a child was in danger. She'd tearfully demanded the judge do as she asked, evidence or not, because she'd had a "feeling."

The judge had cited her for contempt. The child had been sent on an unsupervised visitation with her father and had later been found dead in a dumpster—the father's retaliation for his wife wanting a divorce. The speculation in the papers was that Ms. Carlisle had proven her case, but the judge hadn't wanted to grant her motion because she'd become emotional.

The last thing this case needed was a drama queen.

The bells at St. Anthony's rang.

Grandpa King stood in Mack's doorway. "I found the perfect buckle for your lady friend." He handed Mack a delicately carved wooden shoe box. "And I thought you might deliver it to her."

"This was Grandmother's box." The shoebox had been lined with velvet and had once held his grandmother's wedding shoes, the shoes she'd worn when they met. The box had been stored above Grandpa King's workbench since her death ten years ago.

"I used the buckles from her shoes. Pearls, not rhinestones." Grandpa King winked. "Diamonds aren't always a girl's best friend."

"But…."

Grandpa King didn't wait to argue. He left, and Lovey scuttled after him.

CHAPTER TEN

Mack hadn't seen 3B since the night she'd been stuck on the fire escape. His phone was replaced. His eyes had recovered. He tried not to remember that kiss. He wasn't going to go soft when he saw all that blond hair and those big blue eyes.

Didn't matter how many times he counseled himself, Mack was nervous about seeing her today—her and her divorce lawyer. The Tremaines were going to try and work out the big issues of the divorce for the first time. Mack would wait until another meeting to drop the custody bombshell.

Mack sat with Eddie in the clear glass conference room. Mack tapped his pencil. Eddie stroked his goatee.

In his mind, that room was a fish bowl. How he hated being a fish.

Through the glass walls he could see 3B come into the office, looking like a dream in a tailored blue business suit, a colorful pink and orange scarf around her neck and that bright blond hair swinging. The only difference today was that she wore a pair of black-rimmed glasses. She looked confident, capable, and everything Mack had ever wanted in a woman.

She was followed by her lawyer, who wasn't as tall or as blond or as captivating. In fact, she looked rather bitter. Cynthia Carlisle looked as if she hadn't taken her downfall in the big city well last month. In fact, it was hard to believe she'd be passionate about anything. Cynthia Carlisle was a sour woman who looked like she might not make it through the day.

Lovey gestured toward the conference room and led them over

Mack stood and went to the fish bowl's door, introducing himself. "Thank you for coming…Mrs. Tremaine."

3B blinked behind those thick lenses. And then she chuckled. "I'm Cindy Carlisle. It's nice to finally meet you Mr. Prince. Or should I call you 3A?" She turned to the bitter-looking woman behind her. "This is Anna Tremaine, my step-sister and client."

Mack's ears rang and he didn't think it was the bells of St. Anthony striking this time. 3B was opposing council? Not the woman he planned to cleave from her child. 3B was opposing council? The same woman who was willing to put everything on the line for a stranger's child, even if it meant tarnishing her reputation.

Maybe she had overreacted in the courthouse before, in a moment of weakness, but this was a woman who'd fight for what was right. She'd done so before. And she wasn't a broken thing. She was confident and capable and passionate. For the first time in a long time, Mack wondered if he wanted to win.

"The attorneys need a moment alone." Mack led Cindy out of the conference room and into his office and closed the door behind them. "*You're* Cindy Carlisle?"

"Since the day I was born. Is that why you stopped kissing me the other night? You thought I was Anna?" She chuckled again. "The woman at the farmer's market was right. I almost didn't recognize you now that I can see again."

"I'm so glad you find this amusing. I thought you were a blind woman." Mack hesitated, but Cindy wasn't playing the dragon lady. She was—and always would be—calm 3B. Mack took the wooden shoebox from his desk and presented it to her. "For you." He hoped she loved the new buckles.

Cindy looked perplexed, but opened the box. "My shoes! The buckles aren't the same, but they're beautiful. How did your grandfather ever find these? They look vintage."

"The box and the buckles belonged to my grandmother." He stepped closer, close enough to catch the scent of Cindy's floral perfume. "The pearls are real. Would you put them on?"

Her gaze met his. Accepting. Longing. Hesitating. "But…Our clients…."

"They can wait." He took the box from her and dropped to his knees, encouraging her to lift first one foot and then the other, so he could set them on her feet. He gazed up at her. "I know about your reputation for fighting for what's right. The day we met, I kept thinking you were nearly blind, but you kept smiling and trying and pushing forward. You wouldn't quit or roll over, not even when I surprised you in the park. And yet, you do it with such grace. I envy that."

"My mother used to say I'd persevere if I was barefoot in a snowstorm. I guess that applies to situations where I break my glasses, too." She admired the shoes, and then her gaze turned serious. "But perseverance and determination aren't always enough. It's no guarantee that the courts will see things my way. I…I did quit. I hit a wall in the courtroom and I lost my composure. After that, I couldn't practice there again. Opposing council would always try to rattle me, and judges would always wonder if I needed a recess to stop a meltdown."

"You came here to make a new life."

Her words lacked their usual optimism. "I'll always be known as the attorney who cried. It's horrible that a child died…. She died because of my mistake. And yet her death proved that I was right."

The sunlight through his window caught the highlights in her hair. "You should always follow your intuition."

The smile returned, soft, regretful. "The day we met, I felt the frustration build again. The sense that I couldn't save something as inconsequential as a shoe. But your voice…. It calmed me." She drew Mack to his feet. "And then a woman at the farmer's market told me that my prince was coming and that I'd meet him through these shoes, through the buckles." Her smile was as radiant as a spring flower. "Do you believe in Fairy Godmothers, Mr. Prince?"

"I do now, because you and your shoes…. You must be my Cinderella." He brushed aside a stray strand of hair behind her ear and kissed her, gently, tenderly, as if she was as fragile as the vintage shoes on her feet. Someday, if things worked out between them as he felt they could, she'd work with him as his partner. Together, they'd help each other through life's ups and downs.

"Our clients," Cindy murmured after what seemed like far too short a time.

"Right. Right." Mack straightened his tie and adjusted her scarf. "Dinner? Tonight? My place?"

She blushed. "Yes."

He opened the door and led her to the fish bowl. But their clients were gone.

"Boss?" Lovey stood at her desk. "The Tremaines made up. Couldn't keep their hands off each other. I got tired of watching them, so I kicked them out."

He hoped Lovely never retired.

The clock tower at St. Anthony's chimed.

But it wasn't midnight, and Mack's Cinderella didn't disappear. He had the shoes and the girl and all the time in the world to live happily ever after.

Copyright © 2015 by Melinda Curtis.

Kate Capulet hails from the Pacific Northwest. She likes the smell of books and coffee (together or separate), and bites her lower lip when she's trying not to say something wildly inappropriate. You can reach her at katecapulet@gmail.com.

SUSAN SHAVES

by Kate Capulet

Susan stared at herself in the hotel bathroom mirror, chewing on her lower lip. The bikini fit, but only if she redefined "fit" to mean "covers nipples and crotch." She wanted to take it off and hide under the covers of the hotel room bed.

At least my hair looks good, Susan thought. Her long blonde hair hung over her shoulders, trailing down her back and breasts. *I think my hair would cover more than this bathing suit.*

Claudia called from the other side of the bathroom door.

"Susan are you done in there? Everyone else is down at the beach already."

Claudia, her roommate for the next ten days, was already changed into her bathing suit. She'd changed right there in the room in front of Susan with no regard for modesty.

Susan had blushed furiously at the sight of Claudia's nakedness, and taken the plastic bag with the swim suit she'd just bought into the bathroom. Though she admired Claudia's uninhibited manner, no way was she changing in front of anyone.

Susan studied the little blue bikini and her bits of pale flesh poking out the sides and made a decision.

"I can't wear this," Susan called back through the door. "I'm going back to the store to get a different one."

Claudia sounded irritated. "Susan come out. Just let me see it? I'm sure it's fine."

Susan took a deep breath. Reached for the door handle opened the door and stepped out. Claudia sat on the hotel bed, knees crossed, bouncing one foot impatiently. Susan felt a pang of jealousy. Claudia had naturally tan skin with dark hair and brown eyes. She looked like an exotic super model in her black bikini.

"Ta da," Susan said unenthusiastically. She spread her arms trying to be nonchalant, but failing. She could feel the heat in her cheeks as Claudia studied her.

"You look great!" Claudia smiled.

"It doesn't fit," Susan said fiddling with the small triangle of fabric covering her left nipple trying to get it to stretch further to cover more skin.

"That's how it's *supposed* to fit."

Claudia stood from the bed and walked over to slap Susan's hands away from the swimsuit. Claudia circled Susan, the latter blushing furiously.

"Oh," Claudia said when she got up close. A frown creased her forehead. "You need to take care of that before you leave this room."

The word "that" was punctuated with Claudia pointing her finger at Susan's crotch.

Susan looked down. A bit of pubic hair stuck out on either side of the triangle of blue fabric.

Susan shrugged.

"I told you it doesn't fit. I need to go get the other one. It won't take me long."

Susan bent for a pair of shorts and tank top she'd left in a pile on the floor.

"No," Claudia said. "What you *need* to do is shave. Friends don't let friends grow their bush out. You brought a razor, right?"

Susan nodded, but she was worried. "I've never shaved before. I'd probably just cut myself."

Claudia blinked. "You've never shaved?"

Susan shook her head.

A slow grin spread across Claudia's face.

"You're in for a treat then. Back in the bathroom." Claudia gestured one manicured hand to the bathroom.

"Wouldn't it be faster to just go buy the other one?" Susan said, and her roommate gave her a playful shove.

"Go. Run a bath. Find your razor. Then call me."

Susan trudged into the bathroom, the tile cold against her bare feet. She turned the tap and let the tub fill. She ran her hand under the water until it was a comfortable leg-shaving temperature.

While the tub filled, Susan hooked her thumbs under the strings of the bikini bottoms pausing before sliding the bottoms down. She bit her lower lip.

"Um, can't I just shave around the edges?"

"Take it off," Claudia called back. "All of it. Hurry up, lady. The beach is calling my name."

Susan sighed and slid the bottoms down, stepping out of them and trying to ignore the swarming butterflies inside her. She pulled the strings holding the bikini top on and let the top fall to the floor.

Susan studied her naked body in the mirror while the tub filled.

Her breasts were firm and high, the nipples pink against her pale flesh. Susan watched them grow hard as the cool bathroom air hit them.

"Not even enough for a handful," Adam would have said. He'd never liked the size of her breasts. Come to think of it, Adam hadn't liked much about her at all. He'd never said anything about her pubic hair though. Perhaps if she'd shaved he wouldn't have broken up with her.

Susan heard her friends' words of sympathy after the break up. *Susan, he isn't worth being sad over. Good riddance.*

Susan looked at the triangle of hair between her legs and wondered what she would look like without it. Quite to her surprise, the flesh between her thighs seemed to pulse at the thought.

Why, Susan.... You're horny!

Well so what if she was. Watching herself in the mirror, Susan ran her fingers across the peak of one hard nipple, enjoying the tingles it sent through her body.

"Is the bath filled?" Claudia voice came from the other side of the door. Susan jumped, her hand flying away from her breast.

"Yes, it's filled," she called back. She quickly walked over to the tub and stepped into the warm water, letting her feet adjust to the heat.

"Okay, good," Claudia said. The bathroom doorknob turned and Susan gasped.

"Wait! I'm not dressed!" She plunked her naked body down into the warm water crossing her hands over her breasts.

Claudia walked into the bathroom, tsking at Susan. "Of course you're not dressed. You can't shave if you're dressed. Where's your razor?" Her voice had an echoing quality from where Susan sat in the tub.

Susan pointed at her bathroom bag on the counter then hastily snatched her hand back. The warm water did nothing to relax her as her roommate dug through her bag.

"You have to let your skin acclimate to the water first," Claudia said, her back to Susan.

While she waited, Susan looked Claudia up and down.

Claudia's back and arms were toned, but not overly muscular. Susan let her eyes trail down her roommate's spine to her buttocks. Shapely and curved, the black bikini bottoms dimpling the soft flesh only a little. Her hips were shapely, her legs long and slender. Her black string bikini top cut a straight line into a bow on Claudia's back.

Susan felt her sex pulse again and looked away, disgusted with herself. Claudia was just trying to be helpful.

Claudia finally found the razor. "Here it is."

Susan held out a hand covering her breasts with one arm. "Thanks."

Her roommate grinned. She did not hand her the razor.

"Nope. Your first time should be done right."

Susan frowned pulling her arm back into the water. "What do you mean 'right'?"

Claudia picked up a wrapped bar of hotel soap from the side of the tub. She tore the paper of it and tossed it into the sink. Then she pointed to the far edge of the tub.

"Hop up on the edge there, feet in the tub. Face me."

Susan tried to shrink in on herself. "Why?"

"I need to see what I'm doing."

"Claudia, I really think I should just go get the other suit. This is crazy—"

"Hush. I won't cut you. Now I'd like to get down to the beach sometime today, and this will go faster with my help, so get up there."

Susan reluctantly rose from the water, the drips and splashes drowned out by the thunder of her own heart beat reverberating in her ears.

Claudia leaned over the edge of the tub and handed Susan the soap.

"Lather up," she said. And then Claudia winked at her. Actually winked!

Susan swallowed hard and dipped the soap into the water holding her other hand across her breasts. The bar of soap slipped out of her hand and plunked into cloudy water. She felt around but the soap squirted away from her hand each time and she quickly realized she needed two hands to find it. She'd have to let go of both her breasts and her modesty. She considered bolting for the door and cursed herself a coward.

Just do it, she thought. *Mexico is meant to be crazy.*

Faking a bravado she didn't feel, Susan dropped both hands into the water found the bar and lathered up the soap in her hands. From the corner of her eye she saw Claudia trying to look everywhere but at Susan's exposed breasts.

Susan worked the soap into the top of her pubic hair.

This isn't so bad, she thought.

Claudia cleared her throat.

Susan looked up from where her hands worked in her lap.

"Spread 'em." Claudia said, nodding at Susan's tightly closed knees.

Susan blanched. "Claudia, I can't do this with you in here."

"Bullshit. It's your first time; let me help." She ticked her points off on her fingers. "One, you don't know what you're doing. Two, yours isn't the first pussy I've ever seen." She crossed her arms beneath her breasts. Susan tried not to notice how that pushed them up. "Part your legs and lather up or you're never going to finish."

Feeling embarrassment heat her face Susan spread her knees, feeling the lips between her legs part. And yet somehow there was a wetness down there that had nothing to do with the bath water.

Susan worked the lather into the hair between her legs, trying to ignore both Claudia's scrutiny and the tightening in her belly.

"Okay, good enough," Claudia said, watching Susan like a teacher watches a student. She lifted the razor.

Susan drew back and instinctively closed her legs. Soap squished up between her thighs. A thrill of anticipation wormed through Susan's belly. "Claudia, I don't know about this."

For the first time Claudia looked less certain. "Would you prefer we stop? I can be a bit bullheaded sometimes. I was only trying to help."

Feeling torn, yet more and more curious, Susan opened her legs, but turned her head away, blushing. She heard Claudia splash the razor in the warm bath water and then felt the head of the razor touch the flesh just above the top of her pubic hair. Claudia drew the razor down, slowly.

"See? Nothing to it." Claudia spoke to Susan in soft tones as though talking to a frightened animal. "You're lucky," Claudia continued. "You don't have much hair."

Susan felt the razor moving along her pubic area, stroking gently against her sensitized labia. Claudia's touch was light, but efficient.

"Need some more soap," Claudia said.

Susan lathered more soap in her hands and applied it to the remaining hair. She was surprised when her soapy fingers found long patches of bare flesh beneath the soap. She opened her eyes and looked down, fascinated.

Claudia was concentrating, gently drawing the razor down again and again, rinsing the blade in the bath water every second or third stroke.

Half of Susan's pubic hair was gone. Only a triangular shape remained at the top.

"Wow," Susan said, looking down at herself.

Claudia paused in her work and looked up at Susan between her parted thighs. "Like it?" she asked.

"Yeah. I do."

"Do you want to keep this?" Claudia said, pointing the razor to the patch of hair remaining at the top. "I could make it into a shape for you if you want to keep it."

Susan considered for a moment. She felt rebellion well up in her. "Shave it all," she said, finally.

Claudia quirked one perfect eyebrow at Susan. "Feeling brave, are we?"

Her roommate stroked the razor down the remaining patch of hair. This time Susan did not look away. She watched Claudia work, her breath coming quickly now. It felt strange to have another woman between her thighs, and she was nearly giddy with the naughtiness of being bare down there.

Susan was horrified when she felt her vaginal walls clench.

Claudia paused and Susan knew she had seen the movement. That close there was no way she could *not* see it.

Embarrassment flooded Susan and suddenly she just wanted this over and to never ever, *ever* talk about it again. Hopefully she would just think it was tenseness, not the beginnings of arousal.

She'd talk to one of the other girls tonight and see if she could switch rooms. Claudia wasn't stupid. She'd know Susan was avoiding her, but Susan didn't care as long as she didn't have to look at her again.

One final stroke of the razor and Claudia patted Susan's thigh. She jumped at Claudia's touch.

"Time to rinse off," she said. Susan thought her roommate's voice sounded a little funny. Thicker somehow.

Claudia reached up and detached the shower head from its cradle. She turned on the water and opened the drain. Claudia held the shower head out to Susan."Rinse off."

Susan took the shower head and did as Claudia saidShe watched the flow of water rinse away the remains of the soap. Susan looked down at herself fascinated.

All of her pubic hair was gone. The flow of water parted Susan's labia, and struck the pink nub of flesh. She bit her lip holding back a groan of pleasure.

Susan felt a hand stroking her hair and jumped. She'd been so engrossed in watching the water flow over her body that she'd forgotten Claudia for a moment.

Susan looked up. Claudia was watching her with an intensity that she had never seen on another person's face when focused on her.

"Do you even know how incredible you look right now?" When there was no answer, she added, "No, I suspect you don't."

Susan dipped her head, shy despite the position she was in. Looking at Claudia while the water poured down over her lower body made it hard to breathe.

She could not find words. She could only shake her head. The movement made her breasts jiggle slightly, the nipples hard little rocks. The water coursed over her and if she moved just right—Susan shifted beneath the stream—the water entered her vagina giving her the filling sensation she so badly craved right now.

Claudia leaned in over the edge of the tub, her breasts surging against the black fabric of her swim

suit, her lips touching Susan's lightly before her tongue slipped between Susan's parted lips.

Susan felt Claudia's tongue, warm and soft in her mouth, and gasped. She tentatively touched her tongue against Claudia's, shifting to get more of the kiss as the water struck her clitoris again.

Susan felt torn in half. Between the water pouring over her body, thumping into her opening, and the soft touch of Claudia's tongue against her own, she was almost drowned with unexpected feeling.

An involuntary groan tore from her lips as the sensations built, and she broke the kiss, eyes closed, breathing hard.

Susan felt a warm wet mouth close over one erect nipple and cried out softly.

Claudia released her nipple and Susan opened her eyes long enough to see her roommate lean further into the tub and part her lips over her other breast. When Claudia took the other nipple into her mouth and suckled it, her hips jerked upward, and she wished the water would come down harder, exert more pressure.

"I can't hold myself up anymore," Susan said, gasping. Her arms were shaking uncontrollably. She felt a deep pang of regret when Claudia released her nipple, sitting back.

"Come here then," her roommate said, standing. She turned off the water and extended a hand to Susan.

Susan stood and took her hand, following her into the bedroom, her arms still trembling.

Claudia stopped at the edge of her bed and turned towards her. She took the blonde's face between her hands, gently kissing her lips. Susan froze, not knowing what to do with her hands. She settled for running them tentatively up Claudia's side, then back. Her fingers encountered the string holding her bikini tied up and began to pull it.

Claudia stopped her, breaking the kiss. "Mmmm... tempting. But not this time. We've still got to get to the beach, remember?" Claudia pushed her toward the bed. "Lie down. Let's make your first time shaving memorable."

Susan couldn't help but notice that Claudia was breathing a little heavier than normal. The deep breaths made her breasts rise and fall in an utterly pleasing way.

She fell back on the bed and asked, "But what about you?"

"Later," Claudia said. "Or we'll never leave the room." She grabbed Susan's ankles.

Susan cried out, surprised.

"I think you can be louder than that," Claudia teased, coaxing Susan's legs apart and climbing onto the bed to lie between her thighs.

Claudia placed her lips over Susan's clitoris, kissing lightly. Then Susan felt her tongue, a warm wetness, caress her swollen nub. Her head fell back against the pillow, eyes closed, lips parted.

"I want to hear you, Susan," Claudia said, murmuring the words against Susan's inner thigh. "I want *everyone* to hear you."

Claudia flicked her tongue rapidly against Susan's clitoris and slipped a long finger into her wet vagina.

Susan groaned and threaded her fingers into her roommate's (now lover's?) long dark hair, thrusting her hips upward, wanting more, feeling an undeniable pressure build within her.

"Make some noise, Susan. Make me believe you want this."

Susan cried out and lifted her head to watch the other woman work between her legs. Claudia smiled at her, encouraging.

"That's better," she said. Claudia bent back down, running her tongue into Susan's wet opening.

Susan cried out again, louder this time.

Claudia sucked her clitoris and flicked it with her nimble tongue. She worked a finger in and out of her body and Susan's world seemed to concentrate down to region between her legs. She could think of nothing but the movements of Claudia's lips and tongue and fingers.

"Louder," Claudia said. "I want the neighbors to hear you." She slipped another finger into Susan, worked them in and out.

Susan heard the wetness in the movement. She felt a tightening in her body and surrendered herself to it. She lifted her hips, jerking them up, tightening her hands in her lover's hair, pressing Claudia's face hard between her thighs. The tension built and Claudia sucked on her clitoris relentlessly until something within her seemed to break.

Susan cried out sharply, her whole body clenching into a fist.

"Yes," Claudia said, against her clitoris. "That's it."

To Susan, Claudia sounded very far away. Claudia worked her fingers faster within her and she came again, harder this time, her hips lifting off the bedspread, her orgasm seeming to last an eternity.

Susan was aware of nothing but the tension in her body, of Claudia between her legs, of the pleasure rolling through her in giant waves.

When she collapsed back onto the bed, Susan was covered in a fine sweat, and exhausted.

Claudia sat back on the bed and slapped an open hand playfully against Susan's thigh. "Come on," she said, grinning. "The cool of the beach is calling me. I suddenly feel so very hot."

Claudia disappeared into the bathroom and came out with the bathing suit dangling from her hand.

"Let's try this again," she said. "I'll even tie your strings."

Copyright © 2018 by Kate Capulet.

New York Times & USA Today *Bestselling Author Brenda Novak is the author of sixty books. A five-time RITA nominee, she has won many awards, including the National Reader's Choice, the Bookseller's Best, the Book Buyer's Best, the Daphne, and the Silver Bullet. She also runs Brenda Novak for the Cure, a charity to raise money for diabetes research (her youngest son has this disease). To date, she's raised $2.6 million. For more about Brenda, please visit* www.brendanovak.com.

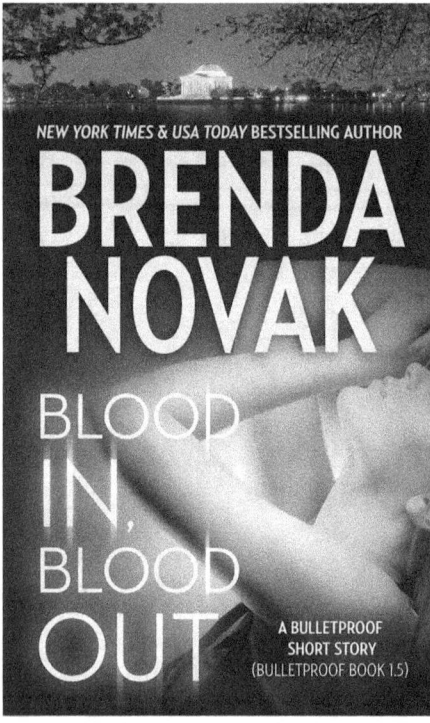

BLOOD IN, BLOOD OUT

by Brenda Novak

A BULLETPROOF SHORT STORY

(Bulletproof book 1.5)

Saturday Afternoon

As he sat in the rundown bar, brooding over a glass of whiskey, Rex McCready decided that his life was a series of battles in a war that would never end, and he wasn't on the winning side very often.

"Hey, thought I'd find you here." Virgil Skinner, his best friend, former cellmate and current business partner in Bodyguards R Us, slid onto the barstool next to him. "What happened *this* time?"

"The same thing that happens every time," he grumbled. He and Laurel Hodges, Virgil's sister, just couldn't get along. They loved each other, but they were both too damaged to make the relationship work, and the stress of having recently entered WITSEC—the witness protection program—together with Virgil and his wife, Peyton, only made matters worse. They all had different identities, his own name one he'd chosen himself but no longer liked. Even after almost two years, whenever someone called him Perry, he looked behind him to see who the hell they were talking to.

It didn't help that they'd been relocated clear across the country, to Washington DC. They'd had to get used to a new place, new names, new backgrounds, all while watching their backs for fear that the people who wanted them dead would find them. Add to that the whiplash effect of his on-again, off-again relationship with Laurel, and it wasn't easy to build a stable life.

Virgil sighed as he pulled a bowl of peanuts toward him. "How bad was it?"

Rex had never struck her. He never would. But her husband, ex-husband now, hadn't hesitated to cross that line, and that was part of her problem. She didn't want to trust the wrong man. And by most people's standards, Rex was definitely "the wrong man." Seeing as how *his* problems were too numerous to list, beginning with the loveless childhood that'd led him into gang life and an eight-year prison term, he couldn't really recommend himself. He'd probably still be a member of The Crew, his conscience conveniently anesthetized by drugs, if not for Virgil. Rex had recruited Virgil while they were serving time in Arizona. It wasn't until Virgil was exonerated for the murder of his stepfather that having joined a violent prison gang became such a problem.

Until then, it was the only way to survive.

After that, it was almost a sure way to die.

Blood in, blood out—or in laymen's terms, "Once a member, always a member—or else." In order to save Laurel, Rex had had had to kill two of the men he'd once called brothers. Kill two and seriously injure a third....

The Crew would never forget what had gone down in Colorado, which meant he, Laurel and Virgil might never be safe.

"We argued. I walked out. That's it." He drained his glass and asked the bartender, a cute blonde with a Southern accent, for another shot.

"Betty," according to her nametag, glanced at Virgil to see if he wanted one, too, and Virgil nodded. "Laurel will cool off," he said when Betty moved away.

Their anger never lasted long. Already Rex wanted to go back. But he wasn't sure how much more he could take. If they weren't having hot, sweaty, full-throttle sex, they were arguing with equal ferocity. There was no middle ground where Laurel was concerned, and if he couldn't have a positive impact on her life he had no business being part of it at all. She had her children—Jake, seven, and Mia, five—to take care of. They didn't need the stress, the disruptions.

"No, man, I'm done. We're just torturing each other. I have to stay away."

Virgil's gaze jerked to his face. "You mean that?"

Rex didn't bother waiting for his second drink. He didn't want to talk about Laurel, didn't want to deal with their problems, not anymore. "Yeah. I mean it," he said and got up and walked out.

He was so upset he almost didn't see the man lingering in the shadow of the building. Out of the corner of his eye, he caught a glimpse of movement, but when he turned, no one was there.

It's nothing. They'd been living in DC for nearly two years, and yet he was still seeing faces he thought he recognized, still feeling as if The Crew was only one step behind him.

Quit being so fucking paranoid.

Despite telling himself that, he tensed, listening closely. He wanted to figure out where the man had gone, get a better look at him. But when Virgil emerged from the bar, Rex took off down the street. He loved Virgil as much as he loved Laurel, but he'd already said all he had to say.

"I found 'em."

It was Mose, the man Horse had sent to Washington DC. Holding his cell phone to his ear, he stared out at the balmy Los Angeles afternoon visible beyond the window of his illegal club and felt a smile stretch across his face. At last! Horse had been waiting to hear those words for twenty-two months, ever since Virgil had emerged from prison and run out on them. Together with the other Crew leaders, he'd been determined to find and stop Virgil, or Skin as they called him, before he could rat anyone out to the cops. But when Rex, formerly known as Pretty Boy, turned on them, too, this became a personal challenge, something that went far deeper than regular gang business. It was partially thanks to Virgil and Rex that Horse held the power he now did inside The Crew, but that didn't mean he wasn't going to avenge those who'd been killed. "*Who*, exactly?"

"Laurel, for one," Mose said. "And I'm pretty sure I saw Rex leaving her place. I followed a guy I think was him to a bar but I was afraid he'd see me, so I couldn't get a good look at his face."

"What about Virgil?"

"Here in DC, too. I got a better view of him than Rex. They were together. I tried to follow Virgil home, see where he lives, but he was on a motorcycle. I couldn't keep up."

The Crew's contact in the Federal Bureau of Prisons had taken a while to deliver the information Horse wanted, but apparently she'd slept with the right U.S. Marshal, one who didn't want the pictures of their time together going home to his wife and kids.

"Virgil, Laurel, Rex. All three of them," Horse mused. "That's good."

"Should I kill the woman tonight?"

"Hell, no! If you do you'll never find Virgil and Rex."

"I just told you, man. They're here in DC."

"But you don't know *exactly* where they live. Not yet. You hurt Laurel, they'll pop you and disappear."

"They won't pop me. When I come after them, they won't know what hit 'em."

Tough talk but Horse wasn't taking any chances. Virgil and Rex were the biggest bad asses he'd ever known. "Don't give me that bullshit," he said. "We have to play this smart."

"Which means what?"

He could hear the frustration in Mose's voice. "It means you grab Laurel, since you know where she lives, and use her as bait to bring the men to you."

There was a brief silence as Mose considered his instructions. "You think they'll come?"

"They'll do anything for her."

"What if they call the cops instead?"

"They won't, because they know you'll kill her if they do. As soon as they arrive, shoot 'em all and get the hell out of DC," he said and hung up.

Was that man following her?

Laurel Hodges stopped in the snack aisle to see if the heavily muscled man she'd spotted two or three times since entering the grocery store would simply walk past.

He didn't. He moved into the same aisle but paused a few feet away and picked up a bag of chocolate chips as if he wanted to study the nutritional information.

"Mommy, what's wrong?"

Laurel forced a smile. Mia was too big for the grocery cart child's seat, so she was riding in the basket while Jake grabbed one item after another and begged Laurel to buy it.

"Can we get this?"

"No." Laurel didn't even look at his latest find. Lowering her head as though taking stock of the contents of her cart, she peeked at the man with the shaved head and the tattoos covering his forearms and tried once again to call Rex on her cell.

She got his voice mail. Damn it. He was really mad at her this time. She couldn't think of any other reason he wouldn't pick up.

She didn't leave a message. If the man was a member of The Crew this would all be over before Rex could do a thing about it. Virgil wouldn't be able to help her, either—not that she'd call him. He had Peyton and his new baby to worry about.

Should she contact the police? They could probably respond faster than her WITSEC handler. But what would she tell the emergency operator? She could imagine the call….

Nine-one-one, what is the nature of your emergency?

There's a man where I'm shopping who reminds me of some violent gang members who once tried to kill me.

Reminds you of some violent gang members?

Yes…

Has he actually done anything to threaten or harm you?

Not yet.

God, would the police even come?

She dialed her WITSEC handler instead, but he didn't pick up, either.

"Who are you trying to call, Mommy?" Mia had been playing with the cans in the cart but tuned in long enough to notice Laurel pressing the End Call button. "The restaurant? Do you have to go to work today?"

Laurel slipped the phone back into her purse. If she had to make a dash for it, she wanted her hands free so she'd be able to hang on to her kids. "No, not today."

"Who will wait on the people?"

"The other servers."

"Oh." Mia went back to playing as Laurel, hands slick with sweat, propelled the shopping cart forward.

The man who'd been making her so uncomfortable didn't follow, but she was afraid he would once she turned the corner. It'd happened twice already. She'd left him in two different aisles only to bump into him a second and a third time.

Unwilling to abandon the treat section quite so soon, Jake slowed their cart to pick up a bottle of soda. "Mom, can we—"

Completely preoccupied with the stranger, and how much he resembled the type of men who belonged to The Crew, she didn't let Jake finish. "No, that has too much sugar."

"Please?" he persisted. "Come on! Other kids drink soda. Look, it's your favorite kind."

"I said no or…okay." Taking it away from him, she added it to the cart and grasped his hand so he had no choice except to keep up with them.

"Mommy?"

It was Mia again. "What honey?"

"Are you upset?"

She'd had a hard lump in her stomach ever since Rex left, and this wasn't helping. "I'm just thinking."

"What about these?" Jake scooped a bag of cheese puffs from the closest display. "Can we have these?"

Laurel managed a tremulous smile as they passed another shopper. "No. We have to go."

"But we just got here!"

She kept moving, so fast he dropped the bag of cheese puffs, and she didn't even stop to pick it up.

"Mom!" He almost tripped as she dragged him along.

"Just do as I say," she snapped, and risked another glance behind them. The man was nowhere to be seen. Was she freaking out for nothing?

Maybe. As busy as the store was, she'd seen several other shoppers more than once. None of them stood out like this guy did, but maybe the argument she'd had with Rex was making her feel extra-vulnerable, making her imagine the stranger was keeping a closer watch on her than he was.

Regardless, she didn't feel safe here and wanted to leave.

Choosing the shortest checkout line, she wheeled her cart into place. The tattooed guy didn't come out of the snack aisle, as she'd expected, but that didn't matter. She was already too worked up to talk herself out of her fear. Suddenly, she couldn't even wait the few minutes it would take to buy the groceries she'd selected. She had to get out of the store.

"Come on." She lifted Mia from the cart.

"Where are we going?" her daughter asked in surprise.

"Home."

"Without our soda?" Jake complained.

"I'll get you an ice cream cone later, I promise. Both of you." *Just cooperate*, she prayed and hurried them out and into the crowded parking lot.

Jake wasn't happy about abandoning their purchases, but he didn't say another word as he climbed into the backseat of her old Volvo and put on his seatbelt. He'd read her anxiety; it was so intense she could no longer hide it. The only other time he'd seen her like this was in Colorado, when she'd made him take his sister and climb out a bedroom window to escape what was about to happen in the house. She'd told both her children that what they'd witnessed that night had been playacting, but she often wondered if Jake, at least, knew better.

Her hands shook as she buckled Mia in. The painful memories were coming in a torrent now, memories of finding the U.S. Marshal assigned to protect them in a puddle of blood on the floor, his throat slit. Memories of Ink, the Crew member who'd survived. Ink, with the devilish tattoos covering his face, breaking into her bedroom, his hands reaching for her, his nails clawing her legs apart. The deafening blast of the gun. The acrid smell of gunpowder....

They'd *all* almost died. If not for Rex, they would have.

"Not again," she whispered. "Please, not again."

She was coming around the car to get behind the wheel when someone called her name. Fear and adrenaline shot through her, and she stiffened, but then she recognized the voice. It was Rex. He was here. *Somehow* he was here.

Turning, she saw him coming toward her and nearly crumpled to the blacktop in relief.

"*There* you are!" As soon as he was close enough, she threw herself into his arms. "What made you come back?"

He stumbled, surprised by her enthusiastic welcome, but caught himself before he could fall, caught them both. "I left my phone at your house, but you have the place locked up so tight I couldn't get in, and I didn't want to scare you by breaking in, so I've been checking all your regular places. You mentioned needing groceries this morning, so...fortunately, I spotted your car."

"That's why you wouldn't answer your phone. You didn't have it. I'm sorry about earlier, Rex. I'm so sorry."

When he hesitated, she feared he wouldn't accept her apology, that he'd continue to be mad. But then his hand went to the back of her head and his body adjusted to hers. "It's okay. I shouldn't have pressured you. We...we were good until I ruined it."

"Last night was special," she admitted. "I've never felt so close to anyone." It wasn't until he'd asked her to marry him that everything had fallen apart. After what she'd been through, she wasn't ready to make that commitment. She'd told him that before. "So don't give up on me," she whispered. "Not yet."

Chin resting on top of her head, he squeezed her tighter. "We'll work it out, huh? Somehow we'll work it out. Don't cry."

She hadn't even realized she was crying. The man in the store had frightened her, but that wasn't the worst of it. She'd been afraid that this time Rex wouldn't come back, that they were really over, and that had sent her reeling.

"You okay?" He pulled back to see her face.

Should she tell him about the panic attack she'd had in the store?

No, she felt silly about that now. The guy who'd spooked her was probably just some biker who liked tattoos and chocolate chips and hadn't meant her any harm. How would The Crew ever find them here? They were in WITSEC, had brand-new identities. *No one* knew where they were. "Yeah, I'm fine. Let's go home." She didn't even want to go back for her groceries.

But the second he released her, the man she'd seen in the store stepped out from behind the van beside her car.

And this time she knew he was dangerous because he shoved the muzzle of a gun into her back.

It took a second for Rex to realize what was going on. He'd been so caught up in his emotional exchange with Laurel, he'd allowed The Crew to get the drop on them. After the uneasy feeling he'd experienced at the bar, he considered this an inexcusable mistake. But he hadn't really believed The Crew could find them, not after everything they'd done to escape. Prison gangs weren't usually that sophisticated, and The Crew was no exception. But they *were* determined and deadly and somehow they'd managed to follow them to DC.

He had no doubt this man would shoot Laurel if he didn't do something. And what about the kids?

"Let her go." He raised his hands to show he was compliant. "I'm the one you want. I'm Rex McCready, Pretty Boy. Horse wants me, not her."

The guy—Mose, according to one tattoo—was six foot, about two hundred pounds and solidly built. His dark eyes focused on Rex, but he had a grip on Laurel. One shot at such close range would almost certainly kill her. "He wants you both. Virgil, too. That's my assignment and I'm gonna fulfill it."

Rex wished he had his own gun. Since he was an ex-con, carrying a firearm or any other weapon violated his parole, but he'd picked up a 9mm on the black market. It was currently stashed under the seat of his truck, which he'd parked along the perimeter of the lot. He'd thought that was close and handy—until this moment, when it might as well be in another state. "You'd be stupid to get greedy. Take me and leave her to her children. She has no part in this, and neither do they."

"Shut up and get in the car." He jerked his head toward Laurel's Volvo.

The kids stared out at them as if they couldn't understand what was wrong. Rex hoped they wouldn't figure it out. They'd already been through more than any kids should have to face.

"Look, you're in over your head here," he said to Mose. "Let her take the kids and go, and I'll do whatever the fuck you tell me to."

"Sorry, not good enough."

Another Hanley's Grocery customer passed by, the wheels of her cart rattling against the pavement. Rex prayed she'd glance up, see the gun and scream or cause some other type of diversion so he could wrest the weapon away. But she was too focused on the baby she had in a carrier. She walked right past them without noticing a thing. That was when the real panic set in, when Rex had to accept that he wasn't sure how to save them, not this time.

"Get in." The guy with the gun indicated Laurel's car again. "Or I'll pop her right here."

Shit! If he resisted, Laurel would be shot. They'd all be shot, along with other innocent people. But if he complied, they'd be abandoning the relative safety of this public parking lot, giving their enemy even more power over them, which didn't seem like the best idea....

In the end, Rex had no choice. He'd do anything to stop Laurel from getting hurt, even if that meant merely delaying it until he could find a better opportunity to save them.

Heart slamming against his chest, he opened the back door, slid Jake to the middle and got in. He hoped Laurel would be able to make a break for safety the second the guy left her side, but she wasn't taking any chances. Mose trained the gun on the kids as he moved around the car—first one, then the other—and Rex knew she wouldn't do anything that might cause him to fire. He couldn't blame her.

"Where are we going?" she asked, once they were all in.

The guy kept his gun low so the people around them couldn't see it. Rex couldn't see it, either, but he had no doubt it was aimed at Laurel because her eyes kept flicking toward it.

"Let's head to Virgil's." Mose tossed a grin over his shoulder for Rex's benefit. "I think it'll be fun to surprise him, don't you?"

Laurel had no intention of leading this man to her brother. Virgil had a wife and a new baby at home. He was finally happy, and she planned to do everything possible to keep it that way. He'd do the same for her if their roles were reversed. She only hoped The Crew didn't already know where he lived, that the man holding the gun wouldn't realize she'd led him to Rex's house instead.

Would Jake or Mia pipe up? It would be so like them, so like any child, to declare that she'd gotten it wrong. They certainly knew one house from the other, but they seemed subdued. They hadn't said a word the entire ride. She wondered if they, too, were reliving what had happened in Colorado....

"Not bad," Mose said, admiring Rex's home as they came to a stop at the curb. "Ratting out your friends must pay well."

Virgil had received nothing from the government for the information he'd provided, except a promise of protection for him and those he loved. He'd been given nearly $700,000 for wrongful imprisonment, however, which he'd insisted on sharing. That money had provided them each with a down payment on a house, but they worked to cover the mortgages. Laurel suspected Rex had bought this house hoping she and the kids would move in with him. Even she'd believed she would live here someday.

She'd never dreamed she'd die here instead.

"Virgil didn't rat anybody out until you tried to kill me," she said. "All he wanted was his life back."

"He swore an oath and then he broke it. That means he pays the price."

"But he should never have gone to prison in the first place!"

"That's *his* problem. We're not gonna sit back while he lives in some fancy-ass house like this. A house he bought with blood money!"

She wasn't going to convince him so she quit trying. She knew what these men were like. "Let my kids go, at least," she said. "Let them walk over to the neighbor's, where they'll be safe." She hoped to win their freedom before he became aware that she'd led him to the wrong house. After that, anything could happen.

Jake whimpered. He was catching on—or what they were saying had confirmed what he'd feared since they left the store.

"Mommy? I want to go home," Mia said and began to cry.

Laurel felt as if she was on fire, burning from the inside out. She'd never experienced such a sensation before—such a mixture of fury, righteous indignation, determination and fear. It was different from the last time she'd faced The Crew because there was a certain amount of resignation involved, too. She'd been expecting this for so long. "You're going to be fine," she said even though it was probably a lie.

The man with the gun twisted around to face them. "Mommy's right—*if* she and your friend here cooperate."

But she wasn't cooperating. She was doing whatever she could to protect Virgil, Peyton and baby Brady. It didn't make sense to put them at risk, too, but the fact that she was endangering her own children in the process made her clammy with sweat. What would this asshole do when he realized? Shoot them all and go after Virgil on his own?

Even if he did, at least Virgil would have a chance to get away....

No longer hiding his weapon, Mose waved the pistol at her door. "Shall we go in?"

Her eyes met Rex's in the rearview mirror, and she hoped he could read the message inside them: *Do whatever you have to.*

Rex made his move as soon as they got out of the car. He couldn't afford to wait, had no idea what might happen if he let this go on. At least outside, the children had room to scatter and hide, and if the gun went off there'd be a greater chance that a neighbor might hear it and call the police.

But the man was prepared. Dodging Rex's blow, he grabbed Mia by the hair and dragged her up against him. "You try that again, and she'll be the first to die," he snapped.

"Run!" Rex stood in front of Jake and tried to shoo him away. He didn't think this man would kill Mia over the loss of her brother. The kids didn't matter that much to him. This wasn't about them. But Jake wouldn't leave—he sidled over to protect his mother.

"Jake, do as I say!"

"No." The boy's chest rose and fell so fast Rex could tell he was terrified, but he was equally resolute. "He'll shoot my sister. Then he'll shoot my mom."

Rex couldn't believe he'd refused to obey. The odds were already stacked against them. He didn't need Jake to get stubborn, even if he couldn't help admiring the boy's courage. "Jake!" He hated the risk he was taking but he had no choice. If they went inside, this man would shoot them all the minute he understood that they weren't giving up Virgil.

Then Jake surprised him. He shoved his mother so hard she stumbled back and fell over the planter behind her, and he started jumping and shouting and waving his arms as if he thought he could force the man to fire at him instead of his sister.

Jake's sudden reversal had taken the bastard off guard. Mose paused for a second. Apparently he couldn't decide whether he should actually fire, or who he should fire at. He even glanced behind him as if he feared Virgil was already on his way out of the house and that was what had set Jake off.

That brief hesitation gave Rex the opportunity he'd been looking for. Launching himself forward, he tackled the guy.

Mia fell when they did, which probably hurt, but it wasn't going to kill her. The man had to let her go in order to keep control of the gun he was trying to turn on Rex.

She wiggled out from between them and ran off crying almost as soon as they hit the ground. While he wrestled Mose, trying to subdue him, Rex didn't know where she went. He didn't care as long as she remained safe. He hoped Laurel was taking her kids and getting them the hell out of here—he trusted she was. He knew how much they meant to her. He knew how much they meant to him, too, all of them, because he felt a huge surge of relief even as the gun went off.

Laurel had a large rock in her hand when she crept toward the two men lying, one atop the other, on the ground. She'd yelled for her children to go next door and call nine-one-one, and they'd dashed off, but she hadn't been able to bring herself to leave Rex.

Tears rolled down her cheeks as she drew closer. He'd been shot. She was pretty sure of that. But where?

"Rex?"

He didn't answer. She got the impression he was struggling just to breathe and felt the tears come faster.

"Rex, answer me."

Finally, he rolled off the guy and lay there, gazing up at her. Blood covered his shirt, but it wasn't *his* blood. It belonged to the man who'd come to kill them. The Crew had lost another member. The sightless eyes of their attacker stared skyward as the red staining his shirt seeped farther and farther from where the bullet had entered his chest.

Dropping the rock, she sagged to her knees at Rex's side and buried her face in his neck.

"Are you okay?" he murmured.

A surplus of adrenaline had left him weak and shaky. She could tell by the limp way he lifted his arm to hold her, and because she felt the same. "I am now."

"I'm glad you changed your mind."

Rex glanced across the table at Virgil, who was watching him with a crooked grin. "What'd you say?" The pizza parlor where they'd met Virgil, Peyton and the baby for dinner was too loud to be able to hear unless he raised his voice a bit more. They were no longer in DC. Now that The Crew had found them, it wasn't safe anymore. They had to decide on a permanent location but for the time being they were in Little Rock, Arkansas.

"I said I'm glad you changed your mind."

Rex drummed his thumbs on the table. "About..."

Virgil jerked his head toward Laurel, who'd left Rex's side to refill her children's glasses. "Staying with Laurel. She loves you, you know."

Leaning back, Rex returned his friend's smile. "I know."

Copyright © 2013 by Brenda Novak.

Read full-length stories featuring these characters with Brenda Novak's exciting trilogy—*Inside, In Seconds* and *In Close.*

Prepare polenta by bringing 2 cups of water to boil in a medium-sized pan. In a small bowl, mix the rest of the water with the cornmeal. Stir mixture into the boiling water. Simmer over medium-level het for 10 minutes, stirring often. Remove from heat and stir in cheese and basil. Spread polenta into a pie pan. Refrigerate until ready to use.

Prepare dressing by combining all ingredients and shaking until mixed. Cut chicken into cubes. Use 1/4 of the dressing to marinade the chicken and refrigerate for 30 minutes.

Place chicken on metal skewers and grill until chicken is cooked. Cut polenta into four squares and lightly brush both sides with olive oil. Grill polenta for about 4-5 minutes until polenta is crispy. Arrange pieces of polenta and chicken over the salad greens. Top with dressing and serve warm.

8 servings.

Copyright © 2015 by Brenda Novak
Chicken should be cooked until internal temprature is at least 165° F

LOVE THAT: BRENDA NOVAK'S EVERY OCCASSION COOKBOOK

by Brenda Novak with Jan Coad

GRILLED CHICKEN SALAD

Each Serving: Cal, 622; Carb, 29g; Fat, 42g; Protein, 35g; Sodium, 794mg; Sugar, 2g

Ingredients

Polenta: 3 cups water, 1 cup cornmeal, 1/2 tsp. salt, 2/3 cup parmesan, cheese (grated), 1/4 cup fresh basil leaves (freshly chopped).

Tomato Dressing: 1/4 cup white wine, vinegar, 1 tbs. Dijon-style mustard, 2 cloves garlic (pressed), 1/4 cup fresh basil (finely chopped), 1/2 sea salt, 1/4 tsp. ground black pepper, 1/2 cup and 2 tbsp. olive oil, 2 plum tomatoes (seeded and finely chopped),

Rest of ingredients: 1 lb. boneless, skinless chicken breasts, 4 cups romaine lettuce (chopped), 2 cups mixed baby greens (chopped), 1 roasted red bell pepper (thinly sliced).

Marie Force is the New York Times *bestselling author of contemporary romance including the indie-published Gansett Island Series and the Fatal Series from Harlequin Books. In addition, she is the author of the Butler, Vermont Series, the Green Mountain Series and the erotic romance Quantum Series. In 2019, her new historical Gilded series from Kensington Books will debut with* Duchess By Deception. *All together, her books have sold 6.5 million copies worldwide, have been translated into over a dozen languages and appear on* New York Times, USA Today *and* Wall Street Journal *bestseller lists. A frequent speaker, publishing workshop presenter, and a publisher through her Jack's House Publishing romance imprint, her goals in life are simple— to finish raising two happy, healthy, productive young adults, to keep writing books for as long as she possibly can and to never be on a flight that makes the news. Join Marie's mailing list at* http://marieforce.com/subscribe/.

HEART'S KISS INTERVIEWS MARIE FORCE

by Lezli Robyn

We'd love to introduce our readers to Marie Force, who is—quite literally—a bright light in our field; a shining example of how to be successful in both the traditional and self-publishing markets, selling millions of books in her popular Gansett Island, Treading Water, Quantum, Fatal, Green Mountain and Butler, VT contemporary romance series. It is a pleasure to welcome her to Heart's Kiss!

Lezli Robyn: Marie, you have said that your mother's pancreatic cancer diagnosis opened the creative floodgates on writing your first novel. I can imagine how important it was for your mom to be the first person to read the opening four chapters of your novel. How important is it for an author to channel their talent through their emotions, or vice versa, especially if they write romance?

Marie Force: People ask me why I didn't start writing fiction until well into my 30s. The answer I always give is because I didn't have anything to say yet. I think you have to live a little and experience

the wide range of emotions life has to offer to bring those emotions to life on the page.

LR: Your first novel took you three years to write (off and on, with rewrites), your second 90 days to write, and you've written a 96,000 word novel within 39 days. Apart from us suspecting you are some kind of Wonder Woman of Words, do you think it is possible for a plotter to write as quickly as a pantser, if they have already planned out the trajectory of their plot? There seem to be pros and cons to both methods.

MF: I honestly have no idea how it works for authors who plot their books. I've never done it, so I can't comment on how the process works for them. But for me, every book is different. Some of them fly off the fingers and others have to be dragged, kicking and screaming, onto the page.

LR: You have self-published your books—to great success—and traditionally published your books— also to great success. Which process has given you the most satisfaction, professionally and personally? There is a certain amount of prestige in selling your book to a traditional publisher, but to also garner such success on your own...that must be a thrill.

MF: Any form of success in this business is thrilling, but there is a particular satisfaction to, for example, making the *New York Times* bestseller list for the first time with a self-published book—and hitting the top ten, no less. I have had great relationships with traditional publishers and continue to work with them to bring my books to a wider audience than I can reach on my own.

LR: You chose to write your erotic Quantum series in first person and from both points of view—the only one of your multiple series in first person. Was it because you thought the sense of immediacy and connection a first person viewpoint provides helped your readers connect to a more erotically intimate plotline? Or was there another reason you made this choice?

MF: Yes, I thought the story I wanted to tell in Quantum required the immediacy that first-person present POV provides. I used to hate first-person books, because most of the time they were told only from the heroine's point of view. I want the hero in there, too, so that's why all my first person books are told from both points of view. I've become a big fan of reading—and writing—first person, but only when done from the dual POV.

LR: In your various series, secondary characters of earlier novels often end up becoming the lead characters in succeeding books. Did you write these secondary characters originally with the aim of eventually elevating them to leading status, or did the character evolve in such a way that you, or your readers, fell in love with them so much you realized they deserved their own story?

MF: I don't plan anything in advance, so I can't say that's intentional, but I do like to create secondary characters that can be used as leads in future books.

LR: If you had to pick *one* heroine from all your novels, across all your series, and *one* hero as your favorites, who would they be? And would you think they'd make a great couple if their paths had crossed between the sheets of the same book?

MF: Sam from the Fatal Series is my favorite character of all of them. She is a total TRIP to write because she's more than a little crazy and funny and passionate about her work and her husband and son. She's extremely entertaining to spend time with. My favorite male character is Mac McCarthy Jr. in the Gansett Island series, for many of the same reasons. If the two of them got together, they'd probably burn down the house with their antics.

LR: And lastly, what is next for you, for 2018? What do your readers have to look forward to?

MF: I have new books coming in all my series, including the long-awaited fifth and final book in my Treading Water Series. I will also be winding down the Quantum Series with the last two books.

Copyright © 2018 by Lezli Robyn.

NEW YORK TIMES BESTSELLING AUTHOR
MARIE FORCE

DELIRIOUS
A Quantum Novel

EXCERPT FROM
DELIRIOUS

by Marie Force

Kristian

Her skin brushing against mine sends a charge of heat through me. Stunned all over again by my unprecedented reaction to her, I pull my hand back, though that's the last thing I want to do. "Aileen...."

"Did I do something wrong, Kristian?"

The question shocks me. "What? Why would you ask that?"

She takes a deep drink of her wine, as if seeking liquid courage. "I can't help but notice that you are, or you *were* before Maddie got hurt...different." She swallows hard. "Toward me. So I wondered if maybe I did something—"

"No." That she could think such a thing is unbearable to me. "*No*," I say again, more emphatically this time. "It's not you. It's me."

"Nothing good ever comes of that statement," she says with an ironic laugh that's followed by a sigh.

I'm making a goddamn mess of this, so I decide to level with her. "You could do so much better than me, Aileen."

She stares at me, her eyes big with shock. "*Why would you say such a thing?*"

I could give her so many reasons, but I decide to go with the most important one. "You deserve better."

"Do you know why I wanted to move here?"

Thrown off by the change in direction, I say, "Because Nat and the others talked you into it?"

She shakes her head. "It was primarily because you live here."

Closing my eyes, I rest my head back against the chair. I shouldn't be here. I don't deserve her sweetness, her honesty or her blatant desire. But God, I want it. I want it all so badly, I burn with the need for more of her.

"Should I not have said that?" she asks in a small voice.

I keep my eyes closed as I shake my head.

"Did I read this wrong?"

"Aileen…."

"I'm sorry. I'll get your shirt into the dryer so you can go." The rustling sound of her getting up has me opening my eyes and reacting.

Like before, when Maddie fell, I'm moving before I decide I should. I grasp Aileen's arm, catch her off balance and bring her down to my lap, my lips landing on hers before either of us can take the time to ponder the massive implications. I cup her face in my hand and try to remember to be gentle with her. My inner Dominant needs to stand the fuck down. There's no place for him here.

When I use my tongue to coax her lips apart, she whimpers, another sound that goes directly to my cock, which has been hard since she moaned about the time. I kiss her with months' worth of pent-up desire that's made all other women pale in comparison to her since the day I met her. I don't want anyone but her, and now that she's warm and soft in my arms, I want to show her what she's come to mean to me.

My heart is pounding and my palms are sweaty. I'm light-headed, off balance and out of whack. Everything about this is new to me, as is the craving desire that swamps me when her tongue brushes against mine for the first time. *Fuck. Fuck. Fuck!* I'm so screwed. One taste of her has me addicted. It's never going to be enough. In the scope of two seconds, everything I want to do with her and to her

runs through my mind like the dirtiest movie I've ever seen.

That has me pulling back from her, gentling the kiss, putting a stop to this before it gets even more out of control. I stare at her swollen lips and the stunned expression on her face. "Does that answer your question?"

"I seem to have forgotten the question."

Smiling at her witty reply, I say, "You asked if you read this wrong." I kiss her again, tipping my head to better the angle. "You didn't. You read it exactly right." I force myself to keep my hands still when they would love to wander. I want to touch her everywhere, but her little girl is sleeping inside, and this is not the time for that. However, in the last five minutes, I've begun to accept that this, whatever it is, is going to happen, whether I think it should or not.

"Something is different, though," she says, her lips hovering near mine, her hand caressing my face as she gazes into my eyes. "*You* are different."

It is both upsetting and exhilarating to realize she already knows me well enough to see that I'm troubled. "I don't mean to be." Nuzzling her neck, I breathe in the fresh, clean scent of her. It's not perfume or anything other than *her*. "I couldn't wait to see you again."

"Then where were you yesterday?"

"I was…." I start to tell her I was sick, but I can't. I can't lie to her. "I had myself convinced that this couldn't happen. I still don't think it should."

"*Why?*" she asks imploringly. "Is it because I have kids? I wouldn't expect you to take them on or—"

And then I'm kissing her again, because I can't bear to hear any more about her being afraid I don't want her because of her kids. I kiss her voraciously, forgetting that I'm supposed to be gentle and soft with her. She makes me so fucking crazy. "Your kids are adorable, well-behaved and beautiful, like their mother."

She snorts with disdain. "I'm not beautiful. I'm scrawny and pale, and my hair is growing back curly, and I have no idea what to do with it."

Her description of herself enrages me. "*You* are *beautiful.*"

"So are you," she says, her voice husky and sexy. "If you knew how much time I've spent thinking about you since the day we met, you'd run away from here and never look back."

"Aileen…." Filled with despair, I drop my head and try to find my resolve. "Sweetheart…."

"What is it? Please tell me what's wrong. I don't understand."

"I want you too much, and I'm all wrong for you—and your kids."

"Shouldn't that be up to me to decide?"

Before I can reply, a soft cry comes from the baby monitor.

Aileen is up and off my lap, gone in a flash to tend to her child.

I take deep breaths of the cool air, trying to find my balance after kissing and holding her. I never should've done that, but I can't wait to do it again. I hear her through the monitor and wallow in the sweet words of comfort she gives her daughter.

I never had that. I don't know how to be soft or sweet or any of the things they'd need me to be. I'm selfish and arrogant and focused on my career. I need dominant, kinky sex the way some people need caffeine to jump-start their day. It's not just what I like. *It's who I am.*

Listening to Aileen softly sing to her baby, I'm stunned when tears sting my eyes. Are you fucking kidding me? I don't *cry.* I haven't cried since the foster family I'd started to love kicked me out to make room for one of their sons who was coming home from college.

I should get up, tell her I'm leaving and get the hell out of there while I still can. But I don't move. I remain riveted by the sound of her voice and the sweet way in which she loves her child. For the little boy in me who never knew softness, sweetness or love from his mother, my emotions are all over the place, listening to her give everything she has to her baby.

I take a deep breath, as if that could slow the wild beat of my heart. Once again, I'm moving before I consciously decide to, drawn to her so powerfully, I can't stay away. I stand in the doorway to the bedroom, watching over them as Aileen soothes Maddie back to sleep.

She sees me there, bends to kiss Maddie and gets up to come to me, her arms sliding around my waist and her head returning to my bare chest. I'm power-less to do anything other than wrap my arms around her and hold her as close to me as I can get her. I don't care that she can feel the obvious proof of my arousal pressing against her.

"I should go." Even my voice sounds different—gruffer, thicker.

"Stay." She holds me tighter and looks up at me with her heart in her eyes. In that one instant, I get why Flynn married Natalie without a prenup. If he feels even a fraction of what I do gazing down at Aileen, I get it. I'd give her everything I have with no questions asked if it meant she would look at me, just like that, every day for the rest of my life.

Without breaking the intense eye contact, I lower my lips to hers, which are swollen from our earlier kisses.

Her hands slide up my chest to link around my neck, trapping me.

I've never let any woman trap me. I do the trapping, not the other way around, but in this case, I can't be bothered to care about details that would've mattered with anyone else. Here with her, the only thing that matters is *more*—of everything. All the reasons why I'd planned to stay away are long gone as I lift her into my arms, carry her to the sofa and come down on top of her, losing my fucking mind in a kiss.

A fucking *kiss.* When was the last time a kiss alone was enough to take me to the brink of release? A million years ago when I was new to such things. But this…. *This* is new to me, the *feeling* that comes from kissing her, the desperation, the craving. I've never experienced anything remotely like it, and I can't get enough.

It's like the highest of highs with no drugs required. That thought is yet another reminder of the many reasons I should not be making out with Aileen on her sofa. But when I pull back from her, she whimpers, her fingers grasping my hair to keep me from getting away. I have zero ability to do what I know I should. Losing the power that saved my life ought to terrify me, but I can't spare the brain cells to think it through, to ponder the implications of what I'm giving up to her.

How can I think of anything but her when she's wrapped around me, the heat of her pussy pressed tight against my cock, which is so hard, it aches?

The one thing I know for certain is I can't let this continue toward its inevitable conclusion, not with her little girl injured and sleeping in the next room. If—or I probably should concede to *when*—this happens, I want to be completely alone with her so I don't have to hold anything back.

"Aileen," I whisper against her lips. "Sweetheart…."

She looks up at me, seeming as dazed as I feel. Her lips are puffy and swollen, her cheeks flushed, and her eyes are wide with wonder that makes me want to say fuck it to propriety and anything else that doesn't have me inside her right fucking now. I'm shaking from the effort it takes to hold back. I can't remember the last time I held back like this. It's far more common for me to take what I want than it is to show restraint.

"What's wrong?"

"Absolutely nothing." Other than the fact that I've lost my mind, my heart and everything else to her, I'm fine. Better than fine. Being with her like this is *amazing*.

"Why did you stop?"

"I didn't stop because I wanted to." I caress her face, my fingertips gliding over her soft skin. She's so incredibly responsive that even a light touch has her hips rising, seeking me out. I bite back a groan of frustration.

"Then why?"

A very good question. "Because when we do this, I want to be completely alone with you so we don't have to be quiet." I nuzzle her neck, and she arches into me. "And I want to take my time."

She trembles, and I feel it everywhere, especially in my cock.

"I should go."

"No." She tightens her hold on me, and I love that. I love that she wants me so much. No one has ever wanted me the way she does. Women want me for what I can do for their careers and the things I can buy for them. They don't want me for *me* the way Aileen seems to. "Don't go. Not yet."

I sag into her, my painfully aroused body molding to hers.

"It feels so good to be held by you. It's been such a long time since anyone held me, and it's never felt as good as it does with you."

And she's so refreshingly honest. If she thinks it, she says it. When she asked me earlier if she'd done something wrong, she nearly broke my heart. I'm not used to refreshing honesty from women. I'm far more accustomed to games, intrigue, cat-and-mouse and hidden agendas. With Aileen, what you see is what you get, and I have a feeling I ain't seen nothing yet.

Our columnist, Julie Pitzel, has been a receptionist, radio DJ, bill collector, telemarketer, administrative assistant, community college instructor, and an expediter (aka professional nag). She's been involved in the Houston writing community for many years including two years as President of a local Romance Writers of America Chapter. She writes paranormal fiction from a geodesic dome south of Houston, where she lives with her husband and a pair of cats. Most recently, her story "The Dance" was published in The Death of All Things" *anthology.*

YOU READ *THAT*?: DARK FANTASIES

by Julie Pitzel

What are your fantasies? I have the standards: win the lottery, travel the world, achieve J. K. Rowling style fame and fortune, eat ice cream and lose weight. You know, the normal daydreams I can talk about at work or with the in-laws.

But I have other fantasies, too. Most of us do. Naughty fantasies with a bit of a dark twist.

According to a report from *Psychology Today* most women—about 90 percent of those surveyed—have sexual fantasies. In a study performed by Notre Dame and the University of North Texas, almost two-thirds of the women reported fantasies of apparent forced encounters. The women who confessed to these types of imaginings tended to be sexually open—they had lots of fantasies about lots of different things. The study found them to be comfortable *dreaming* about situations that they wouldn't want to actually happen.

The key take away is that having erotically risky fantasies is common among women with healthy, normal sex drives. The report went on to state: "*Women who have rape fantasies don't want to be sexually assaulted. They feel comfortable with their own sexuality and are happy to embrace their erotic fantasies—wherever they may lead.*"

The term "rape fantasy" is a bad descriptor. Women aren't dreaming about a violent, negative act. It's more about unbridled desire, imagining that we bring out uncontrolled lust in our *chosen* partner. A better term might be ravishment fantasies. In another *Psychology Today* article, "Don't Call Them 'Rape Fantasies'", the author states they're about voluntarily relinquishing control and choosing to allow our fantasy partner to be dominant. It suggests the act of forfeiting control actually gives us power.

And some of our romance novels play into those riskier fantasies. I always considered them a form of controlled danger—like a riding a roller coaster, watching a horror movie, or shopping for a swimsuit. We can read about women succumbing to the seductive force of a hunky bad boy knowing that he won't hurt her. Because it's a romance, we know he cares for her more than he's willing to admit—yet. We can live the fantasy from a safe distance with the foreknowledge that everything will turn out at least happy-for-now.

The bodice rippers of the 80's and 90's were filled with non-consensual sex. The heroines were abducted and raped, sometimes by the hero. When we talk about those books, we usually focus on how badly the heroines were treated. Today it's difficult to understand why readers put up with that mistreatment. From my own experience, there were a couple reasons. For one, the women in these stories enjoyed sex. The only other books I'd read where that was common were the porn paperbacks I found when my older brother moved out of my parents' house. And the other reason was that at the end of the book, the heroine was in command. She had gained control of her captor. She'd tamed him and won his love. It was very liberating.

That's also a common trope in the Billionaire/CEO/sheikh romances. The heroines in these stories are frequently a secretary or someone without clout or authority. The people who deride these romances see the heroine as weak. They believe the billionaire has all the power. But the lowly shop-girl eventually teaches him how to live and love, and ultimately proves to be as strong—or stronger—than the hero.

Whether the stories include vampires and werewolves or sports figures or the guy next door, the romance genre is about fantasy. It involves the belief that love can overcome conflict. That's a powerful idea because it doesn't come true for everyone in real life. Still, we read romance because we want to live that fantasy for three hundred pages. We want to experience the ups and downs, cry when a character walks away, cry more when that character comes back, and swoon when they ride away into the sunset.

In an article at Jezebel, "The Romance Novelist's Guide to Hot Consent", one of the authors interviewed specifically talks about young readers finding these stories and learning about consensual relationships. And I understand her point, we want to teach the young adults who read these books to have a healthy respect for themselves and to know what a good relationship looks like. But romance novels can also show them that sexual enjoyment comes in many different forms.

We're bombarded by information, especially through social media. Sometimes it's difficult to find out what's normal or acceptable, especially if our interests involve a little kink. A Google search is more apt to provide questionable websites than useful information. But we can search through Goodreads and other book sites for the type of fantasies we want to discover. Books are a safe way to explore darker fantasies, especially if we only want to live those scenes in our imagination.

And sometimes our books can show the negative effects of bad relationships. As a genre, romance covers so many different subjects. Some stories touch on dark subjects that have nothing to do with sexuality. There are stories about addiction and abuse and poverty and bigotry. Ugly things happen to our heroes and heroines and we accept that it's part of the journey. The characters are flawed and need to face internal demons to become the best version of themselves.

If part of the job of a romance novel is to teach about consensual relationships, the presence of non-consensual situations is also called for. Sometimes we need to see the characters misbehave. We need to see the problems that misbehavior creates. And we need to see how the other character reacts. It adds to the lesson to show a lowly secretary tell her boss to keep his hands to himself—and if he's our hero, for him to realize his mistake.

I do believe that consensual sex in my romances is sexy and thrilling. A good hero who can woo and

seduce and make the heroine (and by extension, me) want to jump him, is fun and magical and exciting. We also like our alpha heroes, and some readers like it when the hero takes charge and fulfils our ravishment fantasy. Many women enjoy risky fantasies, and our romances should include them in the mix.

Having a healthy respect for ourselves and our sexuality includes having a healthy respect for our fantasies. All of them, including the darker ones.

Helpful Resources:

https://www.psychologytoday.com/blog/all-about-sex/201508/why-do-women-have-rape-fantasies

https://jezebel.com/the-romance-novelists-guide-to-hot-consent-1822991922

https://www.psychologytoday.com/blog/evolution-the-self/201411/don-t-call-them-rape-fantasies

Copyright © 2018 by Julie Pitzel

C.S. DeAvilla writes award-winning science fiction, fantasy, and romance under another pen name. She has been a romance fan since she sneaked a peek at her mother's massive historical romance bookcase and fell in love with all the characters. She reads every romance genre—as long as two people are falling in love, she'll give it a read. Her favorite authors are Jennifer Crusie, J.R. Ward, Darynda Jones, Suzanne Brockmann, Sarah MacLean, and Kristan Higgins. But she always has room for one more.

RECOMMENDED BOOKS

by C.S. DeAvilla

Title: *Sweet, Filthy Boy*
Author: Christina Lauren
Publisher: Gallery Books (Simon and Schuster)
ISBN: 1476751803
Release Date: May 13th, 2014

Continuing my Christina Lauren kick—I read through Wild Season's series in a few days. It has an irresistible premise. Three friends take a girl's trip to Vegas and meet a group of three guy friends doing the same. They quickly become friends and spend a wild night together in which each pair off and marry by the end of the night. Two of the couples quickly annul their marriages the next morning, but Mia and Ansel do not. Keeping Ansel to a promise she forced him to swear to while drunk, Ansel con-vinces her to join him in Paris, his home city. She declines, but soon decides to throw caution to the wind and surprise him at the airport by using the ticket he's purchased. What follows is a sweet, unex-pectedly easy—yet hot and heavy—romance. But is it too easy? Ansel's past slowly creeps between them and all that perfect Paris love tarnishes too easily as secrets become revealed. Reading through this tale reminded me of another amazing book with similar themes written around the same time, Melanie Har-low's *Frenched*. If you loved *Frenched*, *Sweet, Filthy Boy* is sure to please. Lauren's writing style is fresh. Her characters are real in a flawed and loveable way. And the conflicts pile on just as you're planning the character's wedding (or in this case, brainstorming a way these two can remain married and not get that annulment they've promised each other by sum-mer's end). If you become as obsessed as I did while reading about Mia and Ansel, then you can dive right into the next books in the series and see what the other fated Vegas couples do to find their ways back to each other.

Title: *Dangerous Books for Girls*
Author: Maya Rodale
Publisher: Self-published
ISBN: 0990635627
Release Date: April 21st, 2015

Dangerous Books for Girls is a deviation from my usual review. One, it's non-fiction. Two, I consider it a must-read for all romance readers. I'd read it about a year ago and recently picked it up for a second pass. Each chapter and section is meaty, offering historical references to the romance genre and why romance—more than any other genre—has developed an undeserved reputation in the literary world. Romance remains steady in its ability to be the highest grossing genre. Its readers have proven to be among the smartest and well-read, yet the perception is that readers of romance are uneducated. Critics of romance point out its short-comings, often that the genre is anti-feminist—but that couldn't be further from the truth as romance has and continues to push the boundaries of women's roles. *Dangerous Books for Girls* details each slight presented against the genre and counterpoints it with proof and data to the contrary. I remember my early years as a reader being chastised by my fellow classmates in graduate school for reading Diana Gabaldon's *Outlander*. They'd said it barely counted as an intelligent read. "Don't you think it's an unrealistic view of love and men?" as if I wouldn't be able to tell the difference between fantasy and reality after reading. Had it been a murder mystery, would I then go out and try to solve a murder crime? Accidently fall into the life of a serial killer? I didn't agree and the next class after I finished my book I made sure to bring in Jennifer Crusie's *Bet Me* to prove they wouldn't scare me away from the kinds of books I enjoyed most. If you've ever been put down for the types of fiction you choose, this book is the one you need to bring you confidence and pride in your choice. Women who read romance are truly choosing the most dangerous genre—written mostly by women. One that continues to thrive despite its many, many critics.

Title: ***First Star I See Tonight***
Author: Susan Elizabeth Phillips
Publisher: Avon (Harper Collins)
ISBN: 0062561405
Release Date: June 27th 2017

I have a number of authors I've been following for as long as I've been reading romance and Susan Elizabeth Phillips was an early author discovery I'd made in college. I fell hard for her Chicago Stars series starting with *It Had to Be You* in 2002. If you're new to Phillips, you can start pretty much anywhere, but I recommend *Lady Be Good*. *First Star I See Tonight* has a punchy start, which is the calling card for what I like to think of the romance comedy sub-genre. Piper Dove, the heroine, is following Grant, an ex-football star. Piper is tasked to follow the once-decorated-athlete-turned-club-owner and gain information on his daily routine. In the process she discovers his bartender is skimming from him and so even though she can't seem to keep herself hidden from the football hotty, she does win him over with her ability to see things in places he'd never think to look. It's not long before Piper is pulling him into even more adventures, including tangling with a Middle Eastern royal family to free one of their servants. Phillips delivers fast-paced, humorous, and touching novels and this one is no different. Her characters always spark and the banter in the dialog gives it a rowdy edge. If you're new to Susan Elizabeth Phillips or an old fan who hasn't checked in for a while, it's time to check her out with *First Star I See Tonight*.

Title: ***Blood Fury***
Author: J.R. Ward
Publisher: Ballantine Books
ISBN: 0451475348
Release Date: January 9th, 2018

So, it's no secret I'm obsessed with The Blackdagger Brotherhood. I'm a fan of the rich world Ward has created, and I seriously dig her style. I know for those who have yet to pick up a book in the series it might seem daunting with so many out. Where does one start? For those who have tried it and not liked it (a very tiny percent of the reader population): you may skip to the next review. Everyone else? You are nodding along with me here. These books are pure fun. And vampires. Did I mention that? The spin off series with the new trainees is a good place to start, picking up one of these will give readers a taste of the world, without bogging the reader down with a lot of background information. Each book can stand on its own and *Blood Fury* is no different. This installment features Peyton, self-proclaimed just-for-fun guy. He doesn't take much seriously and as a result he has a lot of growing to do. His love interest is also a recruit, Novo. She's had to be an adult a

little too soon. Her sister snagged Novo's boyfriend, but not before he left her when she was pregnant and later lost the baby—telling no one. Her prickly nature isn't for naught. She's got a thick skin that protects her from emotional harm. But a major bonus for old fans of the series: we get Saxton's story too—our favorite lawyer to the vampire king. Those who don't know, Saxton stepped aside when Quinn and Blaylock got together. He'd been with Blaylock and thought he'd never find true love again. But cue Ruhn—a mysterious soft-spoken civilian who can fight like he's a professional. Sparks are flying all over this book, both couples bring delight and hours of reading pleasure. Sometimes it's awesome to discover a new read, and other times it's reassuring to know our old favorites have still got it. Ward is that consistent hit for me.

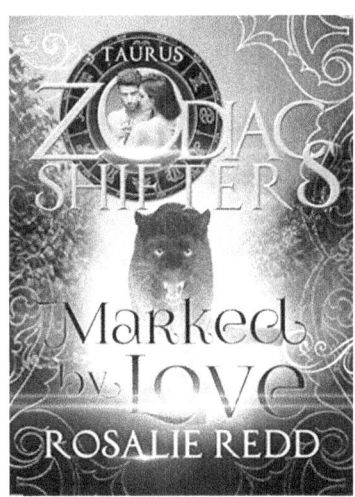

Title: ***Marked by Love: A Zodiac Shifters Paranormal Romance: Taurus***
Author: Rosalie Redd
Publisher: Self Published
AISN: B06XZDC415
Release Date: May 9th, 2017

The world of self-publishing brings about creative projects, like a group of popular authors pooling together and writing a series. Such is the case with

The Zodiac Shifters. Each novella landed in its coordinating zodiac sign during release. In the Taurus installment, Danae, a panther shifter, will do anything never to mate again. After Danae had been forced violently into a mating arranged by her father, she vows to never trust another male again with her heart. Aramond was the panther she was supposed to spend the rest of her long life with, but he's banished soon after her forced mating with another male and she believes her true love is gone forever. Fate has something else in mind for this pair, however, and they meet again a few hundred years later (panther shifters have very long lives) under the backdrop of a war where panther shifters are struggling for survival. They quickly realize the sparks are still between them. This was a delightful, random find. The novella was a quick read, not because of its length, but because the story pulls the reader along with magical narrative and compelling characters. I always love uncovering new series and new authors and these projects are a treasure trove of discovery.

USA Today and national bestselling author Anna J. Stewart writes sweet to sexy romance for Harlequin's Heartwarming and Romantic Suspense lines, but paranormal romance is her first love. Early obsessions with Star Wars, Star Trek, *and* Wonder Woman *set her on the path to creating fun, funny, and family-centric romances with happily ever afters for her independent heroines. Anna lives in Northern California where she deals with a serious* Supernatural *and* Sherlock *addiction and tolerates an overly affectionate cat named Snickers. You can read more about Anna and her books at www.authorannastewart.com.*

WARDEN OF SIGHT

by Anna J. Stewart

"You're sure you told Clara thirty minutes?"

Nellie MacQueen tucked a springy curl behind her ear and bit the inside of her cheek. How her older sister could sound both frustrated and condescending was a question Nellie had been asking herself for twenty-eight years. Ever the peacemaker of the family, Nellie counted to five before answering. "Yes, Amber. This isn't my first go-around with our book obsessed sister. A half-hour. We agreed." And yet it was going on ninety minutes. Unease bubbled low in Nellie's already squirming belly. She knew she should have stuck by Clara's side rather than go rushing off to help a more-than-capable Amber with the car rental. She just hadn't been able to tolerate the idea of yet another dreary, dust infested bookstore.

"Yeah, well, she better get her butt into this car soon." Amber chewed on her thumbnail, a telltale sign her frustration was getting the better of her. "Text her again."

"I've texted Clara twice already." And received no response. Not even Clara's typical "yeah, yeah," brush off. "How about I just go in and get her?" Anything to get away from her increasingly moody sister. It wasn't as if this trip was easy for any of them. Nellie shoved open the passenger door.

"Wait." Amber locked a hand around Nellie's wrist and squeezed. "I'm sorry, Nellie. I'm just wound up about seeing Mom after all these years. I don't mean to take it out on you."

Nellie relaxed a little. At least Amber was finally willing to admit she'd been a bit of a crank ever since they'd left on vacation. Of the three of them, Amber had the strongest and most vivid memories of Shona MacBride, the mother who had abandoned them and their father when Amber had been three, Nellie, two, and Clara barely one. While Clara was the queen of avoidance when it came to talking about their mother, and Nellie turned a deaf ear, Amber was the one who bore the most emotional scars. It was odd that it had been Amber who had pushed so hard for this family reunion.

"What else are sisters for if not to take things out on?" Nellie offered Amber a sympathetic smile as she shoved her purse under the front seat. "We're all anxious about seeing her again. It'll either go well or it won't. No sense worrying it to death. Whatever happens, in another week we'll be back in the States living our mundane, ordinary lives once again."

And Nellie would have to come to public terms with her *ex*-fiancé embarrassing betrayal. Nothing like running halfway around the world to try to forget how desperate she'd been to be with anyone that she'd fallen for a man who'd used her to advance his own career.

"My life is hardly mundane." Amber tilted her chin so her nose went higher up in the air. "Or ordinary. I'm considered one of the—"

"Top ten art buyers in the continental United States." Nellie rolled her eyes and fought a grin. "Seriously, sis, get a new tag line. That one's getting old." But Nellie had accomplished her task. She had a talent for knowing exactly where and how to needle people, especially her sisters. It came with being the unassuming one; the one who blended in with the crowd. Being invisible had turned her into a master observer. Amber's inordinate pride in her job, not to mention her status, always lined her up as the perfect target. Wallowing in uncertainty, however, was never a good state for the eldest and most protective of the MacQueen sisters.

"I'll work on my branding while you drag Clara out of there." Amber leaned forward, her long, wavy red hair spilling over the steering wheel as she peered around Nellie toward the storefront.

"Huh. It does look interesting, though. I love those candlesticks in the window."

"Candlesticks?" Nellie climbed out of the car and followed her sister's gaze, a frown on her face before she found the items that caught Amber's interest. Glistening silver sparkled against the morning sun, through crystal clear glass. Not a smudge in sight. "They must have just put those in there." And cleaned the glass. And…dusted.

"I thought you said this place was a hole," Amber accused with narrowed eyes. "Or was that just your way of trying to keep me out of there as well?"

"I'll plead the fifth." It was the most diplomatic way to end the conversation, especially since Nellie felt the need to double check the sign over the door. *Thistles and Thorns.* No, this was the same shop. Except when she'd stood outside with Clara a little over an hour and a half ago, the place had looked like something out of Dickens's red light district. At least…that's what she'd thought. "Maybe I just need more coffee." She leaned back into the car for Amber's cup.

"Not a chance." Amber knocked Nellie's hand away and scooped up the paper cup to clutch against her chest. "Just because you guzzle your caffeine like a thirsty camel, you don't get to claim mine. I sip. I savor. And I keep, otherwise I'm going to get very testy."

"What do you mean 'going to get'?" Nellie did what she always did when Amber won a round. She stuck her tongue out at her.

Amber laughed as Nellie slammed the door and hurried to the front door of the store. She flipped the collar of her jacket up against the morning chill that was slowly burning away under the rising sun. If there was anything more exhilarating than an early morning in Edinburgh, Scotland, Nellie certainly hadn't found it. This place was otherworldly perfection, mingling her love of history with the excitement of modern day. She could easily set her life aside, or most of it at least, without much regret. Regret was only one of the reasons she was anxious to get this "meeting" with their mother going. If Shona welcomed them with open arms, all would be fine and they'd see life in this beautiful country first hand from the woman who had birthed them. If Shona didn't want to see them…. Nellie caught her lower lip between her teeth. Well, she didn't want to think about that, did she? Being rejected by their mother once had already caused life-long damage. Nellie didn't want to consider what being cast off a second time might do to her sisters. Or to herself.

A horn blared, and Nellie jumped. When she looked back at Amber, she found her sister waving an impatient hand at the door.

"Yeah, yeah." Where was Clara when she needed her? She never let Amber—or anyone else—steam-roll over her. "I'm going." And she might just buy those candlesticks, if for no other reason than to annoy Amber.

Ah, a goal. Excellent.

Nellie's step lightened as she reached for the doorknob—she could have sworn it was a latch handle when Clara entered—and went inside. As she lifted booted feet over the threshold, a jolt of electricity shot through her body. Nothing painful, just enough to set her teeth on edge as she closed the door and turned to face an elegant display of historic-inspired brick-a-brack. There wasn't a speck of dust in sight, not even floating in the air. Everything sparkled and glowed as if she'd stepped into Aladdin's cave. Paintings in ornate frames hung on the walls. Jewelry, from pearls to rings to diamond encrusted brooches, sat housed in thick glass display cases atop lush velvet fabric. Sets of hand-painted bone china were stacked far in the corner, with a delightful collection of teacups hanging from hooks along sections of the opposite wall. And…ooooh. Nellie's fingers itched to touch. A miniature replica of Glamis Castle that included a working drawbridge and hand-stitched coat of arms flags.

Nope. Didn't have time to look closer. Nellie sighed. Not yet, anyway.

"Hello! Clara!" Nellie stepped further inside, spotting the crammed shelves of new and very old books lining the shelves at the back of the store. "Unless you want Amber coming in as backup, we need to go! Oh, hello." Nellie's cheeks went warm as a woman stepped out from behind a beaded curtain at the back of the store.

The woman was tall, almost willowy, with long silver hair that trailed over angular shoulders al-most to her waist. Her bare arms displayed a collection of bracelets and bangles while a shimmering copper amulet hung low around her neck against the black fabric of her dress.

"I'm sorry," Nellie said. "I'm looking for my sister. She came in a little while ago."

"Clara, yes, she was here. Please." The woman turned and motioned for Nellie to follow. It was then Nellie noticed the woman was very pregnant. "I'm Elya." She smoothed one hand over her rounded belly that had Nellie's heart pinging with longing and more than a bit of envy. "Clara was most interested in my collection of books. If you'll follow me, I'll show you what she was looking at."

"Um, actually, I just need to collect my sister." Unease prickled the back of Nellie's neck and she resisted the urge to shiver. She'd learned a long time ago to trust her instincts and right now, those honed alarm bells were ringing louder than a ca-thedral's tower. "We have an appointment and can't be late." The lie slipped easily from her lips. How could they be late when their mother didn't even know they were coming? "Clara!"

Had Nellie not been looking at Elya, she would have missed the flash of irritation that sharpened her features. Silver-grey eyes darkened as if a bank of storm clouds crossed. For a moment, Nellie was reminded of a raven with its sharp talons and even sharper gaze.

"Impertinent." But her thin lips formed into a smile and once again Nellie wondered if she'd imagined the slight. "Clara is in my…private read-ing room. Just back here."

Nellie thought the shopkeeper had said Clara *was* here—past tense. Did that mean she was no longer here?

Her head began to spin the deeper into the store she walked. Her pace slowed, as if she were being held back by something even while feeling com-pelled to move forward. The aroma of nutmeg and incense drifted into her nose, fogging her mind even more. She stumbled clumsily over her own feet, almost falling flat on her face. Typical. She'd always been a klutz of the first order.

The small room ahead didn't have a door. The en-try way was constructed of stacks of thick, leather-bound books with heavy gold embossed spines.

Nellie jumped as candles flickered to life inside the makeshift space. While she didn't see Clara nose deep in a tome as she expected, she did find her sister's purse on the rickety wooden table. "Where is she?" Nellie cleared her throat, uncertain why it was so difficult to push the words out of her mouth.

"She's close." Elya reached for a green book so large she had to step back to set it on the table in front of Nellie. "Clara wanted you to see this." Elya's long fingers trailed across the cover. Beneath her touch the gold lettering shimmered. An image of a walking staff topped with a glowing white orb burst to life before being replaced by a triskele. Mesmerized, Nellie reached out her hand.

"You know *The Bruadarach?*" Elya's question broke through the haze in Nellie's mind.

Nellie nodded. She and her sisters had been obsessed with the stories of three warriors fighting an unstoppable evil in a time of myth and magic. Granted Clara was the expert, probably because the book had been the one gift their mother had left for them. No doubt that was part of the reason Clara had become a librarian and rare book collector. But Nellie would be lying to herself if she didn't admit to having imagined those three heroes—Keane was the only one she could remember by name—well into her older years. The magical warrior with a twinkle in his blue eyes and an unparalleled weapons expertise had had made an indelible impression on Nellie in particular, who at times, especially when dealing with her ex-fiancé, found herself wishing Bruce could be more like the fictional hero. Honest. Loyal. Devoted. Determined.

That Keane was, at least in Nellie's mind, heart-branding handsome hadn't hurt, either. Whatever author had created those characters, this magical world, they had certainly known how to ignite a young girl's heart.

Nellie couldn't remember the last time she even thought about these stories, or Keane. She could only imagine Clara's excitement having come across what looked like a genuine first edition. Nellie, however, wasn't quite as enamored. Men like Keane and his fellow warriors didn't really exist. They were childhood fantasies, imaginings and tales she and Amber and Clara had joked would change depending on their moods and whims. Stories didn't change. Once ink hit paper, the story was set. Forever.

That electrical jolt that had welcomed her at the door zinged through her system once again as her fingers drew close to the brass lock holding the pages closed.

"You wish to see? To read?" Elya's voice echoed as if from a distance. Nellie nodded as her fingers brushed against the bulky finding.

The book burst open.

The pages flipped back and forth as if caught in a windstorm. Nellie clutched a hand to her throat. Unable to look away, her eyes focused on the hand-drawn flickering illustrations as the book settled. Her mind exploded with memory. Her mouth went dry. She trembled at the image of the lake amidst a thicket of trees tumbling with silvery buttercup type flowers reaching and stretching toward the shimmering water. But those woods. How she used to dream of running through the thickets of trees to dip her toes in the glistening water, embracing the creatures that would surround her and envelop her in magic like an animated fairy tale princess.

"Your sister is waiting for you." Elya moved around the table. The lights flickered. Darkness descended and blanketed the room in shadow. From a distance Nellie heard Clara's cell phone ringing its annoying boyband tune.

Clara. Nellie blinked. *Where was Clara?*

"Take my hand," Elya urged as her claw-like fingers wrapped around Nellie's wrist. Nellie's skin burned beneath her touch. "Take me with you."

"Take you where?" Nellie forced herself to turn around but felt as if she'd been caught in a tide of sludge. Every movement she made was a struggle, took effort, even as the power of the book, the image before her, drew her in.

Elya stepped closer, her grip tightening, her protruding belly sinking back into her body as if it had never existed. Before Nellie's disbelieving eyes, Elya transformed into a hunched old woman that called to mind the Wicked Queen with a bit more glamour. The amulet around Elya's neck glowed a brilliant, eye-blinding white. Her long painted black nails dug into Nellie's skin as the odd stench of burning flesh drifted into her nose.

Nellie blinked again, her eyes watering as she stumbled into the table. She twisted her hand, then her entire arm this way and that, but she couldn't break free of Elya's grasp.

The book trembled as the corners of the pages flickered in the dimming candlelight. A wind kicked up and spun like a tornado around them and blew out the last flames. A roar as loud as a jet engine filled the room.

"Let me go!" Nellie threw all her weight forward. She planted her free hand on Elya's chest and shoved. Elya's grip loosened and Nellie took advantage of the woman's shock, her self-defense training kicking in. She dropped down, kicked out her leg and caught Elya at the knees.

The shopkeeper stumbled back, tried to catch her balance, but as she grabbed for a stack of books that created the entrance to the room, Elya sent the entire pile cascading down and around her. Nellie sprang to her feet and reached for Clara's bag and, at the last second, she reached for the book.

The second her hand touched the weathered parchment, her feet whipped off the floor. Nellie cried out as the entire storefront shook. A bright light exploded. Nellie fought to keep her balance and braced herself for the impact. But she didn't land.

She fell and fell and fell.

Everything around her spun and vanished from sight, replaced by a jet black, bone-chilling sky. Nellie couldn't breathe, couldn't scream. Couldn't do anything but plummet and spin as if she'd been tossed out of a plane at fifty-thousand feet without a parachute.

A loud *wumph* rent the air. A spark of heat ignited inside of her, setting her fingers and toes to tingling. She was going to die. For a fraction of a second, she accepted it, didn't fight it.

Her head snapped back hard as her body jerked to a stop. She hung there, suspended in the sky, for countless seconds. Countless minutes. Her breath finally returned in sharp pants. She held herself still, felt her heart hammering so hard against her chest she thought her ribs might explode.

When she gathered the courage to turn her head and open her eyes, she found herself hovering well above the tree tops, like bait dangling from a hook. An invisible vice tightened around her midsection, cutting off her air. Out of the corner of her eye she caught a flash of movement, a group of winged creatures headed right for her. Winged creatures that looked an awful lot like.... Holy crap! Was that a dragon or a really big bird?

Big bird. She swallowed the bubble of hysteria and squeezed her eyes shut. All that was missing from this crazy dream was an eight-foot yellow Muppet. She'd passed out in the shop, hadn't she? Or she was still back at the hotel, dreaming in her feather-soft bed while Amber and Clara banged on her door demanding she wake up.

"Not real," she whispered. "Wake up. Wake up." She scrunched her toes in her boots, fisted her hands. She dropped another few feet and screamed. She held her breath, wanting but unable to prepare for whatever came next.

Voices echoed in the distance, on the wind, deep masculine voices. She couldn't make out the words, but the vice around her ribs tightened. Her head went light as her air vanished. She choked, coughed.

And dropped like an anvil.

Limbs and twigs and branches broke and caught and scraped against her face as she plummeted. She tumbled and somersaulted through the strange, thick trees. Animals screeched and cried out, unfamiliar sounds that only reached her ears as she fell past. Finally, she caught enough air in her lungs to inhale as she heaved her arms and legs up so she could rotate in the air. There! She struggled to shove her body to the side—was she flying?!?—and aimed for the expansive lake below.

She hit the water feet first. Nellie gasped a quick breath before she went completely under. She kicked and moved every part of her body, spinning back and forth, around and around, unable to find the surface. Her lungs burned. Her skin froze. The energy drained from her entire core as her extremities went heavy as stone. The more she struggled, the harder it became to stay buoyant. This was it. She clawed above her head, determined to find air again, determined not to die without having said good bye to her sisters.

Her sisters.

Nellie gasped, water choking her as an image of Amber and Clara floated before her glazed eyes. She stopped fighting. She stopped struggling.

And sank.

"I've lost her!"

From his seat atop his devoted winged pharenta, Seraphim, Keane twisted to look back at Bowen. His friend's face glowed pale in the darkness of perpetual night. Defeat shone in Bowen's glassy eyes as Keane realized Bowen's newly returned magic wasn't close to complete strength. He hadn't been able to stop Clara's sister's descent. Which meant Bowen was more liability than a help.

Astride his own younger pharenta, Bowen slumped forward, his eyes rolling back in his head before he passed out. The creature squawked a warning that something was wrong with its rider and arced its feathered wings up to protect Bowen as it soared through the sky.

"Get him back to Clara!" Keane ordered two of his men who flew beside him, and a bit below, as flank guards. Keane's hand fisted in the soft feathers that shimmered in sea-and-sky-camouflaging colors of Sera's body. The animal knew how to protect itself and a rider, changing colors much like a mood stone did once it connected to its wearer.

"Erian ordered us to stay with you, sir!" One of the men yelled then backed his creature off when the golden orb of Keane's sight staff began to glow white.

"Go!" Keane bellowed. "Seraphim, it's on you and me. Let's get her." The last thing he needed was a distraction; the plan they'd put in place over countless mooncycles had little time for improvisation. His meeting with the resistance was the only chance they had to putting an end to Dracha and his reign of terror over this realm once and for all. But he'd given his word to bring Clara's sister to her.

And Keane was nothing if he didn't keep his word.

He gave a quick glance back to Bowen, assured that his fellow warrior was on his way to safety before he angled Sera into a dive. This close to Dra-cha's stronghold of the Keep, Keane couldn't take any chances, not with strangers arriving with obscure magic that could be used against Keane and his people. Or worse, aid Dracha in his desire to overtake the world Keane and his fellow warriors and prisoners had left behind. Keane needed to get the woman back to the Citadel as fast as possible. It was the only way to keep plans in place. He'd had sacrificed too much, turned his back on too much, to let even the idea of failure seep in.

Her scream sliced through Keane's ears with the force of an arrow shot straight to his heart. He pushed the staff and its glowing light forward in its harness and narrowed his eyes to peer through the foggy mist of grey that had infected his sight the moment he'd arrived in the Forgotten Realm. Without the orb given to him by Miranda, who had a way of conjuring most needed items, he was as blind as a Concavian bat, able only to see faint shadows and outlines. With it, he could see…better.

The woman was going in. His heart froze in his chest. As Sera soared high above and around the perimeter of the lake, Keane watched helplessly as the woman hit the water and sank out of sight. Keane held his breath. Maybe the cherellean water beast hadn't heard. Maybe the same hideously spined and slimy water monster that had once dragged Keane to the bottomless depths of the lake would continue to slumber….

The lake rumbled. The earth quaked. The surrounding trees trembled as animals screeched and scurried deeper into the forest.

Wrong again.

Keane swallowed the terror that climbed into his throat. With a squeeze of his knees, he urged Seraphim through his fear. The wind ripped across his face like tiny obsidian blades, stinging its warning he was taking too many chances, tempting fate one too many times. He'd escaped the lake and its master once. Barely and certainly not intact. To challenge both again seemed reckless even to Keane's radical, impulsive mind. Still he urged Sera on and into a steeper dive.

Seraphim let out a sharp whine as Keane kicked a leg over the saddle, his other foot still securely in the stirrup as he angled the beast down. "Nice and easy, Sera." He gripped the soft feathers between his fingers before aiming the orb out over the water with his other hand.

He blinked fast, able to clear fragments of his vision long enough to see the form of a woman dropping into the depths of the lake. "Head back once I'm gone," Keane told Sera. "Give Erian the staff. He will know what to do."

Sera gave a sharp nod of her head and squawked before she looked at him, the florescent purple of her eyes reminding him of his promise that he would never leave her alone.

Another promise he needed to keep. Soon there wouldn't be enough of him left to keep a fraction of them. Of course, he might not survive the next five minutes, so….

Keane looked down as Sera soared silently around into the clearing above the lake. He locked the staff back into his harness and called on the magic he kept in reserve. He wasn't nearly as powerful as Bowen on his weakest day; he never had been. What magic he did possess was being used to protect the Citadel from their enemies, leaving Keane's power weaker than a warrior of his stature should possess. That said, Keane had never relied on his magic to get him through his existence. Magic could let him down. But extreme times called for a change in plans.

A well-aimed blast of fire energy exposed the section of the lake that held his quarry. And alerted all the creatures within as to his impending invasion. In the distance, a loud rumble echoed as the Citadel's force of protection fluctuated. With a final goodbye squeeze to Sera, Keane took a deep breath and jumped.

He went in tight, arms clasped into his chest and his ankles locked. He closed his eyes against the pulsating magic of the water, magic that could deceive as easy as aid. Lessons he'd learned long ago kicked into place the second the water closed over his head.

He willed time to slow, a feat far beyond his power, and forced himself to calm, waiting for the guiding, glowing light of the shelled and amphibious creatures that called the lake home. Rocky ledges made for dangerous dives but could, when warranted, morph and shift against the elements. Even as the water vibrated below him, he turned his attention to the woman. To her heartbeat. If he could just…pick up….

There! *Thud. Thud thud. Thud. Thud. Th…*

Keane flipped over and dived down, down, down, his lungs tightening as the pressure increased. He couldn't think about what was rising beneath him; the creature that could pinpoint her location far more easily than he ever could. He stroked his arms out and around, feeling for anything unfamiliar. Feeling for….

Thud. Thud thud.

Her heartbeat was slowing. He swept his arms out in wide arcs, squeezing his eyes shut so hard he almost saw stars as he tried to focus.

Lake kelp, slick and slimy, tangled around his wrists and as he freed one hand, he found her. He kicked to a stop, flipped again and tightened his fingers around the rough fabric encasing her arm. The water quaked.

Something whipped up and around his torso. A sharp thorn pierced his skin beneath his ribs and tried to drag him down. He opened his mouth to howl as he twisted and fought his way free, ripping the thorn-tipped tentacle away from his body. Nothing but a bubble of silence erupted from his lips. The last of his air gone, Keane felt his head go light.

Muscles under his grasp tensed and jarred him back to the moment. She was alive. But only barely.

Thud…thud…thud.

Keane focused his energy into kicking to the surface, dragging her with him, the pain in his side settling into a slow, steady burn. The odd muted roar from below sent vibrations of terror through him. The cold water was warming, it's warning against the water beast making its ascent. Tides beneath the surface ran as rough as the ocean at times, tonight being no exception. He'd learned the hard way that a lake as serene as a temple at High Moon was one of the biggest dangers of The Forgotten Realm.

Out of time, his lungs on fire, the wound below his ribcage stinging, Keane used all his strength to shove her up and over him, pushing her toward the surface. In the silence of the night, he heard the muted sound of her breaking free before he followed.

Keane gasped in huge gulps of air and locked his arm under her arms, keeping her head above water as he kicked out, guided by the faint florescence of the Farrengold blossoms lining the west side of the lake.

A loud screech from a Boddinbird on the far end of the bank had Keane kicking double time. The comical looking birds known for tripping over their own webbed feet acted as an early warning system for cherelleans; they could sense when a water beast had awakened and moved within the swirls and fathoms of its watery home.

It seemed an eternity before Keane's feet hit solid ground but the second he could walk, Keane twisted to grab hold of the woman to haul her onto the bank just as the water lapped up over his knees. His side screamed in fiery pain, but he blocked it out. Focused on the woman.

The roar that split the air nearly split Keane's skull. Nausea rolled through him as his chest and torso throbbed. He'd gotten out alive. Again.

He pressed a hand against his lower left side, drew away sticky fingers as his warm blood seeped.

Something told him he would not survive a third attempt.

The irritated howl of disappointment over lost prey broke the surface before the shadow erupted to hover over the lake. Keane shivered and moved further into to the safety of forest. Cherellean water beasts might be death personified in the water, but on land, they were beyond helpless.

"Missed me this time, didn't you?" Keane shoved the woman onto her side and slapped a hand hard against the center of her back. "I've given you enough. You can't have her. Come on. Breathe." The beast gurgled and sank out of sight.

Keane slapped harder, gripping her shoulder. She wasn't dead. He wouldn't allow it. He would not return to the Citadel and tell Clara he'd failed to save her sister. He'd failed enough for ten lifetimes. He would not fail again.

She stiffened a second before she gasped and choked for air. He released her, letting her come back to consciousness on her own. The darkness of the night overtook the residual effects of the orb and Keane's sight vanished once again. Pushing aside the despised helpless feeling, he heard her spitting up water and gagging. He felt her roll away before she retched, and when she collapsed, she nearly knocked him off his knees.

Keane swept his hair off his face, scrubbed at his eyes in a useless attempt to get a better look at her. But all he could see—all he would ever see—was the faint shadowy outline of her most definite feminine form.

He kept a steadying hand on shoulder, attributing the odd warmth weaving its way through his fingers and up his arm to her body temperature coming back to normal. His eyes ached. The throbbing in his chest eased. The tightness in his chest relaxed.

"Th-thank you." Her voice, while raw, zinged through him like the most cultured of music and sang of times and memories long forgotten. A knot inside of him—wedged into the deepest part of his being—loosened.

Keane squeezed her hand when she tried to sit up. "Rest," he ordered gently as his eyes throbbed. "Get your breath."

"Get my breath?" The disbelieving tone had him torn between frowning and laughing. "How about my stomach and heart? I think I left them about five hundred feet that way." He felt her hand shoot past his face as if she gestured to the sky.

"You fell a long way," Keane agreed. "But had you landed anywhere else, you would not have survived." As much as he hated the lake, it had, in essence, saved her life.

"Guess that's good news then." The shadow of her shuffled around him.

He could feel her looking at him and, not for the first time, Keane cursed his fate in not being able to look back. In this world of perpetual darkness, the one bright light would have been the beauty of a woman, but he'd never found complete solace in that distraction. How he missed appreciating every nuanced movement, exploring every…. Well, some things he'd found a way to manage.

"Drowning's always been my second choice for death anyway. Appreciate the save. Got a name, hand—ah, mister?"

Amused at her discomfort, Keane sat back on his heels. "Of course."

The woman snorted, which sent her into another coughing fit. "N-not funny. Oh, ow. I'm going to hurt for weeks. I never should have let my gym membership expire."

She attempted to stand, but her knees folded and she plopped almost on his lap. He folded his arms around her and held her still. Her clothing felt rough, soaked through, but beneath it the warmth of her seeped into him. He resisted the urge to stroke her hair. Her skin. He ducked his head and took a deep breath, smelling the faint hint of wildflowers beneath the briny scent of the lake. His eyes tightened and burned, no doubt displeased by his return to the water that had taken his sight.

"We have medicine back at the Citadel that will help," he told her.

"The Citadel. You mean I ended up at West Point?"

"We are nowhere near the western point of this realm." Keane might need Clara to translate for him. Her sister's vocabulary was so…odd. "I am sure what you need is rest and dry clothes, but we need to get moving. Dracha's men will have no doubt seen your arrival." He rotated his injured arm as stiffness began to set in. "They will come looking for you. This we do not want."

"Dracha." The woman muttered under her breath. "I've heard that name before. That book Clara was always going on about when we were kids. The book Elya showed me in the—"

"Elya?" Keane gripped her shoulders and spun her around to face him. His fingers brushed her face. His eyes flickered and for an instant, he swore he saw…. Keane shook his head, dislodging the thought. Now wasn't the time for hallucinations. "You saw Elya? She lives?"

"Well, I met an Elya." She shrugged. "Last I saw her she had about a thousand books landing on her head, so who knows what…happened. Your eyes are white. You're blind."

As her fingers brushed feather light against his cheek, the constant pain in his eyes, in his head, eased. He sucked in a breath and flinched against a blinding flash of light. As he blinked, for an instant, he saw her: fully and completely. A round, full face framed by tight red curls glistening in the flower-light, and gold-flecked golden eyes that sent him soaring into the past. "Shona."

"Not hardly," she muttered as her face faded from sight again. "Nellie. Shona's my mother. Well, she's the woman who gave birth to me. I wouldn't exactly call her a mother. What do you know about her? Geez. I'm babbling. Hot guys make me babble. Lord, someone stop me."

Keane's soul screamed. What did he know about Shona? Only that he and Bowen and Rivalin had disobeyed their orders in the hopes of protecting the Goddess's only remaining child. The child Dracha was determined to kill once and for all in his final act of vengeance against the Goddess Alastrine. Keane and his three best friends had hidden the girl where—and when—no one would ever be able to find her. "Nell-ee." Her name felt like a balm on his stinging lips.

From the moment he, Bowen, and Rivalin had accepted their punishment to be banished to the Forgotten Realm, Keane had focused whatever energy he had in defeating Dracha and protect his own world. The world duty dictated he leave behind. The world Keane knew he'd never see again.

"We must get you someplace safe." Pushing thoughts of the Goddess's daughter aside, Keane pushed her hand away and plunged himself back into the grey shadows in which he lived. Bowen was right. Elya was alive and plotting, which meant they probably had even less time than Keane had counted on. If the sorceress found her way back to Dracha before he signed the treaty with the resistance….

Keane shoved himself to his feet and hauled Nellie up with him. The sooner he got her back to her sister, back to the protection of the Citadel, the sooner he could finalize plans for the summit. His side burned; his insides tightened.

"Hang on there. Give me a second." She wrenched her arm free. "I'm tired of being man or woman handled. Are you going to tell me where I am or not?"

"When we are safe." Would it not be better to have all this explained by someone she trusted? By her sister? As the shadows in his vision closed in again, he saw her rub at her arm. "Did Elya hurt you?"

"Not really. She tried to hitch a ride to…wherever this is. And are you blind or not?"

Keane caught her wrist as she waved her hand in front of his face. "Nearly." He moved in and heard her breath catch in her chest. The sound shot straight to his groin and had him wishing they had more time to explore more than niceties. Something about this woman elicited every protective instinct inside of him and aroused the rest of him. But he could see potential doors opening before him. He couldn't be certain, not until he heard Clara's story. Bowen's arrival with Nellie's sister at the Citadel had coincided with Nellie's fireball entrance into the Forgotten Realm. There hadn't been time to decipher information of any kind other than to reveal to his brother-in-arms that he was, indeed, alive after being presumed dead at the jaws of the Cherellean. "You and Clara are not of this world." And yet…. "But you are of Shona."

"According to my father and I believe he'd know. You've seen Clara?" Excitement and relief vibrated in the air. "She's here? She's okay?"

"She is under my and Bowen's protection."

"Wait. Bowen. As in the three warriors?" Her arm relaxed beneath his grasp. "That would make you either Rivalin or—"

"Keane. Warden of the Southern Realm." He shifted his hold to clasp her fingers in his palm and lifted her hand to his lips. He smiled at the sharp intake of breath when his lips touched her skin. The sound hit him straight in the heart and melted through him. "It is a pleasure to meet you, Nell-ee."

"Uh-huh. I bet you say that to all the drowned rats you pull out of that lake."

"Drowned…rat?" The bubble of seduction burst as he frowned.

"Consider it self-deprecating humor. And as appealing as the idea of a lakeside make-out session with a hot stranger is, you said something about Clara? Where is she?"

"At the Citadel." He loathed what came next, but he set his pride aside. "But I will need your assistance to find our way back."

❖

Leave it to her to take the blind leading the blind thing a bit too far.

She may as well be tromping through a lost rain forest of the Amazon for all the information she had. Trees that moved? A sky without stars? No moon in sight? Where on earth was she, anyway? And how had she gotten here? Magic? Hallucinogenic drugs? More importantly, when had she turned into a flirt?

On top of being soaked to the skin under wet wool and a too-tight skirt, she'd been babbling almost non-stop. She rubbed her fingers against the raw welt around her wrist, the mark Elya had branded her with back in the store, and tried to focus on the pain rather than the panic threatening to overtake reason.

She'd never had the best imagination. It was one reason she chose to lose herself in logic and the facts of history. But to find herself here—in a world known only in an obscure storybook her mother had given them…how was this even possible? Was this all some crazy dream? Or was she losing her mind?

Real or not, it seemed she was stuck here. There wasn't any use in dwelling or worrying or doing anything other than seeing this adventure to the end. Wherever it might lead. Preferably to a hot bath and soft bed.

She did find a certain irony, however, in her current situation. As a scholar, she lived her life in books and essays and testimonials to history. Why shouldn't she be…trapped in one? She caught a laugh behind trembling fingers. Who was ever going to believe this?

The darkness that encased this world settled around her like a suffocating blanket. Trudging through an unknown forest like Tripsy, Snow White's lesser known eighth dwarf, had her considering investing in inflatable clothing. She'd fallen on her face so much there were more twigs and leaves in her hair than were strewn on the ground. Just as the thought passed through her mind, a small clearing appeared, bathed in that soft, glowing light courtesy of the same luminescent flowers that had surrounded the lake.

She could hear the trickle of water nearby. Her stomach growled around the remnants of the solitary mini scone and coffee she'd had for breakfast. "Not a Starbucks in sight."

"Starbucks?" Keane's voice sounded strained.

"A place that serves coffee." What she wouldn't give to be sipping on a white chocolate mocha about now.

"What is coffee?"

Nellie stopped suddenly, and Keane barreled into her from behind. This time she dug her heels into the ground to stop from falling.

"I might be able to accept a lot of things about this place, but no coffee?" She spun in time to see him sway before he caught his footing. Great. Now her clumsiness was contagious. She squinted into the growing light provided by the flora. Glowing flowers. Who knew? But now, now she could see this place for the beauteous fantasy world it was. Such odd, shimmering colors. Angular shaped leaves and thick branches dripping off trees with trunks thick and wide enough to provide housing for a small family.

But all that scenery was nothing compared to the man who had pulled her out of that swampy lake. He stood tall enough to give her altitude sickness. She had to tip her chin back to look into that stunning, handsome—she hadn't been kidding about that—face that bore tiny scars that hinted of heroism. She could only imagine what tales his body could tell. And what a body it was. Toned and fit, with barely an ounce of fat that she could see, she'd bet he could have easily doubled as a cover model for the romance novels she was addicted to. Hair the color of summer hay hung long enough to brush the top of his ears and the back of his neck, and as it had dried, curled itself into tempting waves she'd bet felt like silk under her curious fingers. Nellie cleared her throat. Yeah, that was appropriate thinking for the situation. "I've read where other senses kick in when you lose your sight? Is that right?"

"If that's your way of asking if I'm always this clumsy, the answer is no. I'm a bit distracted." Keane rubbed his fingers hard against his temple as if he had a headache before slipping his hand into the split of his stained tunic. "It's been a while since I've been around a beautiful woman."

Nellie snorted. Now she knew he was blind. "I'm short, round, and my hair is probably twice as wide as I am right now." Amber was the glamour sister. Clara, the pretty one. Nellie was…the one with the fun personality. She'd stopped trying to smooth her ragged curls. What she wouldn't give for some defrizzer. Or tights that weren't squishing in her waterlogged boots. Or a flashlight. Clara would have had one in her bag, but that and the book were probably on the bottom of that lake by now. Nellie bit her lip. Best not share that bit of information with her sister when they met up. "Are you sure you're all right?" She moved closer to him. He took a step back. "You look awfully pale."

"I am fine." He teetered as he spoke. "Just residual effects from the lake. We should keep moving."

"Yeah, yeah, demon warriors on our trail, right." Not convinced he was telling the truth, she slapped a hand on his chest to hold him in place. He flinched. "Hold on." She caught his chin in her fingers and tilted his head toward the light. "You're bleeding. Your head—"

"Not my head. Please, Nellie." He caught her arm and attempted to turn her around. "We need to—"

"Stop it!" She shrugged off his hand more easily than expected and pulled him over into brighter light. Only then did she see the thick trickle of blood pooling from beneath his shirt. "Keane, holy hell!" She ripped open the fabric. "You are hurt! Why didn't you say anything?"

"Because there's nothing we can do about it until we get back to the Citadel." But he swayed again, this time far enough to the side that Nellie had to catch him. "Your safety is my priority. I promised Clara."

"You let me deal with my sister. And you can't protect anyone in your condition. You need to sit down so I can look at that." She looked around him, spotted an uncomfortable looking rock, and guided him to it.

"We don't have time—"

Nellie moved in, hands gripping his upper arms—wow, did he have well defined biceps—and peered up at him. "Sit on the rock or on the ground. Your choice."

"There is nothing to be done, Nellie." He chose the rock, thankfully, Nellie thought, as she wasn't sure how she'd haul him up off the ground. "I need a healer. Unless you are one?"

"I'm an historian," Nellie mumbled. "And I guess this brings us to our get to know each other portion of our romantic walk through the woods." When she was sure he was steady enough to sit up without assistance, she heeled off her boots so she could shimmy out of her tights. She tossed them to the ground and unbuttoned the wool coat she'd bought the day they'd arrived in Edinburgh.

"What are you doing?"

"Giving you a show, obviously," Nellie said and took some pleasure in the amused light shining in those eerie white eyes of his. Like she'd have had the guts to strip in front of him if he could see her. She'd always been the lights off kinda girl when it came to her very limited intimate experiences. "Kidding, of course. Unless…." She leaned in and stared him right in the eyes. "You weren't lying about being blind, were you?"

He shook his head.

Her jacket hit the ground and she pulled her black turtleneck over her head. The oddly warm air brushed against her bare skin. She watched Keane, shifting on the rock as he tried not to show how much pain he was in. "Of course I'd meet a guy who has no way of appreciating my hidden attributes." She looked down at her bra, half grateful he couldn't see the plain white cotton fabric she wrestled with every day. Nope. No lace and satin for her. Besides, neither would make good bandages anyway. Her overly practical Scottish mind and wallet wouldn't go for such frivolity.

"Nothing hidden from me." Keane held up one hand, wiggled his fingers. "What my eyes don't see, these do."

Nellie laughed, surprised that the sound made her feel better. "Understood, Romeo. Let's see about getting you fixed up here. Shirt, off, please." She returned to his side and pulled his hand away from his side.

"You women and your orders." But he did as she said. He hissed out a breath when she probed around the wound. "Please don't."

"I can't tell if there's something in there. It looks like a bullet wound." She pressed her fingers on either side of the jagged opening, watched the flow of blood and felt a bit relieved when it wasn't running dark and black. She didn't know a lot about triage, but she knew the darker the blood, the worse the condition.

He leaned toward her, his breath warm against her skin. Nellie shivered. "I wouldn't do that. I smell like swamp."

He took a deep breath and sent chills racing down her spine. "Lake and wildflowers. What is a bullet? Some creature from your world?"

"Ah, no." Nellie pushed her hair behind her ears and stooped in front of him. He opened his legs. Her cheeks went warm as knelt between them. He'd asked her a question. What had he…hard to concentrate when she was surrounded by a man who could fry every synapse in a woman's brain. He was as intoxicating as weekend in Cancun. "A bullet is a metal fragment fired from another metal weapon. It's a projectile, I guess you'd call it."

"Dangerous?"

"Can be." Nellie pressed her fingers harder. Keane sank away from her, letting out a string of curses—she assumed they were curses—in a language she didn't recognize. "Sorry. Yeah, I think there's something in the wound."

"Zephyr thorn. Tententacled creature that lives in the lake."

"Killer decipus. Got it. As long as it isn't poisonous…." When Keane didn't respond, she looked up at him. How did a blind man manage to avoid her gaze? "Keane?"

He lifted a bloodstained hand to her face, stroked a solitary finger down the side of her cheek. "I need to get to the Citadel."

"Son of a biscuit maker, you've been poisoned? You've got to be kidding me." She scrambled to her feet and grabbed her turtleneck off the ground. Heading in the direction of the water she'd heard, she found a small stream and dumped her shirt into it, ringing it out a few times before folding it. After a good couple of drinks, she returned to Keane and, bracing one hand on his bare, scarred shoulder, pressed the wet fabric against his injury.

"You're trying to kill me." Keane gritted his teeth and dropped his head back. "And after I saved your life."

"I'm trying to make sure you get us where we need to go." Having him bleed to death on the way wasn't going to do either of them any good. "Let me guess." She grabbed her tights and drew them around his torso to hold the makeshift bandage in place. "You're one of those prideful kind of men, aren't you?" She shoved her feet back into her boots, pulled on and buttoned up her jacket, and wedged herself under his arm to heft him back on his feet. "Not about to show weakness or ask for help."

"I did ask for help." He pressed tentative fingers against the bandage before he drew his shirt closed. "I told you I needed your eyes."

"You need a brain transplant. If we're going to get to this Citadel in one piece, we need to work together. No more holding out on me, Keane, understand?"

"Yes, mistress."

"Okay, wow." Nellie's entire body flushed. "How about you save that talk for when you're feeling better?" There she went again, flirting. What was wrong with her? She never initiated…anything. Clara or Amber? Sure, they didn't have any qualms when it came to the opposite sex. Or sex in general. Nellie, on the other hand?

According to her ex, an igloo registered higher on a thermometer than she did. And didn't that work wonders on a girl's self-esteem.

Cue the over-compensation. Not that she expected a man like Keane to be remotely attracted to a frumpy woman like her. "Any idea how far we have to go?"

"We just have to get close enough for Sera to sense me." Keane leaned on her more than Nellie expected. She stumbled and finally caught her balance.

"Sera, huh?" Nellie sighed. There went any plan of using Keane to get over her…issues. "Yeah, should have figured you'd have someone waiting at home for you. Just my luck."

"Have you no man who calls you his, Nell-ee?"

"Just Nellie. And I did. A fiancé. We were going to be…." Nellie really didn't want to go into the humiliating details. "It didn't work out."

Keane stopped walking and caught her hand in his, drew it to his chest and waited. She looked up

to find him watching her with those oddly blind and penetrating eyes.

"He didn't want me," Nellie admitted out loud for the first time in three months. "He wanted to use my connections. To get a job. Advance his career." And Bruce had advanced, stepping on her heart on his way up the collegiate ladder. "We aren't together anymore."

Because once he'd gotten what he'd wanted, he'd dumped her for his old girlfriend.

"Good." He brushed his lips against her fingers. "He did not deserve a powerful woman like you. You come from a very strange world, Nellie." His arm slid around her shoulders and Nellie grinned into the night. "Are all the men you meet so undeserving?"

"Remains to be seen, Keane." She pulled him along beside her. "That remains to be seen."

❖

"At some point I'll actually be able to see this Citadel of yours, right?"

Keane heard Nellie's voice through a buzzing hum that was growing louder in his head. How long had they been walking? Hours? Days? He'd lost track.

The zephyr poison was wreaking havoc with his magic, what little he had left of it, not to mention his mind. He had to keep present, keep control, otherwise the shielding protecting his people, his men, would collapse and expose them all to their enemies. Another reason to meet with the alliance at the summit. He needed more fighters.

Reality was warping, twisting in on itself. Had he still possessed his sight, he would have been dealing with hallucinations. Instead, he heard voices, ghostly voices screaming at him, accusing him. Condemning him. *Warning him.*

"Hey, stop that, Sparky." Nellie's hand covered his. She squeezed before she stumbled to a stop and pushed him back against a tree. "I'm not fire resistant."

"Stop what?" He'd been shivering so hard his teeth hurt, but the second she touched him, his fever cooled. His head hadn't ached this bad since he'd first lost his sight. Nausea swept over him and he doubled over.

"The fire manicure." She leaned down and touched his face. "It's your magic, isn't it? It's fritzing out on you."

"How do you know about mag—" His mind began to clear and he could breathe without pain. He lifted his head long enough to look around, to attempt to get their bearings. She'd led them into another clearing. He wondered if the lush grass beneath his booted feet was as soft and welcoming as it felt. It was all he could do not to lay down and surrender to the exhaustion creeping over him.

"I have a pretty good memory," Nellie told him. "Don't tell Clara, but I was reading those stories when she wasn't. Bowen has the real magical power. You're more adept with a sword and dagger. And with words. I should find you some more water." She started to leave, abandoning him, removing her hands from his skin. And when she did, the pain, the voices, the dizziness returned. Stronger than before.

"Wait!" Keane grabbed her and hauled her back, slipping his fingers between hers to see if what he believed was true. "Don't leave me." The utterance of weakness nearly drove him to his knees.

"I won't go far. You have to drink something. Who knows how much longer we have to walk." Nellie's entire body went tense. He could feel her hand tighten around his as she stood and turned to face the path. "Um. Keane?"

Keane struggled to keep coherent. While he'd been concentrating on putting one foot in front of the other, the back of his mind had been working on the possibility that there was far more to Nellie than either of them realized. Even more than he could have dreamed. Was it possible…. "I need to do something." He tugged her toward him, tightening his fingers around hers as he drew her into his arms.

"Uh…." She squirmed in his hold as he molded her curves against him. He slid his finger under her chin and tilted her face toward his. "I thought you said we needed to…oh. You're going to kiss me? Really? Figures. You're delirious, aren't you?"

He stopped, feeling her warm breath against his face. Her surprise confused him. "Did this fiancé of yours never kiss you?"

"Yeah, sure. Personally, I never really got what the big deal was. I mean, what can someone do with a kiss? It's just lips and tongue and—" She shrugged. "Never did much for me."

Even in a weakened state, Keane was up for a challenge. "Let's see if that holds, shall we?" He brushed his lips against hers.

"Oh."

Her gasp exhilarated him, the buzz of excitement and attraction masking, at least for a few moments, the effects of the poison coursing through his blood. He felt his strength returning, fighting against the infection even as his desire for more overwhelmed reason.

"Was that all?" she whispered.

"I hadn't planned for it to be." His sight flickered. "Would you like more?"

"Uh-huh." She slipped her hand around to the back of his neck, her fingers pressing into his skin as she urged his head down toward hers. "I think I'm becoming a fan of experimentation."

In the shadow of grey, he saw her tongue flick out to moisten her lips. Had he had his full sight, he might have thrown all reason to the wind and made love to her as his final act of life. Every cell in his body tingled as he dipped his mouth and pressed his lips against hers. Teasing at first, testing. This time when she gasped, he took full advantage and angled his head, diving deeper, pulling her closer, dipping his tongue into her mouth to tempt hers into a dance he found himself wishing would go on forever.

His hand continued to flex around hers, fingers clenching, sliding, rubbing as he continued the kiss, drawing all the tension from her body and leaving her lax and pliant in his arms as his own body grew hard with desire.

When the wound in his side began to throb anew, he knew he'd reached his limit. Knew if he didn't put a stop to this now, he very well never would. Every female he'd ever been with faded from his memory, replaced by the image of a bright, green-eyed smile of a round-faced woman who held no understanding of her own appeal.

"I think this is one time I'm very glad to have been wrong," she murmured against his lips.

"About?" He drew his mouth away and pulled her forehead down against his chest. He was breathing heavy. The pain in his head exploded like a million unseen stars. He squeezed his eyes shut, clung to her as the pain gradually receded.

"Kissing. And if that's what you're capable of while you're injured and bleeding, I can only imagine what might happen once you're well." She stiffened in his hold. "I mean, if it was okay for you. And, you know, might want to do any more kissing. With me." She tried to pull away, but he held on. "Please tell me the ground is soft enough for me to dig a hole to crawl into?"

Keane kissed her again, this time without the pretense of caution, but because he needed to. Needed her. Beyond how she made the darkness recede. She filled an emptiness he hadn't even realized he had. "You will not be needing to crawl into any holes." He stroked his thumb across her face. A face that as he opened his eyes, he could actually see smiling up at him. "Nellie." Her name came out as a whisper, a prayer perhaps. He let his hand drop, released her other hand, moved back so they were no longer touching.

And fell back into the darkness.

"What?" Nellie stepped toward him. "What is it? Is the pain worse?"

"No." He held out his hand and the instant she took it in hers, the darkness eased. "No, it's not worse. Just…different. Come here." He pulled her in again and held her, his mind racing. He'd been told there was no cure to his blindness, that there was no hope that he'd ever regain his sight and yet….

Nausea rolled through him with the force of an undertow. Was it possible this woman could end up being his greatest strength *and* weakness?

"How much further is it?" Nellie guided him to the ground, staying close, her hands on his bare neck, his face, holding his hand. Whenever she touched him, wherever she did, it was as if he'd been released from this prison he'd called home for countless cycles. "Tell me what you need me to do?" She asked. "Go ahead? Find someone?"

"I don't want you out here alone." He shook his head, unable to clear it now of the haze that was overtaking his thoughts despite her touch. "Not

safe." The hallucinations were coming back, the sounds of heavy booted footfalls pounding through the forest. Dracha's soldiers would be looking for her. Looking for *them* as by now, surely, they knew to be searching for two. "Nellie—"

"Quiet! I hear something." Nellie's frantic whisper had him trying to sit up, but he groaned as new pain sliced through him. He could feel the poison moving into his chest, pressing against his heart, his soul. The center of all that made him who he was. "Come on." She shoved him to the side and got behind him to drag him under the arms and deeper into the protection of the woods. "Maybe if we're quiet they'll keep going."

Keane tried to speak, to tell her it wasn't any use. Dracha's men were well-trained. They would search every inch of the Forgotten Realm if even one suspected there was something or someone to aid Dracha's agenda.

He should have sent her on, in the direction of the Citadel. Erian would be watching for him, for them. Erian and Bowen. The only two people he trusted without hesitation. But there were no words to be found. She piled branches and leaves on top of him before moving away, taking the light with her.

But there…in the back of his thoughts, pressing into his mind, he heard a familiar cry. "Sera," he murmured, before he surrendered to the pain.

Nellie remained hidden behind the thick trunk of a tree that's bark molded beneath her touch. She welcomed the unexpected softness as she planted her feet in the ground, keeping one concerned ear on Keane's increasingly uneven breathing, the other on the heavy footfalls echoing through the woods. She gripped the tree hard and as she did, heavy leaf-tipped branches dipped down and around her, as if bending to her thoughts to conceal her. "Keane," Nellie whispered as the tree limbs behind her rustled and shifted and blanketed him from sight. "Thank you." She pressed her forehead against the tree.

Panic and uncertainty set her heart to racing. What had she gotten in to? Trapped in a magical world with telepathic trees and a sexy, blind warrior? It was as if her mind had gone on vacation and chose to reignite the imagination she'd never embraced as a child. Dreams, fantasies, like the ones she had of her mother coming back, had never brought her anything but disappointment. Certainty, facts, those were predictable. Emotionless. Safe.

But now…magic was the only answer she had for so many things, including that mind-blowing, self-esteem building kiss not even her wildest dreams could have conjured. Men like Keane didn't look twice at women like Nellie. How was it he couldn't see her yet couldn't seem to keep his eyes off her?

He certainly couldn't keep his hands off her. She shivered against the thought of what those hands, what those fingers, were capable of in the best of circumstances. She blew her hair out of her eyes. Would that she'd ever get the chance to find out?

Excitement and uncertainty bloomed deep within her, stagnated by her constant companion, self-doubt. Put her in front of a hall filled with lecture attendees, behind a lectern speaking to colleagues with twenty years more experience, and she'd knock it out of the park every time. But relationships? Men? Nellie pressed her lips tight together. She'd had only one serious one: Bruce. And he'd done enough damage to scare her off even trying again. Until Keane. Because of Keane, the doubt was fading…gradually. Because of what Keane—a blind man—saw in her.

Nellie's head shot up as voices echoed beyond the clearing, not in the direction from which they'd come, as if someone was in pursuit, but from where she and Keane had been headed.

Nellie crouched, making herself as small as possible. Gut instinct told her these could well be his own men Keane had referenced, but could she take the chance when he was equally convinced Dracha's soldiers were hunting for them? Keane was in such bad shape that if those approaching weren't the good guys, what could stop them from killing Keane on the spot?

Her muscles tightened. *I will protect him.*

Resolve overtook fear. He'd risked his life to save hers. He'd continued to try to do so even as that poison wreaked havoc with his body. The least she could do was put herself between him and…whatever that approached.

A loud crash followed by an earsplitting shriek had her shrinking back. What the holy hell was that? She peeked out around the tree, lifted her hand to pry apart the branches as an enormous shadow dropped into the darkness and swallowed the small clearing beyond.

Nellie gasped, straining to see, to comprehend what had come from the sky. The creature changed color as it moved its large feathered head like a scanner, aiming its gaze deep into the trees. Copper and gold mingled with yellow and oranges, a brightness she hadn't seen since she'd first arrived in this world. Living fire. The warmth it conveyed drew her to her feet. She took a step forward.

A branch snapped beneath her foot.

The creature whirled around, its body shifting colors once again, this time to a purple that matched its glowing amethyst eyes. Nellie's mind reeled. Not a dragon. Not a bird. But a glorious combination of the two. This was the creature she thought she'd imagined as she'd fallen through the sky. No scales covered its massive body; its feathers appeared as soft as down, its wings held tight against its body as three feet scrambled to face her as it stretched out its short neck and opened its sword-straight beak.

The creature screeched.

Nellie slammed her hands over her ears, squinting against the stinging vibrations moving through the air. But she held her ground, took a step forward and, when the creature closed its mouth, Nellie held her arms out to her sides. "You can't have him."

A squawk this time. The creature moved closer and quirked its head. Its solitary front foot clenched in the ground, the damp grass squelched beneath its six talon-tipped toes.

"He's under my protection." Bravado she'd never felt before swelled within her. If she was going to go out, she might as well make a stand first. "He's sick. Injured. He's no danger to you." Yeah, that was a smart thing to say to a potential enemy. *Move along. This isn't the warrior you're looking for.* Nellie forced herself to keep calm and appear unthreatening. The closer she and the creature got to one another, wonder and amazement overtook the fear.

"Stop!" a male voice blasted, from behind the creature which reared back in response and struck out with its foot. Nellie's heart jumped into her throat, but she rejected the order and kept her eyes pinned to the creature's, determined to find a way to drive it off before it could attack—and probably kill—both her and Keane. She held up her hands in a surrender like gesture, her mind racing for a solution should the creature decide to turn its deadly attention squarely back on her.

"Nellie." Keane's weakened voice broke through the darkness as he came stumbling out. He had one arm wrapped tight around his torso. Blood had begun seeping through the bandage and his tunic, staining his sleeve now, dripping onto the ground.

"No, Keane, stay back. I've got this." That bubble of hysteria she'd been swallowing for hours burst to the surface. "I don't know what I've got, but…stay back!" She moved one hand toward him.

The creature whipped its head and dropped to the ground so hard Nellie stumbled into Keane, who grunted in pain. His free hand grasped her hip, his fingers digging through the fabric of her skirt and jacket.

"No!" Nellie yelled as the creature's head swooped in, hundreds of thin razor-sharp teeth glistening against the darkness of the night only inches from Nellie's face. "You can't have him." Nellie closed her eyes against the hot oily breath the creature expelled.

"Nellie, come away." Keane took a step back and tried to draw her with him.

Nellie dug her heels in. There was nowhere for her to go, nowhere to run. Even if she wanted to.

"No. I can't let it hurt—" She gasped as the creature closed its beak, ducked its head, and pushed its forehead against her outstretched hands. "What. The. Hell?" Nellie didn't know what to do other than sink her fingers into the soft feathers of its head. "Oh, wow. Wow. Keane, this is amazing. It's…." She'd never seen or felt anything so miraculous in all her life. Wonder swelled around apprehension, dulling her fear.

"Seraphim," Keane's hold eased, and he circled around to place a hand on the creature's neck. "She found us."

"Seraphim," Nellie repeated, grateful the darkness would hide the embarrassed blush erupting on her face. "Sera. You weren't talking about another woman. You were talking about *her.*" Nellie took another step closer, lightened her touch on Sera so she could add her other hand. "You are beautiful, aren't you?"

Sera's throat feathers ruffled as she let out a noise that sounded like a chuckle. She lifted amused eyes to Keane who looked as shocked as she felt.

"Keane," Nellie whispered but as she drew her gaze from Sera to him, she saw his grip on the creature tighten before he slumped to the ground. "Keane!"

Nellie dropped to her knees as the forest around her erupted. Dozens of hooded, black-clad figures darted out of the trees, torches and weapons raised, giving a wide berth to Sera, who had extended her wing over both Nellie and Keane. Nellie found herself dragging Keane's limp form across her knees as she leaned back against Sera's leg. He wasn't moving. He was barely breathing, but as she grasped his hand in hers, he squeezed back.

A man carrying a tall walking staff topped with a glowing golden-encased orb emerged from the group, nodding gravely towards Nellie, as if in greeting. "Sera." He pulled off his hood, revealing close-cropped shockingly silver hair and a face weathered by battle and obligation. "Let us help them, Sera." The man dropped to one knee and bowed his head. "Please."

"Are you Erian?" Nellie asked, quietly.

He nodded.

Relief swept over Nellie like a tide going out to sea. No soldier with malicious intent would bow to a creature like this in such a submissive posture. These were Keane's people.

Sera lowered her head and knocked her beak lightly against Nellie.

"It's okay." Tears burning her eyes at the creature's surprising affection toward her, Nellie reached up and patted the side of the creature's face. "I think we can trust them."

Sera squawked and let out what sounded like a huff of irritation, before stomping a few steps away and lowering herself in the middle of the clearing, much like a chicken sitting on her eggs. The other men closed in and bathed the entire glen with welcome light.

The man raised his head and waited an extra beat before he rose and hurried toward them. "I am Erian, Keane's second in command." The words flew at her like bullets as he dropped to his knees in front of them. "You are Nellie or Amber?"

"Nellie. He's hurt." She continued to grip Keane's hand in hers. "He said it's a zephyr thorn. He didn't tell me at first." She didn't know why, but she didn't like the idea of this commanding man blaming her for what had happened to his…whatever Keane was.

"Of course he didn't. Torches!" Erian yelled as he pulled open Keane's shirt. "You did this?" He unknotted the tights and removed the shirt as the light around them increased. Only then did she notice how deathly pale Keane looked.

"It was the only thing I could think to do." Clearly it hadn't been enough.

"You did well." Erian gave her an encouraging nod. "Fresh river water counteracts the infectious property of the thorns. I need you to go with my men."

"No." Nellie tightened her grip on Keane. "No, I'm not leaving him." She couldn't explain it, didn't want to try to, but she was connected to Keane. More connected than she been to anyone in her life other than her sisters.

Erian's silver eyes sharpened as he pressed down on Keane's wound. Keane groaned, and a sheen of perspiration erupted on his face.

"Glare at me all you want," Nellie told Erian. "I'm not leaving. I can help. Tell me what to do."

"We need to get the thorn out." He kicked out a leg and pulled a dagger from the sheath on his calf. He offered it to her, hilt first. "You can either use this or you can hold him down. Your choice."

Not wanting to cause Keane anymore pain, she nodded at the blade. "I'll hold him." She let go of Keane's hand, slid him off her lap and repositioned herself on her knees beside him, pressing her palms flat on his shoulders. "Might want someone else to grab his legs. I can't manage both."

"Taranto." Erian called over his shoulder. One of his dark-clad men joined them, but he didn't remove his hood as he locked his hands firmly around Keane's ankles. He looked like a hovering shadow to Nellie's spinning mind. "Not an inch can he move, understand?" Erian signaled for one of the torches to be brought closer and he plunged the blade into the flame.

Nellie gasped, wondering how the fire didn't burn his hand when it had been fully engulfed.

"The thorns grow tentacles the longer it's left in the body. If anything is left behind, he'll be dead in hours. I need to get it all at once."

"And you were going to let me do it?" Nellie asked.

"No, actually. I wasn't." Erian actually grinned. The expression seemed so odd on such a harsh and scarred face that Nellie felt herself tip even more firmly away from reality. "You ready?"

Nellie leaned more heavily on Keane. "Just do it."

She focused on Keane's face as she heard the blade slice through Keane's skin. The odd ripping sound left her swallowing bile that rose in her throat. She squeezed her eyes shut. Keane jolted beneath her hold. Erian froze.

"Keep. Him. Still." Erian growled.

"Other than sitting on him, what do you suggest?" But even as she muttered the question, she knew. "Oh, what the hell." She leaned down and pressed her lips against Keane's.

She wasn't sure who was more surprised, the men surrounding them; Keane, whose left hand came up to grasp her hip in a gesture she was becoming all too fond of; or herself. She couldn't remember ever initiating anything remotely as intimate as kissing a man in public before. But she did kiss him. She pressed her lips lightly at first, then more persistently until she heard him groan deep in the back of his throat.

"Well, that's working," Erian muttered behind her. "Almost there."

Keane stiffened, his hand gripped her hip tight as Nellie angled her head and dived in deeper, kissing him in the ways she imagined he'd kiss her should the opportunity ever come around again.

She lost herself in the moment, in the feel of his lips against hers, in the lazy, exploring mating dance she encountered when she pressed his mouth open and drew his focus completely on her. Keane jerked again, not a full-body response this time, but forceful enough to nearly dislodge her.

She held on, hands gripping his shoulders, and refused to give up.

"Got it."

Erian's voice echoed in her ears as if from a distance. Keane's hand moved up her back, over her shoulder, stopping only when he brushed fingers against her face. Only then did Nellie lift her mouth. She found Keane blinking slow grey eyes at her with what she could only describe as a smile of male pride curving those luscious lips of his. "Nellie," he whispered.

"You were expecting someone else? Sera maybe?" She couldn't help but tease him for her own misconception.

"Sera doesn't kiss like that." He cupped the side of her face in his hand and as she blinked against relieved tears, she could have sworn his eyes shifted into a pristine, ocean blue.

"Erian?"

"Erian kisses like that?" Nellie laughed.

Erian snorted. "He should be so lucky as to know." He motioned for his men to move closer as he accepted the satchel handed to him. "I have enough Oleoa root to get you back to the Citadel, but you're still going to need to see Gaius. He'll want you resting for a few days."

"Hours maybe," Keane groaned as he pushed up on his elbows and looked down at his seeping wound. "Not any time for more. Merciful heavens, you could have at least tried to carve a straight line. That's going to leave a hideous scar."

"I like scars." Nellie grinned. "They're sexy."

"And it would have been a lot worse if she'd been doing the carving," Erian told him as he drenched a clean rag with a fermented smelling salve and pressed it hard against Keane's torso.

Keane's face lost all its regained color. "Oh, holy—"

Nellie kissed him again.

"Need to suggest Gaius add that technique to his healing journal." Erian muttered. "You okay to walk?"

"Sera can get me back," Keane said as Erian and Nellie helped haul him to his feet.

He pressed a hand hard into his side and took a deeper breath than she'd seen him take in hours. For the first time since she'd arrived in this world, the fear receded.

"Feel better already." His color was still terrible, and his eyes had once again turned that pure white, but he clung to her as if he'd never let her go. "Nellie, would you like to walk of fly?"

"Are you kidding me?" She moved under his outstretched arm and wrapped an arm around his waist. What did she have to be afraid of now? "Fly, of course."

❖

"I can see you smiling, Bowen." Keane fisted one hand in the bed sheet as their healer Gaius pressed prying fingers into the wound Erian had carved into him. Sweat broke out on his forehead as he rested his other hand on the orb beside the bed. At least Nellie's touch had brought a sliver of pleasure beneath the pain. "Are you trying to hollow me out, old man?" Keane gritted his teeth.

"Always were the worst patient," Gaius chided as he withdrew bloodied fingers and retreated to the healing cart he'd wheeled into Keane's quarters minutes after Keane had gotten out of the bath. The former monk was as stooped and bald and fat as he'd been when Keane and Rivalin and Bowen had met him as boys. "Should have had you knock him out so I could aid him in quiet."

"I'd have done it gladly." From a chair across the room, Bowen of the Eastern Realm, mage and disgraced sorcerer of the highest order, sat with an ankle over one knee, a critical finger poised beneath considering lips and an odd smirk on his face. It had been countless mooncyles since the two men had been in the same room, but as with the closest of brothers, it seemed nary a night had passed. "He does seem to have grown more reckless since we last met."

"*He* can still hear every word you're saying. And stop grinning." Keane closed his eyes and turned his head, more to focus on stopping himself from heaving into a bucket than to deal with the suspicion he saw on his friend's face. "Don't you have a wedding to plan?"

"I'm leaving those details to my betrothed."

Keane wondered if Bowen noticed how his voice gentled whenever he spoke of Clara MacQueen. He'd never seen his friend besotted with a woman before. And there had been plenty of women. For both of them. Just never one that left them, for want of a better word, distracted. Or thinking of anything remotely connected to a future.

Once upon a time Keane might have considered the visible emotions on his friend's face a weakness to be exploited, but he couldn't think that way now, could he? Not when Keane was having similar feelings about Clara's sister.

Nellie. Keane squeezed his eyes hard. What was he going to do about Nellie? Even as he asked himself the question, he knew what he wanted; something that wasn't possible. He wanted a different life, one he could share with her and not spend his time warring and plotting and scheming. He wanted her.

"We need you recovered in time to lead the summit."

Keane grunted at Bowen's reminder. "I'll be well enough." Even if he wasn't, nothing would stop him from going. He'd given his word to the resistance. They had to believe he could be trusted otherwise there would be no defeating Dracha. "Is that not correct, Gaius?"

"As I am not one to argue with my patients, of course, my lord."

Bowen chuckled.

Keane growled. How he hated being anyone's Lord, but his people had insisted. Just because he'd saved most of them from sure execution during one of Dracha's men's raids soon after his arrival didn't give him special status. Of course, that he'd done so without a sliver of sight had probably fed into the myth of the three warriors. Guilt bore down on him like an avalanche. If only his intentions had been so pure. He'd wanted to die. Had looked for any way to end this existence now that his sight had been taken from him. Only he hadn't been granted his desire. Instead he'd learned killing was even easier when you weren't staring into the eyes of your adversary.

"You could have died out there," Bowen told him as Gaius washed his hands and prepared a new Oleo root treatment. "And it was unnecessary. You should have allowed Erian to go with us."

"I needed him here." In case Keane didn't return. He might be sightless, but he still craved that exhilarated rush that came with risking his life, an exhilaration intensified by the promise of fulfilling an oath. "And you needed someone to protect Clara in case something happened to you. Which something did, I might add. Ow!" Keane kicked out his leg when something hot struck this thigh.

"Boys, please. No magic in the Citadel," Gaius sighed. "Bowen, if you need to practice with your regenerating magic, might I suggest the training facility on the ground level?"

"You're using me for target practice?" Keane turned to look at his friend who was waving smoking fingers slowing in the air, turning the tendrils into spirals of white.

"If you'd told me you have a death wish perhaps I would have argued against the rescue mission more fervently. Or taken it over myself."

"You falling into the lake wouldn't have gotten us anywhere different. And who says I have a death wish?" He hissed out a breath as Gaius pressed a thicker salve onto his wound. "Other than subjecting myself to this torture, that is."

"Maybe I should have Erian bring Nellie in here," Bowen said. "I'm told she has a special technique for calming you."

Ah, there it was. The reason for the smile on Bowen's normally dour face. Come to think of it, he hadn't seen a hint of sadness or depression since the two warriors had reunited. Another effect of Clara MacQueen. "How do you know about Nellie's technique? Erian wouldn't have said anything."

"Erian didn't have to. She kissed you in front of half your division." Bowen sat forward in his chair. "What magic does she possess?"

"Magic?" Keane choked as Gaius pressed and prodded once more. He didn't want to talk about Nellie's magic. How could he when he'd have to admit it appeared only of benefit to him? That sounded so…dishonorable. "I don't know what you're talking about."

"If she's even half as powerful as Clara—"

"I don't know what she is." Keane cut him off and gave a sigh of relief as Gaius wrapped a bandage around the wound. He could feel the skin beginning to knit already as his magic was nearly at its strongest within the walls of the Citadel. "She doesn't know. Not that it matters. She will remain here, where it's safe. With Clara."

"That will take some convincing." Bowen actually winced. "I haven't told Clara yet that I'm going with you. She's not one to let me out of her sight."

"No need to worry about that." Keane sat up and dropped his legs over the side of the bed, drawing the orb with him to ease the shadows. "Because you're not coming."

"Despite what others may think, you are not my Lord and master, little brother. If you recall I have two cycles on you." Bowen's voice was as tight as a bow as he lounged back in his chair. "I will be going with you to meet with the resistance to plan Dracha's defeat."

"There's no need for you to go." Keane used the explanation he'd been rehearsing in his head for the past hour. "It is a meeting to sign the treaty and to begin final assault plans. There's no role for you to play." A lie. There was always a role for a soldier and mage as talented and devoted as Bowen. But Bowen had someone relying on him now. Someone who loved him. That was enough for Keane to stand in his way.

"And what if you meet resistance on the road to the summit?"

"We'll deal with Dracha's soldiers if we need to." Keane struggled against the exhaustion creeping around the edges of his mind. "My men are stronger."

"Maybe once. Not now." Bowen pinned him with a look that stirred dread into Keane's weariness. "Rivalin's alive. He's one of them."

"I believe that's my cue to leave. I've done all I can," Gaius said and patted Keane's bare shoulder and added a squeeze of assurance, as if to remind Keane that he and Bowen had been friends long before they were warriors. "Please try not to move around too much for a few hours at least. Give the wound time to heal."

"Thank you, Gaius." Even if Keane's mind hadn't cleared of the ghostly voices and cries, he still would have been sent reeling by Bowen's declaration. He waited, sitting stone still as he listened to Gaius wheel his medicine cart out of the room. The door clicked shut behind him. Keane was on his feet an instant later, advancing on Bowen, heart thudding in his chest. "What do you mean Riva-lin's alive? We saw him die, Bowen. We saw Dracha drive that spear through his heart."

"I don't know how. I only know Clara and I saw him. He leads the advance guard. He's one of Dracha's."

"No." Keane shook his head and bypassed Bowen and headed to the basin to splash his face with water. The desire for sleep evaporated like smoke in the air. "No. This world might be capable of many things, many horrible things, but Rivalin can't be alive and defending *him*." He gripped the edge of the counter and bent double, his heart tearing in two. "He would never betray the Goddess in that way. He wouldn't betray his oath." *He would never betray us!*

"He might not be aware he is betraying anyone," Bowen's voice belied the fact he'd been giving this great thought. "The man I saw days ago may very well be only a shell. I saw no hint of the man we knew, the dedicated warrior who would have given his life for either one of us. But even if it is just a shell, we cannot allow him to survive. I will not go into a new life with Clara knowing Rivalin, in some form, is suffering immortal damnation. As important as it is to defeat Dracha and prevent him from returning to our world, we must take Rivalin out."

Keane took long, measured breaths. He thought he'd accounted for every contingency, every possible thing that could go wrong. Never once had it occurred to him that in order to defeat Dracha once and for all he'd have to go through one of the best men he'd ever known.

One of the best warriors who ever lived.

How could he kill his best friend?

"If Rivalin is fighting for and protecting Dracha, we're going to need every advantage we can get." Keane's chest tightened as he realized what he must do. He needed every possible weapon at his disposal. But what he needed most was his sight. "We need a new plan. The one I came up with is based on Rivalin's attack at Dorcaster Castle. If even a bit of the man we knew still exists, we have to do something he never would have thought of. And we need to come up with it soon. Before we meet with the resistance." To change the meeting now would only raise suspicion and erode any confidence the uneasy men and women already felt in working secretly with Keane and his Outsiders.

"Agreed." Bowen came up behind him and lay a strong hand on his shoulder. "Which means you need my help. I believe Clara can be of assistance as well. Her magic is growing by the day; magic we can use to our advantage. Dracha and Rivalin would have no way to prepare for something they don't know exists. Which brings me back to my original question. What magic does Nellie possess? And would it be of help to us?"

"To us?" Keane echoed as a light entered his heart. "I don't know." But for himself? He lifted his gaze into the darkness. Nellie may very well be the answer to everything.

Nellie might have been able to stave off Erian's commands while they'd been in triage in that clearing, but once Sera made her landing on what was apparently her own private perch on the western spire, she lost any say over and sight of Keane. While six men followed Erian's orders to get him to the healer, she found herself standing between Keane's loyal second and his protective—what had Keane called Sera? A pharenta.

"You are injured." Erian's gravely voice sounded oddly concerned as he gestured to Nellie's hand.

"It's nothing." She grabbed the cuff of her jacket and tugged it down over the still throbbing welt. "Elya has a pretty harsh grip." Erian dipped his head, but not before she saw the flash of grief and pain in his eyes. "You know her."

"I did. A long time ago. Before she betrayed her family and people by choosing to follow Dracha." His voice carried the weight of regret and betrayal. "Elya is my sister. My twin sister."

Nellie knew he reminded her of someone. She could see it now, especially in the eyes. But where she'd seen cool calculation and determination in Elya's, she saw despair and loneliness in Erian's. "I'm sorry." What else could she say without prying deeper?

"As am I. I will make certain Gaius attends to you as soon as he's done with Keane."

"That's fine." Agreeing seemed to console him. She wasn't sure why. She'd had worse burns pulling biscuits out of the oven. "Keane's recovery is what's important. He knew you'd find him, Erian. You and Sera."

She couldn't help it; she reached back and, without needing to look, stroked a hand down the pharenta's ivory smooth beak. The creature cooed under her touch.

"You saved his life." Erian inclined his head. "For that we are all in your debt."

"He saved mine first, so I'd say we're all even." Fairly certain the ice was broken, she stepped off the straw strewn perch and followed Erian down the circular stone staircase. She couldn't help but feel an odd excitement walking the halls of buildings that may never have been seen by any others from her world. "How did I not see this place before?" Her stomach dropped as she looked down over the edge to the wooded ground below. "This has to be at least six stories high." She should have spotted this miles before the clearing and certainly more than a few seconds before Sera had begun her descent. As Keane had guided the beast through the sky with a shaking hand holding Sera's rein, he'd whispered something that sounded like *odaria comraich*. Next thing Nellie knew, she found herself staring at a grey stone structure straight out of a medieval fairy tale. "And for the record, this is a castle, not a Citadel."

Erian glanced over his shoulder, a silver eyebrow arched nearly to his hairline.

"As Keane would tell you," Erian said, "he is not royalty. This is a fortress of protection. We provide training for soldiers, plan strikes against our enemies and give shelter and food to those in need or unable to make the journey to *Cosanta Baile*."

"That's the area where the other prisoners live, isn't it?" Keane had pointed out the village from high in the air. "It's designated a protected area for those exiled to this world."

"No one is above anyone else," Erian continued. "Keane is our leader, the chosen one who is destined to defeat the darkness, but he would not place himself higher than a common man. Therefore, this place is a—"

"Castle, technically. But I'll give him and you this one." She tugged the collar of her coat tight at her throat as she shivered against the cold. "Chilly up here."

Erian frowned. "I feel no cold."

"Because you scare away the weather?"

Something told her Erian didn't smile a lot.

But so far she'd gotten two out of him. She supposed she'd have time for exploring the *castle* later. That's what she told herself as Erian escorted her down multiple staircases and through countless corridors. She found herself being watched and followed by curious men, women, and children, who whispered behind their hands and smiled when she met their surprised gazes.

She only got a passing glimpse of the great hall and its oversized hearth and fireplace that housed dancing purple and orange flames that radiated enough heat and light to ease the darkness and damp. Intricate tapestries hung suspended on the walls, dozens of flags displaying coats of arms that awakened the historian within her. Despite the coldness of the stone itself, the cas—Citadel felt surprisingly like a home.

Clutching her jacket closed, she hurried to catch up to Erian who, after exiting the hall, turned left and led her to a carved wooden door twice his height.

"These quarters are across from your sister's and Bowen's." Erian took a step back to motion to the matching door behind them. "Clothing and food have been provided, as has a hot bath."

"Awesome." Nellie bounced on her heels, unsure if she was more anxious about the bath or seeing her sister. At Erian's blank stare, she clarified. "That means great. Thanks. When can I see Keane?"

"You will be sent for when our healer is convinced he is out of danger and can receive visitors." Erian's voice held that air of superiority that suited him and irritated her.

"Meaning I did what you needed me to do and now I'm supposed to stay out of the way like a good girl?"

"Meaning, as you noted earlier, Keane is my priority." Erian snapped his tall, lithe body to stiff attention. "If he sends me for you, I will follow his orders."

"Right. Gotcha." Nellie was already feeling antsy about not being at Keane's side. She straightened

her arms and clenched her fists, giving herself a good mental shake. What was wrong with her? She wasn't one to rely on a man, to feel incomplete without one, even one who sent her pulse to dancing like Keane. Holy hackles, she'd known the man less than a day. Yet she felt as if she'd known him all her life. That she didn't feel quite right without him near unsettled her more than any of his kisses had.

She focused her attention back on Erian. "Sorry to sound like a shrew. I'm sure—"

"Nellie!"

"Clara." Nellie turned in time to be engulfed in her sister's embrace. In that instant, all the terror, the worry, the frantic thoughts that had been spinning through her mind since she'd first fallen through that ridiculous book evaporated as she embraced Clara with a sobbing laugh. "That's the last time I let you go into a bookstore by yourself." Her tears fell onto the beautiful green brocade of the velvet gown Clara wore as Nellie stepped back to look at her. "Holy crap, you look like Maid Marian in Robin Hood."

"The Errol Flynn version I hope." Clara's gold-flecked green eyes, the same eyes Nellie possessed, sparkled against her porcelain skin and intricately braided glossy red hair. Out of the corner of her eye, she saw Erian withdraw from the hallway and disappear down the corridor.

"As if there's any other." Nellie gripped Clara's shoulders so hard her fingers went numb. "I was scared you were gone forever." The confession knitted her fractured heart. She didn't realize how afraid she'd been about never seeing Clara or Amber again.

"I know." Clara rubbed her hands down Nellie's wool clad arms in the comforting way she had while they'd been growing up. The action warmed Nellie faster than a gallon of cream laden hot chocolate. "I know, this is crazy. Insane. But…amazing, too. I have so much to tell you. Come on. Let's get you cleaned up and we can talk."

"Enough already!" Nellie smacked her sister's hands away. "You corset me any tighter and I won't be able to eat, let alone breathe." It was as if they were six years old and playing dress up all over again. Clara always did have precise thoughts on what Nellie should wear, but as her sister turned her toward the mirror beside the metal tub Nellie had to admit, Clara knew what she was doing. "Oh. Wow."

The turquoise gown was cinched in all the right places and flowed lightly around her legs and bare feet like the softest silk. The neckline dipped lower than she liked, but not so low she had to worry about overexposure. Tiny gold rope enhanced every line of the dress, criss-crossing over her breasts and midsection before flowing into a floral-like pattern down the skirt. She scrunched her bare toes into the cool grey stone.

Her curls had been tamed by some concoction Clara had been given back at *Cosanta Baile* by a woman named Miranda; a woman, who by Clara's account, Nellie must meet. Nellie's skin glowed even without a hint of makeup and the soap she'd used smelled of wildflowers and rain. "Wow," she said again. "I look…pretty."

"You *are* pretty." Clara squeezed her shoulders, standing behind her and gazing at the two of them with pride, happiness, and more than a little sadness. "All that's missing is Amber."

"And maybe Scarlett O'Hara." Nellie squirmed in the dress. "Seriously, sis, could you loosen that a little? Otherwise after I eat I'm going to look like an overstuffed pork casing."

"Fine." Clara scrunched her mouth into that disproving expression of hers, but a few seconds later, Nellie could breathe again. "Better?"

"Much. Thank you." She discarded what was left of her old clothes and followed Clara to the table by the window that had been set up with what looked like a feast. The large space wasn't cluttered by any means. One wall was completely taken up by a fireplace and hearth with a roaring fire reminiscent of the one she'd seen in the great hall. The lush four-poster bed was draped with blue and green fabrics dotted with explosions of embroidered color and stood in stark luxurious contrast to the simple wooden table and chairs that awaited them.

The arched window gave her the perfect view of the forest that had been her constant companion since she'd arrived and immediately set her to wondering how Keane was doing.

"I'm sure Keane's fine," Clara told her as she poured herself some wine into a plain silver goblet.

"You read minds now?" Nellie grumbled as she took inventory of the odd food displayed before her. Nothing looked familiar, but her stomach growled in a reminder that she couldn't be picky at this point. "Erian told me I'd be summoned when I could see him. He's an odd one." How could he not be, given who his sister was? It was on the tip of her tongue to ask Clara what she knew about him, about his history and background, but something told her it wasn't common knowledge Elya was his twin.

"Erian?" Clara shrugged. "Yeah. They're all a bit odd. Like Celtic ninjas. They move like smoke. Be warned." Her cheeks went bright pink. "Any one of them can pop up at inopportune times."

Nellie grinned and nibbled on the corner of a chunk of orange-veined cheese. She enjoyed the pungent, salty flavor and took a bigger bite. "Sounds like a story I need to hear. Maybe save it for when Amber gets here."

"That's inevitable, isn't it?" Nellie wasn't certain Clara sounded relieved or concerned their sister remained behind in the real world.

"Last I saw her she was stewing in the car with her coffee. But…yeah." Nellie bit her lip. "I went into that store looking for you. When I don't come out, Amber's going to follow."

Clara's strained smile reflected Nellie's. "Well, you came through okay. Nothing we can do about Amber except sit and wait I suppose. Of all of us, however, I would have expected you'd have kept your clothes on. What happened to your shirt? And your tights?"

Nellie face went hot. "I needed to bandage Keane's wound."

"Uh-huh." Clara chuckled. "That's as good as an excuse as any."

Nellie looked at her sister. Really looked at her. "You seem settled. Happy."

"I am." Clara's eyes sparkled. "I wish I could explain it, I wish I could explain anything that's happened, but as unbelievable as it all is, because of Bowen it all make sense. Whatever happens next, I know as long as I'm with him, everything will be okay."

"He's it for you then?" Nellie's insides tightened when Clara nodded.

"When it's right, you know. Doesn't matter how much time has passed. A day, a month. A year." Clara pushed a plate of odd looking fruit in Nellie's direction. Nellie wrinkled her nose. "Time moves differently here. I've been here nearly a week."

"A week?" To Nellie's mind, her sister had vanished only hours ago. "How long do you think it's been since I got here?"

"Judging by our time? Less than a day. You streaked across the sky just after Bowen and I arrived at the Citadel."

Nellie's stomach twisted. "Lovely. A great big red ball of gas. Talk about a—"

"I'm getting married." Clara's eyes went wide as if she'd shocked herself by the verbal blurt.

Nellie sagged back in the high back wooden chair and gaped. *"Married?* You?" That was fast.

Clara pulled her bare feet up to brace on the edge of her chair as she picked at the fruit and cheese. "From the second I saw him, *bam!*" She flicked out her fingers. Bright blue sparks fired from her fingertips. Nellie nearly dropped out of her chair. Clara gasped, then laughed as she looked at her hand. "Or maybe I should have said *pow!* Bowen told me my powers would grow." She flicked her fingers again—only this time she turned her hand over, palm up, and watched as flames danced on her skin. "Blasted Bowen right off his feet the first time it manifested. I'm still getting the hang of it." She rotated her hand this way and that, controlling the flame as it rolled up and down her arm. "We almost died coming here. Whatever happens next, I don't want to end this life without having been married to him."

"Okay." For the second time, something akin to envy tugged in Nellie's stomach. "Does it hurt?"

"The fire? Not at all. It's comforting actually. What about you?" Clara closed her hand. The flames vanished. She turned amused eyes on Nellie who could only shake her head. "Anything magical going on with you?"

"No." Why would it? Nellie had never been anything but ordinary. "How?"

"How did we get magic? Mom apparently. Get this. She's the only living daughter of the goddess Alastrine, Warden of All. Apparently, whoever wrote those stories didn't give her a name, but it all makes an odd kind of sense. Mom left the book for us, after all."

Left them for us or for Clara? Nellie hadn't felt a flicker of anything other than her growing feelings for Keane. She didn't have fire or power or anything of value they could use in Keane's upcoming battle with Dracha.

"Guess we have something to talk about with her if we ever get home," Nellie mumbled. Her appetite had vanished, but that had never stopped her from eating before. "Since I don't feel like dragging my butt out of this chair, can you float some of that wine over here for me?" She lifted her goblet, her humor returning when Clara stood and retrieved the pitcher the traditional way. "Now what were we talking about before your hand exploded?"

"Bowen." Clara's face softened in a gooey smile. "I was trying to explain something I can't. It just worked with him. We fit. Like we've known each other forever." Clara inclined her head. "Something tells me you know a little something about that."

Could she? What she had with Keane? Was it real? Was any of this real? "How is this even possible?" Nellie whispered, her mind filling with images of Keane, of remembering the feel, the taste of his lips, the gentle protectiveness of his hold. She scrubbed a hand against the center of her chest. "It actually aches not to be with him."

"Then maybe you shouldn't be." But Clara's eyes darkened as uncertainty hovered. "I don't know how long any of this is going to last. If somehow Dracha is going to do something that destroys this…world."

"Don't you mean book?" Nellie corrected with an arched brow. "That's what we're trapped in, right?"

"No." Clara shook her head. "No, I've been giving this a lot of thought. Lots of down time around this place, without Netflix. I think the book that brought me here was a portal. One mom might have created when she left the stories for us. A portal Bowen is convinced Dracha can use to carry out whatever plan he has. It's why he freaked out when we saw Rivalin retrieve it."

"That would be warrior number three." She started eating again—by impulse—and realized she was still hungry after all. Or maybe Nellie was just desperate for a distraction. "Wondered where he might be."

"Well, until a few days ago, everyone thought he was dead. He's not. He's working for Dracha." Clara flinched. "Which means I have no doubt Bowen has some ridiculous plan to do something about it."

"If he's anything like Keane, I'd lay odds you're right." Nellie bit into piece of meat resembling a turkey leg. "If your book was a portal, it wasn't the only one. How do you think I got here?" She ignored the plate of fruit Clara set in front of her when she caught sight of the pastries. "Although I haven't seen the book since I got here. That lake monster probably ate it." She paused, then added, "Elya tried to hitch a ride, by the way."

"Old bat," Clara muttered. "I haven't gotten much out of Bowen about her, but she's like the evil sidekick in this fairy tale. Creepy. Ancient."

Nellie scrunched her mouth. "She looked about our age when I met her. Not to mention pregnant. Until she deflated."

"Deflated?" Clara asked. "How—"

"If we keep asking how for everything, we aren't going to be talking about anything else for the rest of our lives," Nellie told her. "Let's talk about your wedding."

"You're changing the subject." Clara poured more wine for the both of them. "But I will say this. Time might not be on any of our sides when it comes to happily ever after. So, if you have any plans regarding Keane, you might want to act on them sooner than later."

In the great hall, Erian, Bowen, and a dozen of Keane's most trusted Outsiders gathered around the table before the fire and reexamined their plans of attack. Some of his men had families, others had been on their own for most of their lives. They were all, however, first and foremost, determined to protect the world from which they'd been cast out.

"It's not going to work. Not anymore," Bowen declared as he pointed a finger to the structure outside Dracha's keep where he stored the majority of his weapons. "Going after their weapons is the first

thing Rivalin would expect. It's what he would do. And if we don't do that, the entire plan falls apart."

"Then we have to think of things he wouldn't." Not that anyone had come up with an idea in the past two hours. Anxiety crept up Keane's spine. His hand tightened on the staff at his side, as if improving his shadowy vision would somehow provide the answers they sought. "We cannot meet with the resistance and their spies until we at least have an idea of how to defeat Dracha. If we lose their trust, we've lost our only advantage."

"Is there any thought to letting them take the lead on the plan?" Bowen asked. "Rivalin knows how you and I think. He'd have planned for whatever we'd come up with."

"We're putting a lot of stock in what we think Rivalin knows," Taranto pointed out, his glass green eyes narrowing in his round, skeptical face. "Would not taking him out of the equation completely be our best option?"

"It would be, yes." Erian said. "But our sources say Rivalin's now as heavily guarded as Dracha himself. That tells me there's more left of him than we even we thought. He's become both a liability and an asset to both sides."

"Which makes him doubly dangerous," Bowen agreed. "What about the Wargari? Can they be of use to us?"

"Better the fire demons be of use to us than Dracha," Keane agreed. "But communicating with them is impossible now that there aren't any Talkers left. Dracha had them all executed when they refused to convince the Wargari to fight for him."

"There's one left." Erian's tight voice snapped through Keane's growing despair.

"There is?" Keane looked across the table at his second in command. "Who?"

"Trevelyan."

Keane's throat ached. He could only imagine what speaking his former lover's name cost Erian. The two had been inseparable for years, even before they'd both been banished to The Forgotten Realm. Erian had never shared the details of what happened between them, but it had taken Erian many cycles to climb out of the bottle he'd dived into when they'd parted.

"I heard he burned in the purge," one of Erian's soldiers countered. "Witnesses said—"

"He's alive." Erian lifted emotionless eyes to Keane. "I can find him. I can convince him."

Keane shook his head. "I can't ask—"

"You aren't asking," Erian said. "By all rights you should be ordering me to track him down. You don't have to. I'll leave immediately."

"Find us a safe path to the summit," Keane told Bowen as he followed Erian out of the hall. "Erian! Erian, wait. You don't have to do this. We can find another solution."

"We don't have time." Erian stared straight ahead, his gaze never flickering once to Keane's. "We're out of options and we don't have time to let our emotions get in the way. If I'm not at the summit as planned, it's because I'm dead." Now he faced Keane with nary a flicker of despair or sadness. He clasped his hand around Keane's forearm and his leader returned the gesture.

"If that's the case, go with the Goddess."

"He going to be okay?" Bowen asked from the doorway after Erian had gone.

"He'll do what he has to." Keane's thoughts turned to Nellie. In truth, his thoughts hadn't turned away from her since he'd first pulled her out of the Lake of Sherena. The pull of her, the desire for, her hadn't lessened the longer they were apart. It had grown like a hunger, one he could no longer deny himself. "Is there a safe path to take to the summit?"

"There will be by morn."

Keane's hand tightened on the staff as he resisted the urge to see if Bowen was lying. He'd gotten the answer he wanted. "Tell the men I'll join them then. First bell. We leave at midday." With that, he headed for Nellie's quarters.

He finally found her, not in the quarters Erian had arranged for her, and not with her sister, who had a knowing smile on her face when Clara opened her own door to him asking where Nellie had gone. He found her in the last place he expected.

The only place he wanted.

He found her in his bed. Sound asleep.

With a wave of his hand, he locked his door and stood looking down at her. He moved the staff from side to side, hoping to break through the shadows and gray. The need to see her, really see her, all of

her, had him setting the orb against the wall before he sat beside her.

He reached out a hesitant hand, his fingers trembling at the promise of the softness of her skin. The pain behind his eyes was familiar and expected. He closed his eyes, waited for the worst of it to pass, sinking his hand deep into her red hair.

They needed to talk. He had to tell her the truth. That with her touch, he could see again. Could be whole again. But at the same time he had to make her see that that wasn't why he wanted her.

But it was why he needed her.

Which meant touching her was a very bad idea.

He felt her stir, her softness shifting on his bed, her cheek pushing into his hand as if begging for more and when he opened his eyes, he saw only her, in perfect focus, looking up at him, her full, kissable lips curving into a smile.

"If this is a dream, don't wake me up."

"It's not a dream." He couldn't decide what filled him with more promise and hope. Being able to see or looking at her. Keane stopped debating and lent down, pressing his mouth to hers. "I went looking for you."

"Thought I'd beat you to the punch." She reached for him, drew him over her. "You don't mind, do you?"

"Finding you in my bed?" He pressed a trail of kisses along her jawline, under her ear. Down the side of her neck. He inhaled her scent mingling with the soap he'd used on his own skin, the combination arousing him to the point of mindlessness. "I don't mind at all."

"Good. Then I have another surprise for you." She smoothed her hands down his arms to slip her fingers through his. As he drew himself back, she pushed up and, before he realized what she was doing, she flipped him onto his back and straddled him. "I've decided taking chances has been working for me." She gripped his hands tighter and drew them over his head, stretched her body over his until he felt her breasts pressing fully into his chest. She shimmied up, nipped at his chin before she kissed him again. "Fair warning," she whispered as her thighs tightened around him. "I've not done much of this before, so I might need some assistance."

Keane might have laughed if the lower part of her wasn't wreaking havoc with the only part of his body that was doing any thinking.

"I am happy to assist."

"Good." She let go of his hands and sat up, taking his sight with her.

He didn't mind. Not when she began to move above him, twisting and turning and...his entire body felt as if she'd set him on fire.

"Ah, man. I am going to kill Clara."

Keane reached out and stilled her flailing arms. "Why? What's wrong? What are you doing?"

"Failing spectacularly at this whole seduction thing. She trussed me like a holiday turkey." She sagged forward and into his hands. "I can't get out of my dress."

Keane sat up, sliding his hands up to the bare skin above her shoulders, unable to stop the smile from forming on his lips as he saw the frustration and embarrassment flooding her face. She was spectacular in every possible way. He cupped her face in his hand and kissed her while moving the other to her back where he found the laced bow.

He pulled once, whispered a word of magic, and the top of her gown fell away.

"Oh. Well, that's one way to do that, I suppose." Nellie sucked in a breath as he nibbled at the side of her throat. "You, um, sure you want to do this, Romeo?"

Was he sure? Could this be the answer he'd been looking for? Bowen had said when he and Clara made love Bowen's magic had been given back to him. Maybe...maybe Keane would be equally lucky. Maybe Nellie would never have to know.... "I'm in your hands, Nellie. Do with me what you wish."

"When I get back home, I'm sending my ex a registered letter letting him know he's as dumb as a stump." Nellie hadn't meant to speak the words out loud, but when Keane's chest rumbled under her, she flushed a new shade of red.

"Did he not please you in bed?" He stroked his hand down her spine and had her arching against him like a cat.

"Ohhhhh. Mmmm. He didn't please me anywhere." But Keane certainly had. He'd pleased just about every inch of her. Was there a part of her that wasn't still tingling? "You should give lessons in this, except that would be weird."

"It would indeed." He pulled her over him, settling her solidly against him from shoulder to hip and drew the blankets around them. "Sleep, Nellie. I must be up early in the morn, but want to enjoy you again before then."

"Again? Really?" She thought that was only something that happened in books. "Oh, that reminds me, Clara gave me this after sex tea to drink to prevent preg—"

"In the morn. You drink it in the morn." He slipped his free hand into her hair, settled his palm against the back her neck. "Now sleep, my love. And dream only of good things."

My love.

Nellie's eyes filled with tears as she listened to Keane fall asleep. No one had ever said those words to her. He loved her?

And that thought, at least for tonight, was more than enough.

Keane awoke as he usually did, instantly and well before first-bell. Only this morn, something was different. Nellie.

He had Nellie in his arms. Not just now, but all night. Even now he was loathe to let her go. Keane tilted his chin and nuzzled the back of her neck, his hands flat against her stomach, his fingers tempted to dip into the heat of her one more time....

A soft knock sounded on his door.

Nellie groaned and pushed herself deeper into the bed. Keane surrendered to obligation and, with more than a bit of regret, slipped his arms out from around her and sat up.

His heart stuttered as darkness descended immediately. Disappointment mingled with anger as he dragged on his pants, grabbed the staff, and, after he made the preventative tea he kept in supply for her to drink when she awoke, headed to the door.

The second he opened it, he found Bowen, who looked at the glowing orb of the staff and offered a sad smile. "I'm sorry. I had hoped mating with her would restore your—"

"Yeah, me, too." Keane scrubbed a hand down his face and motioned for Bowen to back up so they could talk in the corridor. He kept the door open to listen for Nellie should she awaken. "Did you find safe passage to the summit?"

"Yes. But we'll need to leave sooner than planned. Akarak Falls should provide sufficient cover for our number."

"That's more than six miles out of our way."

"But Dracha's men do all they can to avoid that area. We may even find additional allies to add to our numbers."

"Any word from Erian?"

"He sent word he found Trevelyan. Beyond that, we don't have any information."

"All right." Keane struggled to get his focus back, not easy to do when every one of his senses—well, all but sight, alas—was flooded with Nellie. "All right. Have the kitchen send up something to eat. Make sure the men are well stocked and ready to go at my say-so. I need to talk to her before I leave."

"You're sure her magic only works when she touches you?"

"Yeah, I'm sure." And apparently it didn't matter where she touched him, as long as it was skin on skin. The images of what she'd done to him, with him, last night, would have to last whatever life he had left. "What about you? Did you speak with Clara?"

"I did. Which brings me to my next request. Do you have a priestess at the Citadel?"

"Are you in need of spiritual guidance?" Keane tried to joke.

"I'm in need of a hand-fasting ceremony. That's her condition. I have to marry her before I leave." Given the growing smile on his friend's face, it was obvious Bowen didn't find the condition distasteful in the least. "We'd like you and Nellie to bear witness."

"As long as that's all I'm bearing witness to, I'll be there. Callandria. You'll find her tending the gardens behind the second spire. She has an altar next to the lake that will be perfect for the two of you."

"No Cherellean water beasts then?"

"Only a few boddingbirds and scuttles." The heavily feathered birds would add a bit of elegance to the ceremony. "We'll have the ceremony after I solidify plans with the men."

"Thank you, Keane." Bowen clasped his forearm. "This means the world to both of us."

"I know it does." And the idea of a hand-fasting didn't sound like such a bad one to Keane. He wondered how Nellie would react should he suggest... he stepped back into the room.

The door slammed behind him.

Keane spun around. Nellie standing behind him, in the shadow of the orb, sheet wrapped around her, her sleep-tousled hair an odd contrast to the fire in sensed in her eyes.

"Good morn." But even a blind man could see there was nothing good about it. His mind raced as he wondered how long she'd been awake. How long she'd been standing there.

His heart stuttered. How much she'd heard.

"How're your eyes? Still blind?"

With that one question, he knew. A fear he'd never experienced before swept over him like a rush of fire. "Nellie, let me—"

"What? Explain?" She stood there, in the corner of his room, wrapped in his sheet, shivering. "Explain how you used me to try to get your sight back? That is what's been going on, isn't it? All this touchy-feely thing. The way you just *had* to kiss me back in the forest. That wasn't you wanting me. It was you testing to see if I could bring back your sight!"

"I—" Anything he might add would only be a lie. And he'd already lied to her enough for one lifetime. "At first, yes."

"Tell me the truth, Keane." He felt her walk toward him but stayed a good arms' distance away. He'd never felt so far away from anyone as he did at this moment. "Can you see when I touch you?"

He swallowed hard. "Yes."

"But only when I touch you."

"Yes. But I don't care about that now. I did fine before, I'll manage now."

"Well, that's good to know since I won't be touching you ever again." She swept past him toward the table by the window. "Gah." She slammed a cup down. "Well, that's the perfect bitter taste to end this encounter on." She darted around his room, plucking up her clothes, clutching them against her chest as she stumbled over the sheet tangling around her feet.

"Where are you going?"

"Back to my quarters. So I can forget…this." She swung on him before she reached the door.

"You don't mean that." He caught her arm when she turned away. Only then did he see the tears staining her cheeks. "Nellie, what we have is more important than my lying to you. And it wasn't a lie, exactly. I had to find out for certain. I didn't have anything to lose."

"Wrong. You had me to lose. You didn't tell me the truth because you know what I do now. You were using me for something I don't even have. And that's the one thing I just can't forget. Not again. Now let me go."

He held on, desperate for the right words. Desperate for her to understand. For her to forgive.

"I said let. Me. Go." She wrenched her arm free and yanked open the door.

The second the door closed behind her, he realized what he'd done. What he'd lost. Keane's guilt and anger boiled over, driving the breath from his chest. He spun and whipped the staff and orb down and around.

And shattered it against the wall.

"Congratulations." Nellie rose up on tiptoe to kiss Bowen's cheek, embracing her new brother-in-law with as much enthusiasm as she could muster. The setting beside the lake couldn't have been more beautiful. The Farrengold flowers, as she'd learned they were called, had dipped in to bathe the lake shore in moon-kissed light while colorful birds swam to and fro by the bank.

The priestess quietly withdrew as Bowen reached his hand out to his bride, Nellie's sister, who looked caught between utter bliss and complete terror. The white gown she wore glistened in the darkness, her long red hair worn loose and curling around her shoulders.

"I'll, um, leave you two alone for some private time before you have to go." She squeezed Bowen's arm, purposely avoiding looking at Keane, who was standing near the shoreline with his back to all of them.

"Is there no way you can forgive him?" Bowen asked as he caught her hand. "Nellie—"

"I've really only just met you, Bowen, so please don't make me hit you on your wedding day." Tears burned the back of her throat. Angry tears. Tears she swore she wouldn't shed. "Clara, I'll be in my room whenever you want."

"Okay."

Where Bowen had tried multiple times to convince her to give Keane another chance, Clara had not and stood—or rather sat—silently by as Nellie had ranted and raged and cried out her disappointment and having been deceived. Again.

God, how much more pathetic could she get? Except now what did she do? She was stuck in this magical world with her sister, her sister's new husband, and an ex, that husband's best friend. That wouldn't make for an awkward Thanksgiving and Christmas at all.

As she made her way back to her room, she rubbed at the still throbbing welt on her wrist. She'd left that salve Gaius had given her last night, after he'd tended to Keane, in Keane's room during her quick exodus hours before. Nellie sighed. She didn't want to bother Gaius again, not for something so minor. She wasn't ready to face the evidence of what had happened last night with Keane.

So, she detoured to the library Clara had told her about, to lose herself in the extensive offerings of stories and histories that could keep her occupied for however long she might be stuck here. A little while later, cheers and yells echoing from outside drew her out of her chair and to the window overlooking the drawbridge exit of the Citadel. A hundred or so men, led by Bowen and Keane, headed out on foot while friends and family threw Farrengold flowers at their feet in a gesture of good luck. Nellie tamped down the unease churning inside of her. She didn't know the details of what was going on, but she knew Clara was scared Bowen might not return.

Even if Nellie wasn't worried for Keane, she would have wished them good luck for her sister and she did before returning to her room with an armful of books. Which was where Clara found her a few hours later.

"Are you done wallowing and feeling sorry for yourself?" Clara leaned in the doorway, arms crossed over her chest, peering at Clara in that big-sister way of hers.

"Nope." Just to prove it, Nellie stuffed a sweet fruity pastry into her mouth. "Got a ways to go yet."

Clara smirked and joined her at the table. "What Keane did sucks."

"In a word." She really didn't want to talk about it.

"Bowen agrees he shouldn't have kept that from you. That your magic allows him to see."

"I'd have thought you'd have spent those moments with Bowen having post-hand-fasting sex rather than gossiping about me."

"I can do two things at the same time."

"Oh, ick." Nellie shuddered. "Brain eraser, please. I don't want to talk about it."

"Okay, fine. Maybe it's time you saw Gaius again about that thing on your wrist."

"Yeah." The pain had grown increasingly worse over the past few hours. "I left that salve in Keane's room." She stood up and stretched out the kinks. "Come with me to get it?"

"Like the room's haunted or something?"

"It is in a way." It was a reminder of all the things she'd let herself dream of having last night. "I know it might not be a big deal to you, but he used me, Clara. The same way Bruce did."

"Oh, please. Bruce was a douchebag who never dumped his girlfriend in the first place."

Nellie's eyes went wide as they traversed the corridors and headed for Keane's room. "You knew?"

"Amber and I suspected. Keane didn't set out to lie to you, Nellie. And by the way, did you tell him about Bruce? Did he know why your engagement ended?"

"Yes." She didn't appreciate the doubt that admission brought forth.

"Huh. Bet it made it difficult for him to figure out a way to explain that you had something that would make his life a little easier. Just saying." Clara held up her hand as they reached Keane's door. "Food for thought. So to speak."

"Don't say food." Nellie was already regretting that sandwich she'd fixed for herself. And the wine. And the…. "What the hell happened here?"

She stepped into Keane's room and found his walking staff lying in the middle of the floor, remnants of the orb scattered everywhere. "I don't understand." She bent down and picked up a piece that began to glow in her hand. "He can't see without this. Like at all." She looked over her shoulder at Clara who shrugged.

"Maybe he was trying to prove something to himself. Or you."

"When you fill out your next resume, make sure you add devil's advocate to it, will you? As he told me, he was fine before me. He'll be fine now." She retrieved the salve and rubbed some on her wrist. It didn't help. In fact, it burned even worse. "Crap. I guess I'm going to have to go see Gaius after all."

"Come on." Clara wrapped an arm around Nellie's shoulders and squeezed.

"Nellie, Clara. Have they left yet?" An exhausted looking Erian rounded the corner, another man close at his heels.

"A few hours ago, why?" Clara demanded. "Is this him? Is this Trevelyan?"

"I am." The younger man stepped around Erian and offered his scarred hand. He wasn't nearly as strong a presence as Erian was, but he was a sturdy looking man with more battle wounds than an entire battalion. Given he worked with fire demons, she could only imagine the injuries he'd sustained. "I've already communicated with those fire demons I'm connected to. They're willing to aid Keane should he request it. But there's a catch."

"Isn't there always?" Nellie muttered. "Walk with us. I need to see Gaius."

"What's that on your wrist?" Erian grabbed her arm as she passed.

"Hey! What is it with you men in this world grabbing me? It's just a welt from where Elya…what? What's that look?" She circled a finger in front of Erian's suddenly pale face. "That's a weird look."

"You did not say Elya marked you." He glanced at Trevelyan before he covered the welt completely with his hand. "That's a tracking brand. Dark magic. It allows her and anyone she wants to see what you see. Hear what you hear. Not only that—"

"What?" Nellie suddenly had a very bad feeling about this. "You mean she's been spying on me? Following me? Me and…." She gasped. "Keane. If she's been listening in, she knows their plan." Nausea rolled in her stomach. "She knows they're headed to the summit and what route they're taking."

"We have to stop them." Erian whispered a few unrecognizable words and bent until his forehead brushed his hand.

Nellie cried out as her hand went ice cold. Her fingers turned blue before returning to normal. When Erian released her, the welt, the mark, was gone. Nellie shook her hand as if to rid herself of tingles and sent sparks flying.

"Uh-oh. I know what happens next," Clara said. "Nellie, stop! Stop!"

"Stop what?" She shook both hands, unable to shake the odd sensation prickling her skin.

A force of power erupted from within her, exploded out and sent Trevelyan and Erian flying back off their feet. They crashed into wall at the end of the corridor and slid to the ground.

"Damn it, not again. Put those away!" Clara ordered as she rang the tapestry bell for assistance. Erian and Trevelyan were struggling back to their feet as Nellie stared, disbelieving, at her hands.

"What was that?" Nellie asked.

"That was your magic, little sister," Clara told her as she helped to steady the men. "You didn't get a chance to say what else Elya's mark did, Erian."

"It suppresses magic." He shook his head as if trying to clear it. "Now that it's gone, your powers should fully manifest."

"I have powers?" Nellie couldn't help it. She grinned. "Real magic?"

"I take it she's not from around here?" Trevelyan asked.

Nellie would have responded, but she couldn't. She couldn't speak. Couldn't even blink. Because her mind had been taken over by visions of people running for their lives. Screaming. The sounds of swords striking flesh; blood spattering the ground. Armored soldiers leaping out from trees to ambush—

"It's a trap." Nellie whispered as her mind cleared. "And Keane can't see. No, Clara, I'm not quoting Admiral Akbar. Bowen and Keane are heading right into a trap. The resistance members they were supposed to meet are already dead." Terror she

couldn't describe washed over her. "Dracha's men are waiting for them."

"What can we do?" Clara demanded.

"We'll go," Erian told them. "We'll have to take pharentas and neither of you can fly one. You two stay here."

"I can fly Sera," Nellie stated with confidence she didn't feel. Boy, she hoped her bond with the bird was as strong as she suspected. "Clara will stay."

"Bowen told me if anything went wrong I was to evacuate the families to *Cosanta Baile*." She nodded as certainty overtook fear in her eyes. "I know what to do. Go. Quick. Bring my husband back."

"I will." Suddenly Nellie understood the promise Keane had made only yesterday to Clara. "But first, Erian?"

"Yes?"

"I need a uniform."

❖

"You sure you're okay?"

Keane gnashed his teeth and reminded himself Bowen had every reason to be concerned. It had been a long time since he'd gone out without his orb and staff. But he'd spent enough time without them before to get along without them now. At least he hoped so.

"I'm fine. It's only a few more miles before we reach the rebellion encampment. And the more you ask me that question, the more the others will worry. So stop."

Bowen had taken the lead with Keane, clasping his shoulder for guidance.

"Look on the bright side."

"I can't see the bright side."

"Yeah, I guess not." Bowen stopped suddenly. Keane caught himself before he plowed into him.

"What is it?"

"Shhh." Bowen crouched, and Keane followed suit. He heard the whisper of his men doing the same. "Scatter!" Bowen ordered in as low a voice as he dared before he grabbed Keane's arm and darted into the trees.

"I'm beginning to see why Nellie has issues with being grabbed. What is it you heard?" Keane asked as thick leaves and shrubs encased them.

"I don't know. But it doesn't sound right. You tell me. Open up those ears of yours now that your eyes are useless."

Keane grimaced. Like he needed a lecture at this point. Bowen had called him every kind of stupid when Keane told him he'd destroyed his staff, but nothing could be done about it now. He did as Bowen suggested. And caught what his friend had heard. Footsteps. Frantic, running footsteps. Multiple feet. Small feet. Heading right for them. "Children," he whispered. "Or women. Can't be sure. They're rounding the hill now. They're panicked, Bowen. They don't know where they're going."

Bowen let out a sharp whistle, then another, twice as long.

As the stumbling footfalls grew closer, Keane braced himself. Seconds later, he heard their cries as his men emerged to encircle them, weapons drawn.

"Stop!" Bowen yelled and stepped out from the trees, along with Keane. "Wait. Who are you?"

"Galavar." The young man's voice hadn't yet begun to change. "We were traveling with our fathers from the Keep when we were attacked. We were told to run."

"How many of them are there?" Keane asked Bowen.

"Six," Bowen replied. "All children. Where were your fathers going?"

"To the Stones of Cataputalaus."

"The summit," Keane breathed. "They were ambushed."

"Let's hope not all of them. Taranto? Take two men and get these children to *Cosanta Baile*. Miranda will take care of them."

"Sir." Taranto shuffled about and moved off with the children.

"We can't leave them the rebels on their own," Keane told Bowen. "Even if an alliance is no longer possible, I can't let them be slaughtered by Dracha's men."

"Neither can I. Double time it. You men, up front. Eyes alert." Bowen stopped Keane with a hand on his shoulder. "We take the rear. I'm sorry. I can't let you take the lead."

"Understood." But that didn't mean Keane wasn't ready to fight. He drew his sword and fell into step

behind his men. "However this ends, we end it with honor. Let's go."

❖

"There!"

Nellie had been concentrating so hard on controlling Seraphim she almost missed Erian's cry from ahead. Only twenty men had been left at the Citadel and with only nine pharentas capable of flight, that meant too many men for too little seating available. Especially since Sera wasn't about to let anyone other than Nellie into the saddle.

"It's like riding a horse, only higher," she told herself after she'd earned the creature's permission to mount. Clad in the black leather-like uniform Keane's soldiers wore, she had to admit, she felt more powerful than normal. She could also feel that newfound magic sizzling through her blood like hot oil.

Torch light exploded around her in the sky as the Outsiders lit their flames, aiming them at the ground to where dozens of men were engaged in battle. At least that's what Nellie thought was going on. Silver swords flashed and sparked, men cried out, screamed in pain, in anger, in triumph.

"Dive!" Erian ordered.

"Oh, holy crap." Nellie leaned forward and gripped Sera's feathers as the creature followed Erian's lead. The wind rushed hard into Nellie's face and as they drew closer, she could see Keane's men more clearly. They were outnumbered by armored soldiers at least two to one, but they were holding their own—barely. "I don't suppose you breathe fire, do you, Sera?"

Sera screeched. And when she did, a solitary soldier in the crowd rose up and looked into the sky.

"Keane." The instant she said his name, her body warmed. But not for the reasons she might have expected. "What the hell's happening now?" She released one hand, palm out, as the pressure inside her built to a raging inferno. And exploded straight out of her hand in a blinding white light.

It struck the ground with enough force to explode, sending soldiers on both sides flying into the air. Smoke caked the air, rocks and debris rained down and Nellie stared in wide-eyed shock as Erian circled around to her side.

"What are you doing?"

"I don't know!" But it was building again, the magic, and this time she aimed further out. To where a solitary figure sat on a creature that looked nothing like a horse. "Get them out of there!" She yelled and guided Sera over the battle. "Goddess, guide my hand," she whispered. As the words left her lips, a sense of control descended and she knew exactly what to do. "Let me down, Sera. There. Beyond the fighting." There was a clearing—there was always a clearing—just to the right.

Sera picked up speed, flying faster than Nellie had ever fallen, and skidded to a steep halt just before they hit the ground. Without giving it much thought, Nellie leapt down and, hands out in front of her, aimed directly at the soldier overseeing the attack.

The fire left her body in one stream, white hot and scorching. She walked through the bodies, blanking her mind to the knowledge that they had been alive and breathing only moments before. She could smell blood and death, but she didn't cower. Couldn't cower. Not if she was going to distract this man long enough for Erian to get to Bowen and Keane and the rest of their men to safety.

She didn't expect the man to fall back off his saddle. Or for him to call for a retreat. Or for the fire from her hands to die back as the armored soldiers retreated into the darkness. Just for fun, because she could, she knelt and fired one last shot, exploding a boulder to stop any possibility of them returning. "Holy shit, I'm Ironman!"

Only then did Nellie surrender to the hysterical laughter she'd been holding at bay. Only then did she turn to search the bodies, to find her way back to the path where she'd seen Keane standing only minutes before.

Where he still stood surrounded by his surviving men and, thankfully, Bowen. Erian, astride his pharenta, glided down to the ground, followed by the others who dismounted and began helping the injured.

"Keane." Nellie whispered his name like a prayer as she ran full out, toward him. That he'd lied to her didn't matter. That he'd tried to use her didn't matter. Not anymore. Not when she could have lost him. The only man to ever have really seen her.

"Keane." She leapt into his arms and kissed him as the shock formed on his face.

"Nellie?" His disbelieving voice when he broke away had nearly everyone laughing.

"Don't you know when you're kissing me?" She kissed him again, pressing her hands flat against his cheeks. "This time I got to ride to your rescue. How'd I do?"

"How'd you—" Keane lowered her to the ground, ran his hands up and down the sides of her body. "What are you wearing?"

"One of your uniforms. Stop that! We're in public." That earned her a hearty laugh as the rest of the men broke off to help the wounded and collect the dead.

"I don't know what…." In the torch light, his face went white and he dropped to the ground, gripping his head, the scream of pain ripping out of his throat sending Nellie to her knees.

She grabbed hold of him, caught her face in his hands. "What is it? What's wrong?" Had he been hurt in the battle? Had she been too late? "Keane, talk to me. What's wrong?"

She pushed his head up so she could stare into his beautiful white eyes. Only to find they weren't white any longer. They were a flickering flame blue that settled into the most gorgeous ocean blue she'd ever seen.

"Nellie." He lifted a hand to her face, traced a trembling finger down her cheek. "I can see you." He turned his head, looked at Bowen. "And you. And Erian. And Trevelyan. You came."

"I did." Trevelyan bowed his head.

"Let me go." Keane caught Nellie's hands in his and pushed them down and away. When he let her go, she thought about fighting him, then realized what he needed to know. Once and for all. He got to his feet, pushing aside assistance as he stood there, hands at his side, and tilted his head to the sky. He smiled. Then he laughed. "I can see."

Nellie sobbed, tried to catch the sound behind her hands, but failed miserably. "I guess I managed to heal you after all." Before he could stop her, she moved in and as he folded his arms around her, she knew she'd finally found where she belonged.

"Clara?" Bowen asked.

"She took the families to Miranda," Nellie told him. "She said you'd know where."

"We do." Keane squeezed her tight. "Let's say we get everyone home."

"Wait. What's that?" Trevelyan stretched his hand out to the sky as a bright blue explosion erupted in the distance.

She'd heard that sound before. Just as she'd fallen through the book. "Amber," Nellie whispered. "It's Amber. She's coming through."

"She certainly is." Keane shifted her against his side as the blue streak descended. "That's the good news."

"What's the bad?" Nellie wasn't sure she wanted to know. "Is she headed for the lake?"

"No," Bowen moved in and rested a hand on her shoulder. "She's headed straight for Dracha and the Keep."

Copyright © 2018 by Anna J. Stewart.

CLOSING EDITORIAL

by Tina Smith

Thank you, dear readers, for joining us in another issue of *Heart's Kiss*. Lezli and I are absolutely delighted to bring you great romance fiction and fun non-fiction in each installment. We love hearing from readers and if you have suggestions or requests for stories, let us know your favorites! We are dedicated to bringing you more of what you want to read. And as always reviews on the magazine are always appreciated. In the next issue we are excited to have another story from Leslye Penelope in her *Before I* series and the last installment of Anna J. Stewart's Warden novella series. We have an interview with multiple award winning and *USA Today* bestselling author Beverly Jenkins. Brenda Novak also has more yummy recipes for us from her kitchen! We will welcome back Petronella Glover with another tale that celebrates smart, resourceful heroines. Historical romance author, *USA Today* Bestseller, and RITA nominated Anthea Lawson will be joining us as a *Heart's Kiss* newcomer as well. Again, it's been a pleasure—but sadly it's time to go. We invite you to join us in June, or better yet, *Heart's Kiss* joins *you* on some tropical beach outing. Toes in sand and the pages of our magazine spread out on your beach towel. Or maybe a on a hike. Or maybe tucked away in your kindle on a camping trip. You provide the setting and we bring you the entertainment.